ALSO BY EDWARD ASHTON

Three Days in April

The End of Ordinary

Mickey7

ANTIMATTER BLUES

Edward Ashton

ST. MARTIN'S GRIFFIN
NEW YORK

Published in the United States by St. Martin's Griffin, an imprint of St. Martin's Publishing Group

ANTIMATTER BLUES. Copyright © 2023 by Edward Ashton. All rights reserved. Printed in the United States of America. For information, address St. Martin's Publishing Group, 120 Broadway, New York, NY 10271.

www.stmartins.com

The Library of Congress has cataloged the hardcover edition as follows:

Names: Ashton, Edward (Science fiction writer), author.
Title: Antimatter blues / Edward Ashton.
Description: First edition. | New York : St. Martin's Press, 2023. | Series: [Mickey 7] ; [2]
Identifiers: LCCN 2022051601 | ISBN 9781250275059 (hardcover) |
    ISBN 9781250275066 (ebook)
Subjects: LCGFT: Science fiction. | Novels.
Classification: LCC PS3601.S567 A85 2023 | DDC 813/.6—dc23/eng/20221028
LC record available at https://lccn.loc.gov/2022051601

ISBN 978-1-250-32201-2 (trade paperback)

Our books may be purchased in bulk for promotional, educational, or business use. Please contact your local bookseller or the Macmillan Corporate and Premium Sales Department at 1-800-221-7945, extension 5442, or by email at MacmillanSpecialMarkets@macmillan.com.

First St. Martin's Griffin Edition: 2024

10 9 8 7 6 5 4 3 2 1

For Jack.
You taught me what it means to be an artist.
I truly hope you're pleased with the result.

ANTIMATTER BLUES

001

"I just saw myself in the corridor."

Nasha looks up from her tablet. She's sitting in our desk chair, feet propped up on our bed, wearing nothing but underwear and boots. That's not a look that many people can pull off, but Nasha manages it with aplomb. She pushes her braids back from her face and drops her feet to the floor.

"Nice to see you too," she says. "Close the door."

I step into the room and let the door latch behind me. My rack looks a lot smaller than it did before Nasha moved in. The first thing she did when she got here was shove her bed in beside mine to make an almost-double, and the second was to fill up most of the remaining floor space with a meter-long footlocker that I'm not allowed to go into. Also, for some reason Nasha herself takes up a lot more space than her actual size would lead you to believe.

To be clear: I am not complaining about any of this.

I sit down on the bed and take the tablet from her hands. A look of annoyance flashes across her face, but she doesn't resist.

"Did you hear me? *I saw another me.* He was on the bottom

level, near the cycler. I think Marshall has started pulling new copies of me out of the tank."

Nasha sighs. "That's impossible, Mickey. Marshall wiped your patterns when you resigned, right?"

"Yeah," I say. "I mean, I think so. He said he was going to."

"And he hasn't pulled anyone out of the tank in the meantime, right?"

"I don't think so. Berto told me they wound up burning two drones when they shoved the fuel from my bubble bomb back into the reactor. I doubt they would have wasted those kinds of resources if they'd had a bunch of extra Mickeys lying around."

She leans back and props her feet up on the bed beside me. "Right. So unless Eight's really been hanging out with the creepers for the last two years and just decided to rejoin us, you couldn't have seen yourself wandering around the corridors. Are you sure it wasn't Harrison?"

"Harrison? You mean Jamie Harrison?"

She grins. "Yeah. He's like your doppelgänger, right? I could definitely see you mistaking him for you."

Jamie Harrison works in Agriculture. He takes care of the rabbits, mostly. He's short and skinny, with mousy brown hair that sticks up from his head in tufts, a perpetual nervous squint, and a prominent overbite. He looks *nothing* like me.

I don't think he looks anything like me, anyway.

"Look," I say. "I know what I saw, and what I saw was me. Maggie Ling was hustling him down Spoke Three toward the hub. They crossed in front of me just past Medical. They were probably twenty meters away and I only saw them for a second, but I know what I look like. It was definitely me."

Nasha's grin fades. "The hub, huh? And he was with Maggie?"

Maggie Ling is head of Systems Engineering. The last couple of times she hustled me somewhere, I wound up dying of radiation poisoning within the hour.

"You believe me now?"

She shakes her head. "Didn't say that. Let's assume you're right, though. After two years, however he managed it and for whatever reason, Marshall decided to pull Mickey9 out of the tank. What would he be doing with Maggie Ling, on the bottom level, headed toward the hub?"

I can feel my face twisting into a scowl. "The reactor."

"Yeah," she says. "That seems like the most likely bet, doesn't it?"

Mucking around inside the antimatter reactor is a prime job for an Expendable. We can withstand the neutron flux in there for longer than a drone can, and when we die, we're a hell of a lot easier to replace. Just chuck the old body in the cycler, fire up the bio-printer, and wait a few hours.

Of course, I'm not an Expendable anymore. I'm retired.

Unless I'm not, I guess.

"Anyway," Nasha says, "whatever's going on, it's not really your problem, is it?"

I've got a lot to say to that. What's my obligation to care about what happens to another instantiation of me? Is that *me* getting irradiated, or is it just some other guy who looks like me? What does the Ship of Theseus have to say about a damaged hull that gets left behind on an island somewhere and forgotten? But after five seconds of opening my mouth, changing my mind, and then closing it again, all I manage to come out with is, "What?"

"Think about it," Nasha says. "What's the worst-case scenario here?"

"Um . . . that Maggie Ling just sent a copy of me into the reactor core?"

"Right. So something needed to get done, and she did it. If she hadn't pulled a *new* Mickey out of the tank to do it, what would her alternative have been?"

I know the answer to this one. Nasha stands, then pulls me to my feet and into a kiss.

"Worst case," she says, "is that somebody just got sent into the core, *and that somebody wasn't you.* I don't know about you, babe, but you know what? I'll take it."

So HERE'S A solid fact: Warm Niflheim is a much nicer place than Cold Niflheim. It's green and wet and covered with all manner of crawly things. You can even go outside now without wrapping yourself up in six layers of thermals. You'll still need a rebreather, but the partial pressure of oxygen is almost twenty percent higher now than it was when we made landfall, so you won't feel quite so much like you're drowning while you're walking around. On a good day, you can almost imagine that we've found the sort of place that they promised us when we boarded the *Drakkar.*

Here's another solid fact: Warm Niflheim isn't going to last forever. Winter is coming.

Miko Berrigan and his minions in Physics have spent most of the summer poring over records of the thirty years of observations that were made of Niflheim's sun before the *Drakkar* boosted out. There were three warm spells in that period. The longest lasted seven years. The shortest was eleven months. The four winters that surrounded them ranged from two years to nine. The transitions weren't abrupt, and they weren't smooth. They were marked by lengthening oscillations between hot and cold that eventually stabilized into one steady state or the other. The season we're in now went through a half dozen false starts before it really settled in.

The physicists back on Midgard thought what they were see-ing was all due to interference from interstellar dust. Cute, right?

We haven't been wasting the summer. Hieronymus Marshall is a jackass, but he isn't stupid, and he wants this colony to live. We've been stockpiling food, studying the local fauna to figure out how they survive the winters, building out the dome to ac-commodate the first round of decanted embryos, releasing en-gineered algae that are supposed to begin the work of pushing the atmosphere further toward something we can breathe, etc., etc., etc.

The problem is that it all takes time, and that's something we don't have an infinite supply of. All the things that keep us alive here take enormous amounts of power, and right now the only real power source we have is the *Drakkar*'s antimatter reactor, still spinning away under the hub, slowly drawing down the last of the fuel supply that brought us here.

Which brings me back to Maggie Ling, hustling another me down Spoke Three toward the hub. Without the reactor, we might just barely be able to get by, as long as the weather holds.

That's the thing, though. The weather is not going to hold.

I'VE SPENT ALMOST all of my work shifts since my resignation with Agriculture. This isn't because I have a green thumb or any-thing. It's mostly by default. I don't have the qualifications to do anything useful for Physics or Biology or Engineering. Amundsen in Security is tight with Marshall and also is still down on me for losing consciousness while Cat and I were fighting creepers on the perimeter two years ago, so he mostly wants nothing to do with me these days. I'll probably get to spend some time chang-ing diapers in the crèche once they start pulling babies out of cold storage, but that's still on hold at the moment, pending a bit more confidence that we can keep them alive once they're decanted.

So, that leaves me with Agriculture. On this day, in fact, I'm hanging with Jamie Harrison, taking care of the rabbits.

You might be wondering why we keep rabbits in a closed-loop ecological system. Raising animals for meat can be a net source of calories in a place where they can more or less fend for themselves, staying alive by eating things like grass and weeds that we wouldn't or couldn't eat. On Niflheim, though, that kind of thing is still entirely aspirational. Rabbits can't eat the lichen and ferns that surround the dome now. The proteins that the natives use here are folded the wrong way for Union life. Instead we feed them tomato vines and potato greens and protein slurry, some of which gets converted into edible rabbit parts but most of which just gets burned up by their stupid mammalian metabolisms or turned into poop. At the end of the day, every kcal of edible rabbit meat costs us about three kcal of other stuff that we could conceivably have just eaten ourselves, as well as a huge pile of stuff that we can't eat, but that could have gone back into the cycler. Rabbits are a massive luxury item in a place that is notably short on pretty much any other type of luxury. So, why do we do it?

Well, for one, rabbits are cute. Numerous psychological studies over the past thousand years of the diaspora have shown that humans need a certain amount of cuddliness in their lives, and rabbits are the only things on Niflheim that provide that for us.

Of course, they're also delicious. As soon as they reach full growth, it's off to the kitchen with these guys. In the meantime, though, they're a lot more fun to hang around with than most of the people in this colony.

Jamie, on the other hand, is neither cute nor fun to hang around with.

Rabbits on Niflheim are treated essentially the same way maximum-security prisoners were treated back on Midgard.

They spend the vast majority of their time crammed into three small hutches pushed up against a wall next to the hydroponics tanks. Once a day, we let them out one hutch at a time into a slightly larger space bounded by a bulkhead on two sides and a short white wire fence on the other. They hop around a little, get whatever exercise they can, hang out with anyone who (a) needs a cuteness fix and (b) has sterilized themselves to Jamie's satisfaction, and then get plopped back into the hutch for another day, where they while away the time eating, pooping, and making more rabbits.

It's not a terrible life.

It's better than mine in a lot of ways, if I'm being honest.

If I had any choice about my duty cycles, I'd probably spend most of them here. I don't, though. I get to hang with the rabbits during working hours when Jamie puts in a request for my services, and that only happens on two occasions. One is culling day, which is when I get to go through the hutches and pick out the males who are big enough for eating and the females who are old enough that their reproduction has started to slow down. The other, like today, is hutch-cleaning day.

The good thing about hutch-cleaning day is that Jamie doesn't trust me to do it properly. That means I get to spend the day wrangling the rabbits while he does most of the actual work.

I've just finished pulling the last of the kits out of Hutch One and dropping them off in the exercise yard when the door to the corridor slides open and Berto steps through.

Great.

"Hey," he says. "How's my dinner doing?"

I sigh, straighten, and turn to face him. He steps over the fence and crouches down to stroke a kit's ears with one finger.

"Hands off, Gomez," Jamie says without turning away from whatever he's doing in the hutch. "You're not sterile."

Berto laughs. "Sterile? These things are rats in fancy suits, Jamie. You're literally scooping piles of shit out of their house right now. If anyone should be worried about contamination, it's me."

"This is not a debate," Jamie says. "Get your hands off of my animals or get out of my space. I can have Security down here in less than a minute."

Berto's smile disappears, and it looks like he's going to argue. In the end, though, he shakes his head and stands.

"Jamie's right," I say. "You know that, don't you? These poor guys spend nine-tenths of their time crawling all over each other in the hutches. If you get one of them sick, they'll all be dead in a week, and it's not like we have a backup supply around here anywhere."

"Whatever," Berto says. "I didn't come down here to play with the bunnies."

I wait for him to go on. After a long five seconds, I raise one eyebrow and say, "So . . ."

His expression shifts from annoyed to confused. "So, what?"

I roll my eyes. "Why *did* you come down here, Berto?"

He grins. "Oh. I was bored, mostly. Didn't Nasha tell you?"

Now it's my turn to be confused. "Tell me what?"

"We're grounded," he says. "No more aerial reconnaissance until further notice."

Huh.

"No," I say. "Nasha didn't mention that. When did this happen?"

"I found out this morning when I showed up for my shift. Maybe they haven't told her yet?"

"Yeah. Maybe. Did they tell you why?"

He shakes his head. "Not really. The tech on duty said something about not being able to charge the gravitic grids, but that doesn't make any sense. We've got an antimatter reactor, right? It's not like we need to ration power."

"Yeah," I say. "You wouldn't think so."

"Not like it matters. I'm pretty confident at this point that there's nothing out there that's a threat to us other than the creepers, and I haven't seen one of them within five klicks of the dome since the weather turned. Don't get me wrong. I'd rather be flying than . . . well, than pretty much anything, I guess. I'm not kidding myself, though. Aerial reconnaissance at this point is a waste of time and resources."

One of the rabbits is nosing at my boot. I crouch down to give his ears a scratch. "So if, just hypothetically speaking, we did have some kind of issue with power generation, grounding you and Nasha might be a good place to cut back, huh?"

He shrugs. "I guess so. Gravitic grids are power hogs. Those lifters use an ungodly amount of juice." He hesitates, and his grin fades. "Do you know something, Mickey?"

The rabbit nips at my finger. I guess he wasn't looking for affection after all. I nudge him away with one hand, then stand again and glance back at Jamie. He's head and shoulders deep in the hutch, scrubbing at something with a disinfectant sponge.

"Look," I say, "have you seen me around recently?"

His mouth opens, then closes again. He shakes his head. "What?"

"Have you seen me?" I say. "Maybe with someone from Engineering? Maybe looking kind of confused?"

His eyes narrow. "What are you saying, Mickey?"

I sigh. "I'm saying I think I saw another me this morning. I think Marshall is pulling Mickeys out of the tank again."

He tilts his head to one side and folds his arms across his chest. "You're saying that you think Hieronymus Marshall, Niflheim's high priest of Natalism, is deliberately creating multiples?"

I hesitate, then shake my head. "It sounds stupid when you say it like that."

"Yeah," he says. "That's because it *is* stupid. Did you actually see another Mickey somewhere? Did you talk to him?"

"I didn't talk to him, but I saw him. For a second. From about twenty meters away."

Berto rolls his eyes. "So you got a glance of someone from twenty meters off that kind of looked like you, and from that you've concluded that our commander, who has a visceral, religiously motivated hatred of multiples in general, and of you in particular, is secretly making more of you because . . ."

"Look," I say, "I know what I saw."

"You don't," he says, and gestures toward the hutch. "It was probably just Jamie. You two are like twins."

Et tu, Berto?

I open my mouth to argue, or maybe to tell him to go fuck himself, but before I can decide which one he smacks me on the shoulder and says, "Anyway, it doesn't matter, does it? What do you care if Marshall is pulling copies of you out of the tank and . . . I don't know . . . making them fight to the death while he and Amundsen take bets on the winner? You're retired, remember? How is this any skin off of your nose?"

That's a good question, actually. I've given it some thought since Nasha asked me the same basic question. If there's one thing I'm sure of after what happened with Eight two years ago, it's that I'm the only me there's ever going to be, no matter what Nine or Ten or whatever number they've gotten to by now might think about it. By that logic, if Marshall is pulling bodies out of the tank and throwing them into the reactor or making them play gladiator or whatever, it doesn't actually have anything to do with me, but . . .

But still.

It kind of does.

"Look," I say. "Forget about the whole morality thing. The person I thought was me was with Maggie Ling, and they were headed toward the reactor."

Berto starts to reply, but then his smile fades and I can see the wheels turning.

"Oh," he says finally.

"Yeah. And you just got grounded."

"Right," he says. "That might be a problem."

"You think? How long would we last here without power?"

"Depends," he says. "Are we without power because the reactor shut down gracefully and got decommissioned like it's eventually supposed to, or are we without power because the reactor overloaded and vaporized everything in a fifty-klick radius?"

"Let's assume option one."

He scratches the back of his head. "We'd probably be okay for the moment. We're still getting a fair amount of our calories from the cycler, I think, but that's something we can work on if we start throwing bodies at Agriculture. There's not much else going on around here that requires a ton of power and is also absolutely essential for our survival."

"That's for now. What about when the cold comes back?"

"Oh," Berto says. "When that happens we're totally fucked."

"Yeah," I say. "That's pretty much where I wound up."

He grimaces. "Okay. So what do we do?"

"I'm not sure we do anything. We've still got power at the moment and we haven't been vaporized, so obviously the reactor is still functioning. I guess default is to hope that Maggie knows what she's doing and that whatever's going on is just a temporary glitch."

Berto grimaces. "I've got plenty of confidence in Maggie, but if somebody's screwing around with the insides of the reactor, it's not her, is it?"

"Now, wait a minute," I say. "I hope you're not questioning *my* competence. If there's one thing I've proved I'm good at around here, it's fixing crap while picking up fatal doses of radiation."

"Yeah," Berto says. "That's a fair point. Still, I've got to say— just the thought of something glitching in the reactor is enough to spook me. Any thoughts on how we can figure out what the hell's going on?"

"Don't mean to interrupt," Jamie says from behind me, "but I'm finished here. If you hens are done clucking, would you mind getting these guys back into One so we can get started on Two?"

I look back at him. He scowls and points to the hutch.

"Sorry," I say to Berto. "Duty calls."

"Yeah," he says. "You do your bunny thing. I think I'm gonna do a little poking around. Ping me when you're off-shift, huh?"

"Sometime today," Jamie says.

Berto shoots him a glare, then steps back over the fence and goes.

WE'RE JUST GETTING the last of the rabbits back into Hutch Three when Jamie says, "You know, I heard what you and Gomez were saying earlier."

I turn to look at him. "Really? So what do you think?"

He shrugs. "I think Gomez can go screw. You don't look anything like me."

I open my mouth to reply, then shut it again as my brain processes what he just said.

"I'm not saying I'm *better*-looking than you," he says. "We're just different."

"So," I finally manage. "Out of all the stuff Berto and I were talking about, *that's* what you fixated on?"

"Yeah," he says. "Pretty much. Why? Was there something else that I ought to give a shit about?"

I know the screening process to get involved with this mission back on Midgard was incredibly rigorous. I know they only selected the best and the brightest. Jamie, though . . .

Maybe he was somebody's nephew?

I'm about to say something along the lines of, *Yes, I agree that we look nothing alike*, when my ocular pings.

> <Command1>: You are required to report to the Commander's
> office immediately.
> <Command1>: Failure to do so by 17:30 will be construed as
> insubordination.

Okay, then. Here we go.

IT'S PROBABLY BEST at this point if I explain the current state of my relationship with Hieronymus Marshall.

To summarize: it's not great.

On the plus side, he hasn't actually tried to kill me since I resigned my position as Mission Expendable. That's been refreshing. He hasn't been particularly friendly, though. The first thing he did when I told him I wasn't going to die for him anymore, pretty much before his office door had closed behind me, was to cut my rations to base minimum, which at the time was twelve hundred kcal per day. His argument for doing so was that I no longer deserved any service bonuses, since I technically no longer had a job. My counterargument was that if I attempted to live on twelve hundred kcal per day long-term, I would die. His counter-counterargument was that he didn't remotely give a shit. My counter-counter-counterargument was that I was still in close contact with the creepers, and that if I died, they would be sorely put out, and might be tempted to express their displeasure using the antimatter bomb he'd so helpfully provided to them.

He allocated me an extra three hundred kcal then, but he

clearly wasn't happy about it. This still left me pretty hungry, but I decided to let it lie there, for what I thought were some fairly compelling reasons:

1. I don't have a ton of friends, but the ones that I do have seem to actually like me, and they're pretty good about spotting me a mug of cycler paste here and there when I'm looking particularly gaunt.

2. The creepers do not actually have an antimatter bomb.

3. Even if they did, *I have not really been in contact with them.* I've told Marshall that they're staying clear of the dome because of my ongoing brilliant diplomacy, and he seems to be buying it, but the truth is that I haven't heard a whisper from them in almost two years. For all I know, they hibernate over the summer and when winter comes again they're going to pop up through the floor of the dome and kill us all.

So, to sum up, my continued survival is based almost entirely on an extremely shaky tower of lies. Given that, I'm not too inclined to blow a fit over a few hundred kcal.

"Barnes," Marshall says. "Have a seat."

I let the door swing shut behind me and settle into one of the chairs across the desk from him. This is the first time I've spoken to Marshall, let alone been in his office, in almost two standard years. The last time, I resigned my post and he threatened to have me killed. I'm hoping that this meeting goes at least marginally better.

Marshall leans forward, plants his elbows on his desk, and stares me down for a solid ten seconds, which gives me time to reflect on how little he's changed in the eleven years since I first met him. The brush cut and mustache have a bit more gray in them than they did then, but other than that? Hieronymus Marshall is probably the oldest human on Niflheim. Even back on Midgard he'd be well into middle age—but looking at him now, I have a sudden premonition that he might outlive us all.

"So," he says. "It's been a while since we've had a chance to catch up. How's retirement treating you, Barnes?"

Huh. That's not what I expected.

"Oh," I say after a short, awkward pause. "It's great. Thanks for asking. I've been playing pog-ball, mostly, and doing a little traveling. The grandkids don't call as often as I'd like, but what can you do?"

He leans back, and his face twists into a scowl.

"Fine," he says. "So much for pleasantries. Do you have any idea why I called you in today?"

I shrug. I have my suspicions, but I'm not sure this is the time to voice them. Marshall's scowl deepens. "Before we get into that, let's get this on the table right up front: You're not pulling your weight, Barnes. You haven't been since the day you decided that the job you'd agreed to do, the job that got your unqualified ass onto this mission in the first place, the job that you fully understood at the time you agreed to take it on was a lifetime appointment, was no longer to your liking. For the past two years, you have not been a colonist. You have been a freeloader—and while that sort of thing may have been fine back on Midgard, where I'm quite sure you were perfectly content to drift through life as a subsidy brat, you know as well as I do that freeloading is not permissible on a beachhead colony."

I open my mouth to say something sarcastic about how, sure, I might have been a subsidy brat and I might not exactly be doing the things I signed on for at the moment, but that on the other hand as far as I can tell he hasn't done an honest day's work since we boosted out of orbit eleven years ago—but then I remember at the last moment that this man actually does have the power to have me killed if I push him to it. I back up, clear my throat, and start again.

"I hear you, sir. However, I do feel that I should point out that I have not, in fact, been freeloading. I pull a duty shift every day, just like everyone else on Niflheim. I'm basically doing exactly what I was doing before I resigned, give or take the occasional gruesome death."

"Yes," Marshall says. "I've reviewed your duty schedule. Tending the tomatoes. Cleaning floors in the chem lab. Playing with bunnies. You're doing make-work, Barnes. The occasional gruesome death, as you put it, was what you were brought here to do. The rest was just killing time in between your assignments. The honest fact, and I think if you examine yourself you'll be forced to agree, is that nothing you've done over the past two years has contributed anything of any actual value to this colony. The survival of a beachhead is a knife's-edge thing, and every day that you continue to exist here, eating and excreting, drawing resources and putting nothing back, tips us that much further toward failure."

"Okay," I say. "So you're suggesting I should . . . kill myself? Because I have to tell you, sir, that's going to require a lot more convincing than what you've done so far."

Marshall leans forward again, and his voice drops to a growl. "No, Barnes. Much though I might appreciate that, I am not suggesting that you kill yourself. I am suggesting that you consider the burden that your existence has been to your fellow colonists since your *retirement,* and that you then make a decision to do something that will even the scales." After a painfully awkward pause, Marshall leans back in his chair and folds his arms across his chest. "You're obviously thinking that I'm asking you to return to your previous position. To be clear: I am not. As I just said, I am not asking you to kill yourself. In fact, I'm asking you to consider doing what is necessary to save yourself, as well as everyone else in this colony."

"Riiiiight," I say. "And this thing you're asking me to do, it really doesn't involve me dying in some incredibly painful way?"

"No," he says. "Not necessarily, in any case."

I roll my eyes, push back from the desk, and get to my feet.

"Look," I say, "I don't know what you've got in mind here, sir, but I've honestly got a pretty full plate at the moment, what with the bunnies and the tomatoes and, let's not forget, the creepers. So unless there's anything else . . ."

"Barnes," he says. "Sit down. Please."

It's the *please* that gets me. I don't know that Marshall has ever used that word with me before. I sigh, and drop back into the chair.

"Fine," I say. "What's the ask? Clearing a jam in the reactor core?"

His eyes widen slightly, and I can see the muscles in his jaw bunch.

"What do you know about the reactor core?"

Huh. That's interesting.

"Well," I say, "for one thing, I know you've grounded Berto and Nasha to conserve power."

His eyes narrow. "That was a routine measure. Aerial reconnaissance is not productive at this time. The lifters were grounded as a matter of basic efficiency."

"I also know that you've been pulling copies of me out of the tank, and I know you've been throwing them into the core. Is that routine?"

That brings Marshall to a full stop. When he finally speaks again, his voice is a flat monotone.

"Who told you that?"

I give him a tight-lipped smile. "Nobody told me. I saw one of them in the corridor yesterday. He was with Maggie Ling. They were clearly in a hurry. I wasn't one hundred percent sure where they were going, but your reaction pretty much confirms it, huh?"

Marshall stares me down for what feels like a very long time.

"Once again, to be clear," he says finally, "I have confirmed nothing. Do you understand?"

I hesitate, then shake my head. I'm honestly not sure that I do.

"As I said before," Marshall says, his voice now low and even, "this colony exists on a knife's edge. This is true of all beachhead colonies, but given our unique circumstances, perhaps even more so for us." He pauses then, and I consider mentioning how many of our current unique circumstances are the direct consequences of his decisions. Discretion is the better part of valor, though, so I hold my silence until he goes on. "Many elements could finally be responsible for pushing us over the edge, Barnes. Crop failure. Equipment failure. Hostile action. Do you know what the most common cause of colony failure is, though?"

It takes me a moment to realize that this isn't a rhetorical question.

"No, sir," I say. "Please. Enlighten me."

His jaw tightens at my tone, but otherwise he doesn't react.

"Panic," he says. "The most common cause of colony failure is panic. Every beachhead encounters difficulties. Many encounter disasters. The ones who face these setbacks with calm leadership and courage survive. The ones who succumb to rumors and viral fear? They die. Do you understand what I'm saying to you, Barnes?"

"Um," I say. "I think you're telling me to keep my mouth shut about the reactor?"

He leans forward in his chair, hands flat on the desk in front of him. "I'm telling you there is nothing wrong with this colony's antimatter reactor. It has sustained us for eleven standard years now, and it will continue to do so for as long as we require it. I am also telling you that we have not been pulling expendables out of the tank. To say that we have is inflammatory, and could lead to exactly the sort of panic reaction among the general colonists that we need to avoid. Again, do you understand?"

"Yes," I say slowly. "I think so."

"You *think* so?"

"No, sir. Not think. I do. I understand."

His face relaxes, and he gives me what might even be the hint of a smile.

"Excellent. So I can rely on you to avoid spreading these types of rumors?"

I've already spread them to Nasha and Berto, of course, and would have to Jamie as well if he had the cranial capacity to understand them. This probably isn't the time to mention that, though.

"Yes, sir. I'll be sure to keep my thoughts on these topics to myself."

"Excellent," he says. "I'm happy that you understand the necessity of discretion."

I nod.

He nods.

I glance over my shoulder. The door is still closed behind me.

"So," I say. "This was very helpful. Can I go, then?"

"What?" Marshall says. "No. Do you think I called you down here to talk about these ridiculous rumors? I told you, we have a job for you."

Right. That.

"Two years ago," he says, "you went down into the creepers' labyrinth with two antimatter bombs. When you came back, you only had one."

I shake my head. "I only carried one. Eight had the other one, and Eight was not me. I thought we'd established that."

Marshall's mouth twists in disgust. There must have been a really good reason for him to start pulling Mickeys out of the tank again. He can't even talk about multiples without looking like he's about to be sick.

"I'm not interested in semantics," he says. "The two of you left this dome with two bombs, and you only returned with one."

I shrug. "Okay. So?"

"So," Marshall says. "I need you to go back to the creepers now. I need you to get that bomb back."

I let that hang between us for a beat. Marshall's belief that the creepers have possession of that bomb is the thing that's guaranteed my continued survival for the past two years. I do not want to disabuse him of that notion, and even more than that I really do not want to bring that bomb back to the dome.

"I'm sorry, sir," I say finally. "I don't think that's possible."

"Think again," Marshall says, his voice suddenly flat and cold. "When you sat in that same chair two years ago and announced that you were refusing to do your job, when you *resigned* from a position that you had no right whatsoever to resign from, we were forced to send a drone into the core in your place to attempt to reload the fuel from your bomb. The drone malfunctioned. Ling believes that the intensity of the neutron flux in the core damaged the damned thing's brain. It, in turn, severely damaged the antimatter feed mechanism, although that did not become apparent until very recently. Six days ago, we came within ten seconds of an uncontrolled chain reaction that would have turned this colony into a smoking crater a hundred kilometers across."

"Oh. But you did shut it down, right?"

He rolls his eyes. "Yes, Barnes. The fact that you are sitting here in one piece and not dispersed into your component elements and drifting through the stratosphere right now is a strong indication that we were able to bring the situation under control. In order to do so, however, we were forced to spoil over ninety percent of our remaining fuel stores. Do you understand what that means?"

"Um . . ."

"What it means, Barnes, is that we do not currently have the necessary energy reserves to survive another winter."

Oh. That's not good.

"But . . . I mean, there are ways other than antimatter annihilation to keep warm, right? Humans survived weather as cold as Niflheim's back on Earth, back when all they had to keep them warm were animal skins and fires."

Marshall sighs. "Setting aside the advisability of starting a fire inside the dome, or the possibility of doing so outside in an atmosphere consisting of less than ten percent oxygen, or the practicality of making a warm winter cloak out of a creeper's chitin—what do you suppose those hardy humans back on old Earth were eating?"

I actually have no idea what prehistoric humans ate. Probably not creepers? I've already had this conversation twice, though. I know where he's going.

"Even with what we're managing to grow outside right now," he says, "the cycler is still responsible for over a quarter of the calories our population consumes. Moreover, our population cannot remain static. At some point relatively soon, we need to begin decanting babies. If we wait too long, there will not be enough adults left to raise them when we do. There have been extensive studies done to determine the optimal number of infants per caretaker, and that number is closer to one than to a thousand. In order to feed those babies that will need to start coming out of storage soon, we will absolutely need the cycler. Do you have any idea how much power that system draws?"

I do, actually. That was one of the things Jemma Abera covered in detail during my training back on Himmel Station prior to boost.

The answer, in case you were wondering, is a hell of a lot.

"Look," Marshall says. "I don't particularly like you, Barnes. This shouldn't come as a surprise to you. I objected to the inclusion of an Expendable on this mission on principle, but I was overruled on that point. I objected to not throwing you out of the air lock after we boosted out from Himmel Station, but I was overruled on that as well. I was extremely displeased that you returned from your mission to the creepers alive and with your weapon still on your back, and I was even more so when it became apparent that I would not be able to shove you into the cycler face-first afterward. Are we clear on all of this?"

Again, this is apparently not a rhetorical question. After a long, awkward silence, I nod. Marshall leans across the desk, and for an instant I think he's going to kill me where I sit.

"Good," he says, "because I want you to understand how much it hurts me to say this: Get me that bomb back, and *everything* is forgiven. I will not ask you to perform the duties you signed onto this mission to perform, ever again. I will sit quietly and watch you tend tomatoes and play with bunnies until the end of your days, if that is what you choose to do. Without that antimatter, we are lost. Once the weather turns, our reliance on the cycler will jump to nearly fifty percent of our total caloric requirements. Under that load, our current remaining fuel stores will last for a year—maybe two if we cut rations to an absolute minimum, reduce the base temperature in the dome, and minimize waste cycling. Berrigan in Physics tells me this star's next down cycle may last for seven years or more. If that is true, and if you cannot retrieve the antimatter that we require, I tell you that there will be nothing in this dome but starved and frozen corpses when the weather finally warms again."

He leans back and looks down at his hands.

"Well," he says. "Actually, I don't suppose that's entirely true. Once the last natural colonist is dead, the central processor will start pulling copies of you out of the tank, and it will presumably continue doing so for as long as it is able." He looks up again, and gives me a grim half smile. "So, that's what you have to look forward to, Barnes. A series of brief, painful lives, wandering the dark, frozen, empty corridors of a dead colony. How does that sound? Are you feeling a bit more motivated now?"

003

"You were right," Berto says. "We're totally boned."

He ducks into our room and lets the door swing closed behind him. Nasha and I are on the bed, which is pretty close to the only place it's possible to be in our room. Nasha is leaning against the wall with her knees drawn up to her chest. I'm stretched out beside her with my hands folded behind my head. Berto drops into the desk chair and leans forward with his elbows on his knees.

"I talked to my pal Dani in Engineering. There's definitely something up with the reactor. She wouldn't say what the problem was, exactly, but she said they're cutting power usage to the bare minimum across the board until they can get whatever it is fixed. The thing is, though—we don't have redundancy for a lot of the critical reactor components. If it's the feed mechanism, they might be able to get something replaced, but if there's an issue with the reaction chamber or the generation system—"

"It's not any of that," I say. "It's worse. We're running out of fuel."

Berto opens his mouth, hesitates, then closes it again.

"Yeah," Nasha says. "That's pretty much what I said."

"No," Berto says. "That's not possible. Even with what you handed over to the creepers, we should have enough antimatter in the tanks for another ten years."

I shrug. "Apparently there was an accident. Something went wrong when they fed the fuel from my bomb back into the system two years ago, and I guess it just came to a head last week. Marshall said we came within ten seconds of a completely uncontrolled reaction, and by the time they'd gotten the situation back under control they'd spoiled most of our remaining stores."

Berto's eyebrows come together at the bridge of his nose. "Spoiled? That doesn't make sense. How do you spoil antimatter?"

I sigh, sit up, and scoot back until I'm sitting next to Nasha. "I don't know, man. Leave it out in the sun too long? I'm just repeating what Marshall told me."

Berto leans back, almost tips the chair over backward before catching himself on the desk, then folds his arms across his chest and pretends that didn't just happen. "And why would Marshall be talking to you about this? For that matter, why would Marshall be talking to you about anything? Aren't you still on his shit list?"

"Oh yeah, he's definitely still on the shit list," Nasha says. "Best I can guess, Marshall is seeing this as a two-birds kind of situation. He wants Mickey to get the second bomb back from the creepers so we don't all starve to death when the weather turns, and if that means he gets to kill him afterwards, that's just gravy."

"Huh," Berto says, and turns to look at me. "So you're gonna do it, right?"

Nasha and I trade a quick glance. I still haven't told Berto what really happened to that bomb, and I'm not thinking this is a good time to change that.

"It's complicated," Nasha says. "Remember, that bomb is the

only thing that's been keeping Mickey out of the corpse hole for the last two years. If he brings it back, there's nothing keeping Marshall from ending him."

"That's great," Berto says, "but that fuel is the only thing that's going to keep the rest of us out of the corpse hole for the *next* two years."

"Actually," I say, "the corpse hole draws more power than any other single system in the dome. If it comes to that, we'll probably just wind up going old school and burying each other."

"Doubtful," Nasha says. "We'll be starving by then. Eating each other is more likely."

Berto straightens now, and scoots a half meter back toward the door. "I don't think I like how comfortable you are with saying that."

Nasha grins. "Don't worry, Berto. I promise to save you for last."

"Anyway," I say, "cannibalism aside, this whole thing hinges on one question: Do we believe what Marshall is telling us? I'm no Miko Berrigan, admittedly, but this whole business about antimatter spoiling sounds kind of made up to me—and I don't exactly feel a bond of trust with the commander these days."

"What?" Berto says. "You think he's lying?"

Nasha shrugs. "The thought had crossed our minds."

Berto shakes his head. "The power restrictions are real. He's not faking our grounding."

"Come on," I say. "You said yourself that your sorties have been a complete waste of time and energy. If Marshall is up to something, shutting those down would be a pretty painless way to make it seem like there was a problem, no?"

"Maybe," Berto says. "What about Dani, though?"

Nasha shakes her head. "From what you said, Dani didn't tell you jack shit. All she said was that they're cutting power until they can get something fixed, right? That doesn't sound like what Marshall told Mickey."

"Huh." Berto leans back again, more gently this time, then reaches up to scratch the back of his head. "So you think Marshall is ginning up a fake emergency? Why would he do that?"

Nasha rolls her eyes. "That's the easy part, Berto. He wants the bomb back, and he wants to kill Mickey. Like I said—two birds."

Berto looks to me, then to Nasha, then back to me. "So you think Marshall is screwing with the entire colony's power supply, spreading rumors that are likely to start a panic if they get around, just so he can murder Mickey one more time?"

"You have to admit," Nasha says, "murdering Mickey is one of his favorite things to do."

"Look," I say, "we're not saying this is definitely what's happening—just that it's a possibility. I saw the way he reacted when I told him that I knew something was up with the reactor. Unless he's a world-class actor, it wasn't fake. I believe there's something going on. I'm just not sure I totally believe it's exactly what he's saying it is. If I bring that bomb back here, I'm basically putting my head on the block. I'd rather not do that unless I'm one hundred percent sure it's necessary."

Berto shrugs. "It's probably a moot point anyway, isn't it? I mean, what are the odds the creepers actually turn that thing back over to you? I sure as hell wouldn't if I were them."

"I . . . think I can convince them to give it up."

"Truth," Nasha says. "Mickey's very persuasive."

Berto's eyes narrow. "I feel like I'm missing something."

"Really?" I say. "You think I'm not being totally honest with you? Like maybe . . . I don't know . . . I'm hiding critical information related directly to your survival from you because I think it might make me look bad?"

Berto sighs. "Are we back on that again?"

"I don't know," I say. "Are we?"

"It was two years ago, Mickey. I said I was sorry. I let you punch me in the face."

"Oh no," I say. "You didn't let me."

He leans forward, and one corner of his mouth twists up.

"Yeah," he says. "I did."

That hangs between us, until finally Nasha heaves a sigh and says, "Are you two done now? Because if you're not, you need to either start throwing hands, or else bang each other and get it over with."

Berto's eyes shift to her, then back to me.

"Your call," I say. "As far as I'm concerned, they're both good choices."

"Okay," Berto says, and gets to his feet. "You guys are nasty, and I'm out. I'll see if Dani wants to grab lunch. Maybe I can get some more details out of her. In the meantime, I guess you need to figure out who you'd rather roll the dice with—Marshall, or the creepers."

After he's gone, Nasha elbows me in the ribs. "Dang, babe. That was some first-class deflecting you just did."

I lean into her. "Thanks. When you know what buttons to push, Berto's actually pretty easy to deflect."

She cups my cheek with one hand and kisses me. When she pulls back, though, her grin has faded. "We still need to decide what you're going to do."

"I know. Unless Berto can get something definitive out of Dani, I need to . . ."

"What?" Nasha says. "Did you just have an idea, or are you having a stroke?"

"Not a stroke," I say. "I'm not sure it's a good idea, but . . . I think I know what I need to do."

*   *   *

THERE ARE A lot of profoundly shitty things about being an Expendable. Start with the way people treat you. The Natalists are bad enough. They think the whole process of memory uploads and bio-printed bodies is an abomination, and that anyone who's come out of the tank is basically a soulless monster. In a way, though, they're easier to deal with than the rest of the general population. With the Natalists, I know where I stand. Take Marshall, for example. He wants to kill me. I know it. He knows I know it. It lends a certain amount of refreshing honesty to our relationship.

With the others, though?

Everybody knows what Expendables are for. We die, over and over, so you don't have to. You'd think maybe folks would be grateful for that, but that's not how the human brain works. Watching someone else run into a fire while you stand safe and sound on the sidewalk outside doesn't make you feel grateful. It makes you feel guilty. Nobody likes feeling guilty, so on some level you convince yourself that your Expendable *deserves* what he's getting.

That was easier back on Midgard. We didn't use many Expendables on the surface, and the ones we had on the orbital stations were mostly conscripted criminals. Plenty of people here on Niflheim still assume that's how I wound up with this job, and they mostly treat me accordingly. Even the ones who believe me when I say that I volunteered to be here tend to keep their distance, because, really, what kind of nutjob would do that? Back on Midgard, I had friends. Here on Niflheim, outside of Nasha, Berto, and Cat Chen, I really don't.

I know what you're thinking. Boo-hoo, right? Jamie Harrison doesn't have many friends either. And you're right, of course. The worst part about being an Expendable is not the social isolation. It's all the dying.

That's closer to the truth, but still not quite right. Everybody has to die. We've figured out a lot of neat stuff on the science side, but we still haven't managed to get around that one. The worst thing about being an Expendable, the thing that separates me from everybody else, is that I have to die over and over again, and more importantly, I have to *remember* all that dying. When an Expendable goes down, his handlers make every possible effort to make sure he uploads the experience. Because of that, I know what it feels like to be ripped to shreds on a cellular level by high-energy subatomic particles. I know what it feels like to go through the end stages of infection by brain parasites, and lung parasites, and gut parasites. I have nightmares about those things, but the nightmares are nowhere near as bad as the actual memories.

Which makes what I need to do now absolutely terrifying. If I'm right about what's happening, there's only one person who really knows exactly what's going on in the reactor core.

It's me.

If Marshall has really been throwing Mickeys into the core, he's probably been forcing them to upload before they die. I need to see what they saw. I wish there were a way to do that without also feeling what they felt, but . . .

Yeah, there's not.

Fuck me. This is gonna suck.

"QUINN?"

Quinn Brock, Medical Technologist Grade II, glances up from his vat steak, a look of annoyance on his face that fades into confusion when he sees who I am.

"Barnes? Aren't you . . ."

He trails off and takes a quick look around. We're on the early side for dinner, and the caf is mostly empty. I step over the bench and take a seat across from him. It's been a while since I've seen him other than passing in the corridors. His hair is longer now. He's dyed it blond and parted it down the middle so that it hangs down like a pair of limp, oily parentheses on either side of his narrow face. It's not a good look for him, but this is probably not the time to point that out.

"So," I say. "Long time, huh?"

"Uh," he says. "Yeah. I guess so?"

The door to the corridor slides open behind him, and two Security goons enter. They glance our way, and I'm pretty sure one of them shoots me a look before turning away. I spend about a half second wondering what his problem is, but not more than that. I've got bigger fish to fry at the moment.

"You seem confused," I say. "Two years, right? That's the last time I uploaded. Pretty sure that's the last time we talked."

His eyes slide to the side, then back up to mine.

"Yeah," he says. "That sounds about right."

"Two years. That's crazy, isn't it? What have you been doing with yourself? Not much work for an upload tech when nobody's uploading, right?"

His face hardens. "I'm a MedTech, Mickey. Just because all I ever did for you was uploads and downloads doesn't mean that's all I ever did. I've had plenty of work to do since you went AWOL." He takes a bite of his steak, chews, and swallows. "Unlike you, from what I hear."

My head snaps back as if he'd taken a swing at me. "Ouch! Sir, you wound me."

He glances around again, and his face twists into a scowl. "Look, Barnes, I'm really not in the mood for banter right now. What do you want?"

This is where I remember that I'm here to ask him for something, and that I probably should have been nicer from the jump. Time to backpedal.

"Right," I say. "Quinn. Friend. I was wondering—"

"No."

"No? I didn't even say what I wanted."

He leans back from his tray and folds his arms across his chest. "I don't need you to tell me what you want. I already know that I don't want to give it to you. You're visibly nervous, Barnes, and you're dancing around the topic. That tells me that you're about to ask for something big. Also, we're not friends, and you haven't spoken to me since the last time you came in for an upload two years ago. That tells me that whatever you're going to ask me for isn't personal. Ergo, you're about to ask me for something related to my job, and it's definitely something that's going to get me into serious trouble."

"No, I'm not . . . wait, why aren't we friends?"

Quinn tilts his head to one side and stares at me for an uncomfortably long time. Finally, he says, "Do you remember what happened the last time you uploaded?"

I have to think about that.

"Kind of? It was a long time ago."

"Yeah," he says. "It was right before all this bullshit with the creepers got started. You came in because you were going on some kind of reconnaissance thing with Gomez and you wanted to be current if you didn't make it back."

"I didn't, by the way."

He scowls. "Whatever. Point is, I tried to chat with you while I was setting up the rig—you know, like a friend would. Remember what you said to me?"

Okay, this is coming back to me now. "Look, Quinn—"

"You told me to shut the hell up and just do my goddamned job. Not really what a friend would say, is it?"

I sigh. "That was a long time ago, and it wasn't even me. That was Six. He's been dead for over two years now."

"Looked like you. Sounded like you. Acted like you. I'm gonna say it was you."

"Did I ever tell you about the Ship of Theseus?"

That stops him for a moment. "The what? No. No, and I don't want to hear about it. I also don't want to hear about whatever you're trying to weasel out of me now. Let me guess, though. You're bored, because unlike everyone else on this planet you've got no job, and you want me to swipe some drugs from the pharmacy to help you pass the time. Am I right?"

I open my mouth to reply, hesitate, then close it again.

"Right," he says. "Thought so. Piss off, Barnes."

"I am *not* looking for drugs."

He rolls his eyes. "Then what? Want a look at someone's medical records? Trying to figure out if some ghost chaser you banged has an STI?"

"No, and no. Look, Quinn, I think we got off on the wrong foot here—"

"You're not hearing me, Barnes. Whatever it is you want, I do not care. Let me repeat that. I. Do. Not. Care. You're so deep into Marshall's doghouse that you can't see the exit, and from where I sit it doesn't look like that's changing anytime soon. He can't shove you down the corpse hole because of whatever it is you've got hanging over his head. Fine. Good for you—but I've got no such protection. I'm just like everybody else but you on this rock. If I do something shady and it comes out, I'm screwed. More than that, if it comes out that whatever shady thing I did was for your benefit, Marshall is liable to take out all of that frustration about not being able to kill you by *double*-killing me. So, in short, my answer is no. Forget it. Screw off. Go to hell. Whatever it is you're looking for, you're going to have to look for it somewhere else. Are we clear on this, or do I need to call those Security guys over here to physically drag you away from my table? Not sure what their issue with you is, but when they came in I got the distinct impression that they wouldn't mind taking a chunk out of you."

"Um . . ."

He raises one eyebrow, and I find myself wondering if he really would try to get those guys to lay hands on me.

Probably best not to find out.

"Yeah, Quinn. We're clear. Have a nice day, huh?"

"WAIT," NASHA SAYS. "So you just asked him? Like, *Hey, there, Mr. Brock. Mind hooking me up with an illegal download of whatever stored memories you've got from the Expendables you've been illegally pulling out of the tank? I know Marshall probably told you he'd kill you if you told anybody that those memories even exist, but still. Can I get a peek?*"

"No," I say. "That's not what I said. I mean, that's kind of the gist of what I was planning to say, but I would have been a lot more eloquent."

We're back in our room now, huddled together on the bed. Nasha's sitting up, leaning into a pillow propped against the wall. I'm curled on my side with my head in her lap. We're in that weird time of day where unless you're on third shift it's too late for eating but too early to go to sleep. Back on Midgard this would be the time when you'd go for a walk, or see a show, or go to a club, or maybe just stream a vid. Here, though?

"Anyway, I didn't even get to the ask. He shut me down before I could work my way around to the question."

Nasha snickers, which I do not like, but at the same time she absently runs her fingers through my hair, which I do. "Didn't even let you get two words out, huh? How does that work? Much time as the two of you spent together, I thought you'd be friends."

I turn my head to look up at her. She's smirking.

"Apparently we are not friends. I'm not sure I've ever really told you how weird the whole upload process is, even setting aside the fact that it seemed like half the time I was uploading because I was dying. I never liked it, I got anxious bordering on panicky every time I had to do it—even the times that I wasn't bleeding out or choking on blood or dying of radiation poisoning—and I'm sure I probably took some of that out on Quinn over the years. Apparently I was particularly obnoxious the last time I came in, when I was Six. I had completely forgotten about that, but I guess Quinn hasn't."

"This should teach you, Mickey. It never hurts to be nice."

I bite her leg. She smacks the back of my head hard enough to briefly fuzz my vision, but she's laughing.

"Anyway," I say, "apparently Quinn has noticed that I'm an asshole when I upload, and he doesn't like it."

"Fine. But this isn't an upload you want, right? It's a download."

I snug my head back into her lap. "Yeah, and that's worse. I've never been conscious for a download before. Ordinarily you only download when you're trying to fill an empty head. I know it's possible to download into an active mind. They did forced learning that way back on Midgard. Not often, though, because it's super-unpleasant and also sometimes results in permanent psychosis."

Nasha's hand drops away from my head. "Permanent psychosis?"

"Only sometimes. Laying a whole new set of memories over top of the ones you already have isn't for the faint of heart, I guess."

"And you still want to do this?"

I roll over onto my back. "No, I don't *want* to." I sit up, and then scoot back until we're sitting shoulder to shoulder. "We've been through this, right? If I've got to put my head on Marshall's chopping block to keep the colony from going down, then I guess that's what I'll do. I couldn't give a rat's ass for most of the people in this dome, but you know I wouldn't let anything happen to you, or to Cat, or to Berto, even. I've got to know, though. I've got to know for sure. If I bring that bomb back here and it turns out that this was all some bullshit play to get me back under Marshall's thumb, I'm gonna be really, really pissed."

Nasha takes my hand and leans her head on my shoulder.

"I know, babe," she says. "Believe me, so am I."

THAT NIGHT, I dream about Eight.

More accurately, I dream about *being* Eight.

Most of my dreams are weird, fleeting things. This one is not. This one is photorealistic, more like a memory than a dream. I'm down in the creepers' labyrinth, wandering lost with an apocalypse bomb on my back.

The tunnels are just as I remember them—pitted bedrock, cut through with cross-trails, coal black in the visible spectrum, but glowing faintly in the infrared. I wind my way deeper, one hand on the bomb's trigger, wondering what I'm looking for, wondering whether I should just pull the rip cord and be done with it. Every few minutes, Seven checks in with me, tries to talk me out of what we're doing—but I believe what Marshall told me, and I want Nine to come out of the tank when this is done.

Did I actually try to talk him out of it? At this point, I can't remember.

Finally, I stumble through an arched opening and out onto a ledge overlooking the crèche. It's a nightmare pit, a space half the size of the dome, illuminated by a dull orange glow that seems to come from everywhere and nowhere, swarming with creepers. There are thousands of them, tens of thousands, crawling over and under one another, up the walls and across the ceiling. I snap a still frame and shoot it to Seven. This is the time, right? This has to be the time. My hand tightens on the trigger. I . . .

Wake up.

"Mickey?" Nasha whispers, her lips brushing my ear. "You okay?"

"Yeah," I roll over in the darkness until our foreheads are touching. "Was I talking?"

"No. Just breathing hard and twitching. Bad dream?"

"Sort of." I reach up to touch her cheek. She puts her hand over mine and squirms closer. "I was Eight, down in the labyrinth."

"Oh," she says. "Oh gods. Did you . . ."

"What? Die? No, I woke up right before."

She kisses me. "Good. You've got enough of your own deaths to dream about without having to worry about his too."

I roll over onto my back and sigh. "It was weird. It wasn't really like a dream. It was . . ."

She slides her arm across my belly and rests her head on my chest. "It was what?"

"Real," I say. "It was real. Like I was remembering it. Like it happened to me."

"Well," she says. "It kind of did, right?"

I pull her closer. "We've been over this. I wasn't Eight. Eight wasn't me. He was just a guy who looked like me and talked like me and put his hands all over my stuff."

"Maybe," she says, and I can hear in her voice that she's

already sliding back into sleep. "It kind of seems like your brain disagrees, though."

I GET A ping from Berto the next morning. He's bored, and he wants to know if I'm up for some hiking. I blink to my duty roster.

It's empty.

That's weird. I thought I was on tomato duty today.

I check tomorrow.

Empty.

Next day?

Empty.

Now I'm spooked. The only time you get three straight days duty-free on Niflheim is when you're dead. I send a query to the AI that runs human resources. A half second later it bounces back a note letting me know that my schedule has been cleared for the indefinite future, by order of Commander Marshall.

Oh well. After a quick check to make sure he hasn't canceled my rations as well, I bounce back to Berto and let him know I'm game.

"INDEFINITE LEAVE FROM duty? That sounds fantastic."

I glance over at Berto. I can't read his expression behind his rebreather, but there's no mockery in his voice.

"Does it, though? Because, to me, it kind of sounds like a threat."

Berto clambers up onto a block of broken stone jutting out from the fern-covered slope we've been climbing, then turns and offers me a hand up. He's carrying a pack bigger than the one I took down into the labyrinth, but for some reason I'm the one who can't seem to get enough air into his lungs.

"I don't follow," he says as he pulls me up beside him. "I'm basically on indefinite leave. I don't feel threatened at all."

We sit down on the edge of the block with our legs dangling, facing back toward the dome. I don't know how Berto is doing this, but even though I'm carrying nothing but a water bottle, I need a few minutes to breathe. For me, at least, climbing even a shallow grade while wearing a rebreather in an atmosphere that's less than ten percent oxygen is a workout.

That said, this is a beautiful day. It's hard to believe this is the same planet where we made landfall thirty months ago. The sun is a yellow ball in a pinkish-blue sky dotted with white puffs of clouds, and the terrain between here and the dome is a rolling blanket of green and purple vegetation, studded with the occasional granite outcrop or scrubby tree. The dome itself looks like a toy from this distance, an inverted cereal bowl surrounded by a ring of gossamer fairy towers. Days like this, I could almost start to like it here.

Unfortunately, days like this aren't going to last.

"I'm sure you're loving this," I say, and I'm not sure if I mean the time off or the climb or just the fact that we're stuck on this planet for the rest of our lives, however long that turns out to be. "But you and I are in very different situations, Berto. There's a reason you're on indefinite leave, and when that reason is over, you'll be back on regular duty. Not so for me."

"Yeah," he says. "I guess that's true. Also, so far as I know, Marshall doesn't actively want to kill me."

I sigh. "Also true. Even if he didn't want to kill *me*, though, there's no such thing as a permanent basic subsidy on a beachhead colony. Everybody knows that. If you don't work, you don't eat."

"So has he cut your rations?"

"Not yet. I think the implication is that my only duty right now is to retrieve that bomb."

"Okay," he says. "That sounds about right. So when are you going to do that?"

"Better question," I say. "*Am* I going to do that?"

He turns to look at me, shakes his head, then looks back toward the dome. "I had dinner with Dani last night. According to her, there's nothing wrong with the reactor itself. They ran a full diagnostic yesterday, and everything came back green. They're only running at eight percent of full capacity, though. I tried to get her to tell me why, but I honestly don't think she knows. All she said was that they'd been ordered to reduce fuel usage to the minimum necessary to sustain current operations."

"That's not really helpful, is it?"

"No," Berto says. "I guess not. Could mean we're actually running out of fuel, but yeah, could also mean Marshall is trying to manipulate you, if you're really feeling paranoid."

"Right—and I'm not going after the bomb until I know which one of those is true."

Berto pulls a protein bar from his vest pocket, peels off the wrapping, then lifts his rebreather and takes half of it in one bite. He offers the rest to me, but those things are nothing but compressed cycler paste, and I've had more of that in its original form than I want to remember. I shake my head. He shrugs, swallows, and then shoves the rest into his mouth.

"Well," he says with his mouth still full, then gags and has to pause to crack open a water bottle and wash the remains of the bar down his throat. "Wow. Those things are . . . not great."

I roll my eyes. "No shit."

"Anyway, as I was trying to say, you said yourself that Marshall's reaction seemed genuine when you talked to him about the reactor. Between that, what you saw in the corridor the other day, and what I've gotten from Dani, it seems pretty likely that something really is wrong, doesn't it? Is it exactly what Marshall says it is? Who knows? Hard to figure what else it could be, though, isn't it?" He pauses then, and stares off toward the dome. I can see his jaw working under the rebreather, muscles bunching and relaxing. Finally, he turns to me again. "Look, Mickey. I get why you don't want to do this, and I get why you want to know exactly what's going on—but really, you're just delaying at this point. You can keep doing that for a while, I guess. I mean, if you wanted to push it, you could just wait until the weather turns and things actually start going to pieces. Marshall's not about to let people start dying just to screw with you. If the reactor miraculously ramps back up to full capacity then, you'll have your answer."

"Uh-huh. And if it doesn't?"

He shrugs. "If it doesn't, you hustle over to your creeper pals and get that bomb back before anybody you actually like goes down, I guess."

We're only a klick or so from the bomb's hiding place right now. Fifteen minutes, and we could be there. Another hour, and we could be back to the dome. I could hand the damn thing over to Marshall and be done with it. And then . . .

Would he really kill me? At this point, I honestly don't know.

I'm about to say we should probably get going when Berto says, "What's Nasha think?"

I turn to look at him. "About what?"

He rolls his eyes. "About my new haircut, Mickey. About romantic poetry. About the price of tomatoes in the caf. What were we just talking about?"

"Right. The bomb."

"Yeah, Mickey. The bomb."

I shrug. "It's complicated. I mean, she doesn't want Marshall to get the opportunity to shove me down the corpse hole any more than I do."

"But?"

"But, yeah. She doesn't want to starve to death in the dark either."

"Well," Berto says, "it kinda seems like those are our two choices. Which way is she leaning?"

"I think she's pretty much where I am. If it's really me or the colony, I'll do what I have to do, but . . ."

"She wants to be sure."

"Yeah," I say. "She wants to be sure."

SITTING THERE ON that rock, sucking stale air through a rebreather and waiting for my blood oxygenation to get back up to something close to a normal range, I've got some time to actually contemplate the question of what Nasha might want. She loves me. I know that. She doesn't want bad things to happen to me.

But . . .

She's seen me die before. She's held my hand through it three times. Every time, I was back in a few hours, good as new. She can't help thinking about that, can she? Whatever she says about it being up to me and her not wanting me to lose the shield that's kept me alive for the past two years, there's no way it's not ticking over in the back of her head that I could just do it, could just go and get the bomb and hand it over and then whatever Marshall did to me there's at least a chance that I'd be right back there with her the next day. There's no way she's not at least contemplating the idea that me weighing my personal survival against the entire colony's is just a monumental act of selfishness, is there?

WHEN WE FINALLY get moving again, Berto drags me to the top of the hill, over the crest, and then partway down the back side.

We're well out of sight of the dome now, farther out than I've gone on foot since my days doing crevasse recon just after landfall. I'm just working up to asking Berto if he actually has a plan for the day or if we're just doing a random walk when we round a rocky outcrop and I find myself looking at a vista that stretches out so far that it fades out into atmospheric haze in the distance. Ten meters in front of us, the ground drops away. I walk up to the edge. It's an almost sheer drop-off for the first fifty meters or so. Below that is a long, steep slope of jagged rocks that goes on for another three or four hundred meters before it flattens out into grasslands again. If I had to guess, I'd say this is a place where the freeze-thaw cycle split a pretty sizable chunk of rock away from the hillside and dumped it into the valley not too long ago.

I wish I'd been there to see it. It must have been apocalyptic.

"Wow," I say. "Nice view. How did I not know this was here?"

Berto shoots me a grin. "I don't think we ever came this way on our bug hunts. I've been overflying this spot almost since landfall, though. Sweet, right?"

I sit down on the edge and lean forward to look down past my feet. There were plenty of bigger, better views back on Midgard, but this is one of the best things I've seen on this rock.

"Seriously, Berto. This is beautiful. I wouldn't have thought you were the type to spend a day walking to get to one good overlook, but I've got to tell you, I'm glad to be wrong."

Berto snorts, and I hear a thump as his pack hits the ground. When I turn, he's got it open and is starting to pull things out. "You're kidding, right? We didn't come here to sightsee, Mickey."

He's got a bundle of thin metal rods in his hands now. As I watch, he pulls them out and begins snapping them together. Eventually he's built a broad skeletal frame spanning seven or eight meters from tip to tip, propped up by a wide triangular grip attached to the underside.

"Berto? What are you doing?"

He looks up at me, grins, and hefts the thing he's built by the grip. "Come on, Mickey. Don't you recognize what this is?"

I give it one more once-over, then shake my head. "Honestly? I do not."

He sighs, sets the frame down, and pulls a bundle of fabric from the pack. It takes me until he's almost finished stretching it across the frame to realize what he's making.

"Is that a hang glider?"

He finishes making some final attachments before looking up again. "Brilliant! For that, you get to be the first to try it out."

I'm opening my mouth to say something along the lines of, *You've got to be freaking kidding me,* when he laughs and shakes his head. "I'm just yanking your chain, Mickey. There's no way I'm letting you pilot this thing. You're strictly here to record this moment for posterity."

There's a sling hanging from the frame now, just behind the grip. Berto steps through it, pulls a harness up between his legs and cinches it at his waist, then clips into the sling with a pair of carabiners and lifts the glider onto his shoulders.

"Technically," he says, "this isn't actually a hang glider. It's a powered ultralight." He gestures toward two metallic disks fixed to the frame on either side of him. "I managed to get hold of a couple of miniature Casimir drive units. They're only good for a few hours per charge, but if they die mid-flight, I figure I can always fly it the old-fashioned way, right?"

"How . . ." I begin, then hesitate, shake my head, and try again. "Where did you find a hang glider, Berto? Marshall wouldn't let me bring a tablet onto the *Drakkar* because of cargo restrictions. Did you really pack that thing all the way from Midgard?"

Berto laughs. "Find it? No, Mickey. I *built* it. The spars and fabric are from emergency bivouac kits. The drive units are from a mini-drone I scavenged from my lifter. Nice, right?"

"You built it. When? When did you have time to do this?"

His grin widens. "Yesterday afternoon."

I have a lot more questions, starting with, *What makes you think that thing will actually fly?* and ending with, *Are you insane?* Before I can get any of them out, though, Berto whoops, takes a running start, and flings himself off the cliff.

Years ago, back on Midgard, I watched a documentary about a guy named Jan Larsen. He'd managed to turn himself into a minor celebrity when I was in school by doing a series of increasingly stupid things. He started with BASE jumping off of buildings in downtown Kiruna. From there he moved on to stunts with a wing suit—flying through narrow gaps, waiting to pull his rescue chute until he was practically plowing into the ground, etc., etc. He finally killed himself while trying to do a solo jump out of a suborbital transport right at the apex of its hop, a hundred and eighty kilometers over the Northern Sea. His homemade heat shield failed, and he wound up turning himself into a shooting star.

Anyway, at one point they did a functional brain scan on him while subjecting him to different kinds of fear stimuli. They showed a side-by-side of his brain next to a normal person's. The normie's fear center was going crazy, flaring orange and red, but Jan's just sat there, flat, cold, and blue. Something wasn't hooked up right in there, and that part of his brain just wasn't functioning.

I've sometimes wondered if he and Berto might have been separated at birth.

For a solid second, maybe two, I'm convinced that I'm about to watch my best friend die. Berto turns nose-down and drops like a stone, and I have time to picture him broken on the rocks below before the glider catches air. He's still dropping, but increasingly slowly as he levels out and soars away from the cliff and over the grassland. Finally, when he's far enough away that I can barely separate his body from the glider, he banks to the left and begins to climb.

He stays up for a half hour or so, taking the glider through a series of increasingly terrifying maneuvers, ending with a wide loop before dropping down to skim by maybe twenty meters over my head and past the outcrop behind me. A few seconds later I hear another whoop, and then he's calling to me.

"Mickey! Did you see that? I pulled a full inside loop! Aaaaaahh! I can't believe I waited so long to do this!"

I round the outcrop to see him on the ground, thirty or forty meters away. He unclips his harness, turns to pump both fists in my direction, then crouches down to begin disassembling the glider as I make my way over to stand beside him.

"That was incredible," he says without looking up. "In-freaking-credible. I think what I just did was the closest that a human can come to being a bird without a whooooole lot of surgery."

"You could have died," I say. "You know that, right?"

He waves me off. "Nah. I knew this thing would work. Wasn't sure the airframe would stand up to that loop, but—"

"What if it hadn't?"

He stops working long enough to glance up at me. "Hadn't what?"

"What if the airframe hadn't stood up to the loop?"

"Oh." He shrugs. "Then I would have died." He folds the fabric carefully, then sets it aside and starts pulling the spars apart. "I didn't, though. You saw that, right? This is my new recon platform, my friend. These Casimir drives draw practically zero power, so there's really no way Marshall can object. Now that I know it works, I can launch under power from the roof of the dome. This is gonna be *awesome*."

I could object. I should object. This is a homemade, practically untested aircraft. Yeah, he made it through one thirty-minute shakedown flight, but if he actually starts taking this thing up on the regular, I can't believe that there's any possible way that it ends well for him.

On the other hand, this is the happiest I've seen Berto since . . .

Well, since forever, I guess.

"Come on," he says. "Help me get this stowed away."

His grin is infectious. I smile, and sigh, and fetch him his pack.

WE'RE JUST PAST the crest of the hill, almost back within sight of the dome, when we see the creeper.

Berto spots it first. He's walking ahead of me, practically bouncing with every step and saying something about seeing if he can knock another glider together for Nasha, and I'm just about to tell him to fuck right off with that idea when he freezes so abruptly that I almost walk into his pack.

"What?" I begin, but he holds up one hand and points with the other, and there it is, maybe eighty meters off. It's perched on top of a boulder, rear segments curled under it, front segments lifted up. This isn't one of the giants, but it's not an ancillary either. It looks to be maybe three meters long, with a half dozen or so brown-and-gold-mottled segments and two perpendicular sets of mandibles. It's facing away from us at the moment, looking down toward the dome.

"Mickey," Berto whispers. "You see that?"

"Yeah," I say. "I see it."

"Can you talk to it?"

I look up at him. I'm about to say something sarcastic when I remember that he thinks I've been in regular contact with the creepers for the past two years. He thinks I've been negotiating with them. Nasha's the only one who knows I'm completely full of shit.

Well. This is likely to be disappointing.

"Dunno," I say. "Let me give it a shot."

I step in front of Berto. The creeper is moving now, its head weaving slowly back and forth. What would it look like if I were actually communicating with this thing? I clench my jaw, squint my eyes, and lean forward slightly.

"Are you okay?" Berto asks. "You look like you've got the runs."

I shoot him a quick glare, then relax my face and turn back to the creeper. Just for yucks and grins, I blink to a chat window.

> <Mickey7>: Hello?
> <Mickey7>: Are you seeing this?
> <Mickey7>: If you are, we're not here to fight. Just passing
>   through, okay?

It stops moving.

Its head swivels around to face us.

"Is it talking to you?" Berto whispers. "What's it saying?"

I wave him off. The creeper and I stare each other down, and I have time to wonder what I'll do if it comes for us. Run, I guess? I'm pretty sure I could outrun one of the little ones. Not so sure about this guy, though.

Fortunately, I don't have to find out. After a long ten seconds, the creeper ducks behind the boulder and disappears.

When it's been gone long enough that we're sure it's not coming back, Berto lets his breath out in a rush, claps one hand to my shoulder, and says, "Nice work, Mick. What did you say to it?"

I look back at him and grin behind my rebreather.

"Honestly, Berto? You probably don't want to know."

THERE ARE LOTS of things to like about Union technology. It's allowed us to spread across our spiral arm like seeds on the wind. It keeps us warm and safe (mostly) in the cold vacuum of interstellar space. It takes in our garbage and spits out barely edible food. It allows us to live on planets like Niflheim, places where we honestly probably have no business living. There is one factor above all, though, that defines nearly every gadget and whatzit that the Union produces.

It's idiot-proof.

Nearly every device we brought with us to Niflheim is imbued with enough AI to allow it to be operated by almost anyone. If you think about it, this is an absolute necessity, given the way we travel. The typical crew complement on a colony mission is under two hundred adults, who are responsible for shepherding and protecting several thousand frozen embryos. That group has to include the seeds of everything that you'll need to form a fully functional technological society: administrators, doctors, lawyers, engineers, farmers, etc., etc., etc.

There's not a lot of room there for a guy who has an intimate knowledge of how to work the espresso machine. That thing needs to pretty much run itself.

That principle extends to just about every piece of tech on Niflheim. The agricultural specialists, the engineers, the medicos—they know what their equipment is for, and they hopefully know what to do with it and when, but when it comes down to it, making the machines work is mostly just a matter of telling them to go. The main limiting factor isn't expertise, in other words. It's having the appropriate permissions to turn things on.

All of which is just to say: technically, I don't really need Quinn to help me do a download. I know how to strap the helmet on. When I've done uploads, the only thing Quinn has actually done once I'm strapped in is to press his thumb to the authentication pad and tell it to do its thing.

That means, of course, that I do in fact need Quinn's thumb.

"No," Nasha says. "No way, Mickey. I am not stealing a man's thumb for you."

"Oh, come on." I lean my head against her shoulder and look up at her. "It's just one thumb. It's not like I need you to steal his whole hand."

We're back at the overlook that Berto launched himself from yesterday afternoon. I wanted Nasha to see this place. Unlike Berto, I thought she'd appreciate it as something more than a convenient place to kill yourself. I used to do a lot of backpacking back on Midgard, wandering around in the wilderness and looking for places like this to sit and think. I wanted to give Nasha a glimpse of that part of me.

Also, of course, I wanted to bring her someplace where we could talk without being overheard.

"Seriously," she says. "How do you expect this to work,

Mickey? I sneak up behind him with a pair of pinking shears? Snip, grab, and run?"

"Look, I haven't thought through all the details."

She laughs behind her rebreather, shakes her head, and leans back on her elbows. "Babe, the fact that you're here on this planet tells me everything I ever needed to know about your ability to think through all the details."

Yeah, that's a fair point.

"Look," she says. "What do you actually know about the lock on the download system? I mean, do we need his entire thumb? Is it a print reader? A DNA sniffer? Both?"

I shrug. "No idea. All I know is that he always had to put his thumb to the pad before it would go."

Nasha rolls her eyes. "You're hopeless, you know that?" She lolls her head back and looks up into the clear pink-blue sky. "If it's just a print reader, we could maybe . . . I don't know . . . get a scan of his thumbprint somehow? If we had that, we could mock up a duplicate with one of the small-bore printers."

"Huh." Down below us, something leaps from the cliff face, spreads two meters' worth of spidery wings, and soars off into the distance. "That's . . ."

Nasha sits up again and turns to look at me. "That's what?"

I point to the dwindling black vee out over the grassland.

"That's the first flying thing I've seen on Niflheim," I say. "Do you see it?"

"I see it," she says. "Can we focus, though?"

"I am focused. One of the things I'm focused on is that there's a ton of stuff on this planet that we have no idea about. I mean, what was that thing? It looked like what you'd get if a tarantula fucked a bat. What else are we missing, you know? The more of that kind of stuff I see, the less I want to kill myself based on a bunch of Miko Berrigan's assumptions."

She tilts her head to one side. "Assumptions? Like what?"

"I don't know. Like that it's gonna get cold again, and stay that way. Like that we actually need that antimatter back."

"That's not an assumption, Mickey. That's a science fact. This place was a snowball when we got here, remember? What possible reason would we have to think that it's not gonna be that way again?"

"I don't know. What reason would we have to think that it *will* be that way again?"

Her eyes narrow, and her cadence becomes slow and deliberate. "Thirty years' worth of observations, Mickey. Thirty years of watching this place from Midgard, and then two years of modeling from Berrigan's people since we got here, and also the basic fact that if it was cold as hell two years ago it's definitely going to be cold again someday because that's just how planets work. You're not making sense, babe."

"Thirty years' worth of observations from Midgard had them thinking this place was warm and wet, remember?"

She shakes her head. "Their observations were spot-on. They just blew the explanation. You know this, Mickey."

"Okay. So who's to say they're not blowing their predictions now?"

Nasha pulls her legs up under her, rocks back, and then pushes to her feet. "Look," she says. "I'm trying to be helpful here, but if you don't want to be serious about this, I'm out."

"No," I say. "Wait." I catch her hand. She makes a halfhearted effort to pull away, then sighs and sits back down. "I'm sorry. It's just . . ."

"Just what, Mickey?"

Just that I don't want to be serious about this. I don't want a solution to the problem of not knowing, because if we manage to steal Quinn's thumb or whatever and I find out that what Marshall told me is true, I'm gonna have to dig that bomb up and hand it over to him.

Can't say that, though.

"Just that I get off onto tangents sometimes and lose track of what we're actually supposed to be talking about," I say. "I'm focused now, though. Fake thumbs, right? So we don't actually need pinking shears?"

Nasha shrugs. "Maybe not. Depends on how serious they are about security on the download system."

"Why would they put heavy security on something like that? It's not like people are dying to find out what it's like to have terminal radiation poisoning."

"Yeah," Nasha says. "That's probably true. Fine. You get something with Quinn's print on it, and I'll see if I can figure out how to make us a thumb."

She gets to her feet again, then takes my hand and pulls me up beside her.

"Okay," I say. "What if it doesn't work?"

"Well," she says, "I guess then we can talk about breaking out the pinking shears."

On the way back to the dome, I almost hope to see the creeper again. Even though it didn't respond to my ping, there was something about our run-in with it yesterday that made me feel like we had some kind of connection. We don't, but as we crest the hill and start back down toward the dome, I'm pretty sure I see the spider-bat thing drift by, so high overhead that it's barely more than a black smudge against the light pink sky.

Getting Quinn's thumbprint turns out to be surprisingly easy. All it requires is me hanging around the caf for two hours like a homeless person, which I have no problem doing because as of two days ago I have no job. Around 14:00, Quinn comes in to get his lunch. He sits at a bench on the opposite side of the room, pretty much as far away from me as he can possibly be. There are a few other groups scattered around the room, but nobody seems to be paying either one of us much attention. Quinn eats his food, downs his recommended daily shot of vitamin/protein slurry, gets to his feet, and deposits his tray on the conveyor that will carry it back into the bowels of the food prep system. All I have to do is get to the conveyor after he's turned away and before his tray disappears, carefully grab his slurry cup, drop it into a medical sample bag, and make my escape.

This all goes swimmingly until I'm two steps from the corridor.

"Mickey? What are you doing?"

I stop and turn. Cat is sitting at a table with a bunch of other Security goons. She's staring at me.

"Oh," I say. "Hey, Cat."

I try to keep moving, but she's on her feet now and crossing the room toward me. I'm barely into the corridor before she catches my sleeve from behind.

"Hey," she says. "What the hell, Mickey? Hold up."

For one adrenaline-fueled moment I seriously consider yanking my arm free and running.

"Cat," I say. "I don't mean to be rude, but I've got a thing—"

She points to the jacket pocket where I stashed Quinn's mug. "Yeah. The thing you've got is a slurry cup you stole from somebody else's caf tray. What are you doing?"

I open my mouth, hesitate, then close it again. Cat takes a half step closer. "You know I'm legally authorized to beat this information out of you, right?"

I'm not sure that's true, but I've known Cat long enough to know that she could definitely do it if she wanted to.

"I needed something with Quinn's fingerprints on it. That's why I took the cup. I'll bring it back as soon as I'm done with it."

She tilts her head to one side. "You needed Quinn Brock's fingerprints. Why, exactly?"

I sigh. "So I can make a fake thumb."

She stares me down for a long five seconds.

"Fine," she says finally. "Don't tell me. When Marshall hauls you in for making voodoo dolls or love potions or whatever you're up to, though, don't expect me to vouch for you."

I force a laugh. She gives me one last look, then turns and heads back into the caf. I stand there for thirty seconds or so, half expecting her to come back out with her friends and haul me off to cup jail. She doesn't, though, and eventually I give a mental shrug, and I go.

"So that's it, huh?"

"Yeah," Nasha says. "That's it."

I turn the thumb over in my hand.

"It doesn't look like Quinn's thumb." I look at Nasha's hand, then back at the thing in my palm. "It looks like your thumb."

Nasha snatches it back from me. "Look, Mickey, this is the best I could do, okay? I didn't have Brock's thumb for a model, so I used mine. I had to call in a bunch of favors and throw down a couple of threats that I probably couldn't actually follow through on to get twenty minutes alone with the printer to make this thing. If it's not good enough, then I guess you're out of luck."

I stare at her. She stares at me.

"I'm sorry," I say finally. "It's a beautiful thumb, Nasha. In fact, it's probably the nicest thumb anyone has ever given me. Thank you."

At first her glare doesn't break, and I have two or three seconds to wonder whether I'm going to need to shift from mock-apology to groveling—but then she smiles, shoves me hard enough to knock me back onto our bed, and says, "Damn right it is. You need to work on your gratitude, boy."

She crosses the space between us in one quick stride, climbs onto the bed, and crouches over me. I pull her down on top of me and wrap my arms around her. She rolls us onto our sides, kisses me quickly, then pulls her face back far enough to look at me.

"If we do this," she says, "you really think you'll learn what you need to know?"

I close my eyes. When I open them again, the smile is gone from her face.

"I don't know. If they've really been sending copies of me into the reactor, then maybe?"

She leans her forehead against mine. "And what if you don't?"

I sigh. "If I don't, then I guess we're right back where we started."

She pushes me onto my back, then settles her head into the nook between my shoulder and neck. Somehow, despite the fact that this entire dome smells like body odor eighty percent of the time, her hair smells of jasmine.

"By the way," I say. "How did you do it?"

She stretches her arm across my chest. "Do what?"

"Convince somebody to let you make that thing. What possible reason could you give them for making a human thumb that wouldn't have them pinging Security?"

She nuzzles a little deeper into me. "It was Rosales. We've always been friendly, and she's been single since Midgard. She knows how it is."

"Oh." I run my hand down her back, then hesitate. "Wait, I think I missed something. She knows how what is?"

Nasha lifts her head. She's grinning.

"I told her it was a sex toy."

I DON'T REMEMBER a ton of stuff from the survey of ancient philosophy that I took during my first year at university, but there was one bit that stuck with me. It was about the execution of Socrates. He's been ordered to drink hemlock, because apparently the ancient Greeks didn't have access to cyanide and Socrates was too classy for a regular stabbing, and he's got until sundown to do it. His friends all want him to wait until the last possible minute, but Socrates? He chugs it down. If you've got to go, there's no point in waiting, right?

That's basically how I feel about using a fake thumb to possibly fry my brain. No point in putting it off. We catch a quick nap, Nasha and I, then wake just after midnight and head down to the med labs.

Medical is on the bottom level, not too far from the cycler. We don't talk on the way down. Nasha walks as if she's got somewhere important to be, and I follow along behind, head down, eyes darting from side to side, probably looking like an escaped criminal. When we reach the entrance to Medical, Nasha turns to me and says, "Do I need to use the thumb now?"

I shake my head. "I don't think so. I used to have unlimited access for uploads. Should still be active unless someone went to the trouble of locking me out."

I step past her and show my ocular to the scanner. The door slides open. We step through, and it slides shut behind us. We have to pass through two more doors and a short corridor to get to the regen room. It's a space a little bigger than a walk-in closet, crowded with equipment. Half the floor space is taken up by the tank, a gray metal coffin that can be programmed to churn out pretty much any kind of organic matter, but to my knowledge has never actually made anything other than copies of me. The rest is filled by a chair with binding straps for my forehead, wrists, and ankles, and the command console. The squid array sits on the seat of the chair, cables dangling to the floor.

"So," Nasha says. "This is it, huh?"

"Yeah," I say. "This is where the magic happens."

I pick up the helmet, turn it over in my hands, and then settle it onto my head. The contacts scrape against my scalp. I've never had to deal with the cables before, but I've seen Quinn do it enough times. There are two of them, both braided microfiber, one red and one green. They plug into the console. There are two slots there, just to the right of the thumb pad that makes the whole thing go.

The slots are identical.

Which cable goes to which slot?

"Mickey?" Nasha says. "You're not looking confident right now. Do you know what you're doing?"

"Yeah," I say. "Of course."

I look at the ends of the cables. Identical. I look at the slots. Identical.

Maybe it doesn't matter?

With a mental shrug, I shove the red lead into the top slot, and the green lead into the other. What's the worst that could happen?

I could fry my brain. That's the worst, I guess.

I take a seat.

"Okay," I say. "Strap me in."

Her face has taken on a look of concern, bordering on alarm.

"You sure about this, babe? This is starting to look an awful lot like an execution."

I force a grin. "I'm sure. This is all routine, Nasha. Let's do it."

So, she does. First ankles, then wrists, then forehead, closing the buckle around the front of the helmet.

"You good?"

I give the straps a tug.

"Yeah," I say. "I'm good."

She leans down to kiss me.

"Love you," she whispers.

"Yeah," I say. "I know."

She straightens then, and pulls the thumb from her pocket.

"Ready to see if this thing works?"

I close my eyes.

"Hit me."

So here's a fun story about live memory downloads. Eleven years, seven-plus lights, and six deaths ago, I asked Jemma Abera why I was wasting my time studying schematics and procedures and technical specifications. We had a memory download system. I'd be using it every time I took a trip to the tank anyway. Why not just pull up an archived memory from some other Expendable who knew all this stuff, and drop it into my skull?

"That's an excellent question," Jemma said. This was something that Jemma said frequently, despite the fact that her answers made it crystal clear that ninety percent of my questions were absolute garbage. We were in the storage closet that she'd converted into a classroom for me at the time, sitting across from one another at a tiny metal table with a tablet open between us. "Why don't you think about what you've been taught about memory downloads, and then tell me why that's not what we're going to do?"

I rolled my eyes. "Look, if it's a stupid idea, just say so."

"Okay," she said. "It's a stupid idea."

She looked at me, a smug smile tugging at the corners of her mouth.

"You know you can't leave it at that," I said. "You're dying to tell me exactly *why* it's a stupid idea."

Her face split into a grin. "You know me too well, Mickey. The reason it's a dumb idea is that memory uploads and downloads aren't selective. We don't know how to just pluck one thing out of your head—the schematics for an antimatter reaction chamber, for example—and we don't know how to put just one thing into your brain either. We could give you a download that we'd recorded from some other person who already knew all this stuff, but you wouldn't just get his technical knowledge. You'd get his favorite ice-cream flavor. You'd get his first kiss. You'd get the one thing in his life that he's most ashamed of. You'd get everything, Mickey—his entire personality. And, sad though it may be, the fact is that you've already got one of those. His memories and knowledge would be overlaid onto yours, which would probably be confusing at worst, but you get a lot more than memories with a download. You get a worldview, you get opinions, you get biases—and what happens if those fundamental beliefs about how the world works conflict with yours?"

"Oh, right. I guess that might be a problem, huh?"

She laughed. "You think? It's hard enough navigating this world with just one personality inside your skull. Nobody likes a rear-seat pilot."

I smiled. She smiled. I was about to say that we could go back to talking about antimatter rockets when she said, "I actually did try it once, you know."

"Tried? That doesn't sound promising."

She grinned and leaned back in her chair. "Depends on what you consider promising. This was maybe six years ago, just about a year after I signed on as a trainer here. We got clipped by a micrometeorite, and we needed someone to do an emergency patch job near one of the power cores. Problem was, the strike had punctured the radiation shielding, and the hole was wicked hot. Physics said it would be survivable, but none of the techs were willing to take on the gamma dose that would have been required to make the fix.

"Our Expendable at the time was a guy named Doran Gauss—a real prince, by the way. He came to us by way of a diversion program after his second conviction for sexual assault, and at one point during one of our training sessions he tried to . . . anyway, let's just say I wasn't too worried about frying his cortex. We had our chief technician do a full upload, then ran the download on Doran. The results were interesting."

"I'm going to assume you don't mean *interesting* in the sense that it worked great and everyone was really happy?"

She laughed then. Jemma had a great laugh. It's one of the few things I miss about my time on Himmel Station.

"Well," she said. "He got the patch done, and it held, so I guess Command was mostly happy. Doran, though . . . as far as I could tell, he had two different people in his head after that, and the part of him that was Chief Yahontov really, really didn't like the part of him that was Doran Gauss. At first he just had trouble sleeping. After a while, though, he started hurting himself. If he didn't pay attention all the time, his hands would creep up on him and go for his throat. A week or so after the download he managed to gouge one of his eyes out with a shrimp fork while he was supposed to be in his rack. After that, we had to sedate him and put him into restraints while he slept. It took about a month for him to walk out of an air lock in his underwear."

She looked at me. I looked at her.

"So," I said. "What you're saying is, this is not actually a good idea?"

She shrugged. "Not necessarily. You're no Doran Gauss. That man was a monster, and I can see why Yahontov's personality

wouldn't want to share a skull with him. The way that mani-
fested was pretty surprising—the case wound up getting a big
write-up in the scientific press, and for a while they were even
talking about trying to replicate the experiment with our next
Expendable, before the bioethicists shut that idea down—but the
basic problem was pretty predictable. What I'm saying, mostly, is
that you wouldn't invite someone to live in your apartment without making sure you're going to get along first, right? You should
probably apply at least that much thought to inviting someone to
live in your head."

So THAT'S WHAT I'm thinking about when Nasha mashes the
pad with her fake Quinn thumb: I wonder if these other Mickeys
are going to hate me. It's not like they wouldn't have totally valid
reasons to. I resigned, after all. If I hadn't, I would have been
the one going into the reactor to do whatever it was that Ling
and Marshall wanted done, and at least one of them would have
gotten to take over my life. From their perspective I'm the worst
kind of shirker—the Expendable who decided he didn't want to
die. I've been spending the past two years tending bunnies and
picking tomatoes and snuggling with Nasha. Their entire lives
probably consisted of coming out of the tank, getting irradiated,
and bleeding out. If I were in their shoes, I could see wanting to
borrow one of my hands one night to shank me in my sleep.

I'm just starting to think that maybe this isn't such a great idea
after all, that maybe I should tell her to stop, when she says,
"Should something be happening right now?"

I open my eyes. The restraints won't let me turn my head far
enough to see her. "Did you press the thumb onto the pad?"

"Yeah," she says. "I'm doing it right now."

I've never been conscious for a download, but I'm pretty sure
this isn't it.

"Sorry," I say. "I guess it's not a print reader after all. What now?"

She sighs. "Time to get the pinking shears, I guess."

The door slides open behind me.

"Pinking shears?"

"Oh shit," Nasha says. "Hey, Quinn."

I try to turn my head again, but the restraints are cranked down tight and the helmet won't budge. Doesn't matter, though. Quinn comes around and squats down in front of me.

"Mickey? What the hell are you doing here?"

"Oh," I say. "Hello, Quinn. What, ah . . . what brings you here?"

He glares at me. "*You* brought me here, idiot. The AI that monitors the facility pinged me to tell me that you'd come in for an upload." He looks up at Nasha. "Is that a thumb?"

"Not a real one," she says, and slides it into her pocket.

"Seriously," Quinn says. "What are you doing?" He stands and walks around behind me. "You've got the cables wrong, you know. They're set for *download*. What the hell, man? Are you trying to fry your brain?"

I hear the click of the restraints releasing, and my head comes free. Quinn pulls the helmet off of me, stows the cables, and then squats again to open the straps on my wrists and ankles.

"Look," I say. "I know this looks weird, but . . ."

Quinn stands and looks down at me. "But what, Mickey? If you wanted to upload for the first time in two years, why didn't you just ask me? That's my job, you know. And if you were actually trying to do a download . . . well, I have no idea what to say to that except that you need to get some help." He turns to Nasha. "And you, Adjaya. You're supposed to actually like this guy, right? You should have been talking him out of . . . whatever this is. Instead, you . . . actually, I don't know what you're doing here. And seriously, was that a fucking thumb?"

Storm clouds are gathering on Nasha's face, and it occurs to me that if I don't step in here it's likely that I'm about to see a man get beaten to death. I get to my feet and step between them.

"Look, Quinn. You're right, I should have asked you about this. The thing is, though—I actually tried to, the other day in the cafeteria. You remember? You wouldn't even let me get the question out."

His face goes blank for a moment.

"The caf? You didn't ask about an upload. You wanted drugs."

I roll my eyes. "No, Quinn. I did not want drugs. I told you that. I also didn't want an upload, though. I wanted a download."

Quinn looks at me, then over at Nasha, then back at me.

"A download."

"Yeah," I say. "A download."

"I . . . what the hell, Mickey? What the actual hell? You want to do a download into an active cortex—and it's *of your own memories*. For what possible reason could you want that? You've got early-onset dementia? You forgot where you left your wallet two years ago? You want to reminisce about freezing your ass off? What?"

I shake my head. "I don't want my own memories, Quinn."

"You . . ." He stops, glances over at Nasha again, then back to me. "Oh."

"What are we on by now? Nine? Ten? More?"

Quinn sighs. "Marshall would probably kill me if he knew I was telling you this, but I guess you've got the right to know. We've pulled two copies out of the tank since you quit—five days ago, both within a couple hours of each other."

"Right," I say. "I want one of their memories. The second one, I guess—Mickey10, right?"

Quinn shrugs apologetically. "Sorry, Mickey. Can't do that."

"They're his memories," Nasha says. "You've been using his body to do whatever you've been doing. You owe him this, Quinn."

Quinn turns to her. "First of all, *I* haven't been doing anything with Mickey's body. Marshall and Ling come in here and say they need a copy pulled, and I do what they tell me to do. That's my job. Once they walk out that door, it's out of my hands. Second, I don't disagree with you, okay? I didn't say I *won't* give you their memories back. I said I *can't*. The fact is, neither of them made it back here for an upload. Whatever Marshall needed them for, I can only assume that it killed them in a hurry." He turns back to me. "I'm sorry, man. I've got no memories to give you."

I meet Nasha's eyes. She pulls the thumb out of her pocket and holds it out to Quinn. "Prove it."

Quinn's eyebrows meet at the bridge of his nose. "What the hell?"

"He doesn't need that," I say. "He's got his own thumb, re-member?"

"Oh," Nasha says. "Right."

Quinn sidles past Nasha to the control panel and puts his thumb to the reader. The display panel lights up. "You know how to read this, right, Mickey?"

I move over to stand beside him. He's pulled up a menu of available downloads. The most recent time stamp is from over two years ago—the last time I uploaded, six weeks before Berto abandoned me in the creepers' labyrinth and Eight came out of the tank.

"I don't understand. They always made me upload before I died. Even after I took a beam of ions moving at point-nine-*c* to the back of the skull they managed to get me into the helmet before they let me go."

Quinn shrugs. "Like I said, these guys must have died quick."

"Maybe," Nasha says. "Or maybe Marshall doesn't want a record of what they were doing."

I shake my head. "Doesn't matter. They're not here. Sorry to get you out of bed for nothing, Quinn."

He looks back and forth between us. He really does look sorry, and I'm starting to wonder if maybe I should have given him a bit more of a chance over the years.

"No problem," he says. "I can't honestly say I'm sorry that there's nothing here to download, because I'd hate to be responsible for turning you into a raving psychotic, but I'm sorry I can't give you what you need. You're right. You ought to be able to find out what they're doing with your body."

"Thanks," I say. "Seriously, Quinn. I appreciate it."

I pat him on the shoulder and turn to go. Nasha and I are halfway out the door when he says, "Hey, that thumb—it's got my print on it, right? You thought you could use it to run the download without me."

Nasha stops and half-turns. "Maybe?"

"You can't. I mean, obviously. What kind of idiot would secure something this sensitive with a thumbprint? Still, though—can I have it back, please?"

Nasha looks at me. I shrug.

"Fine," she says. She pulls the thumb out of her pocket and tosses it to him.

"Thanks," he says. "I'm not sure what you could have done with it, honestly, but it seemed weird to have you running around with this thing."

Fair enough. I take Nasha's hand, and we go.

"So what now?"

We're back in our rack, curled up naked together in the sweaty half-dark.

"I don't know," Nasha says. "Seems like a dead end, doesn't it?"

"Berto said I should just wait until the weather turns. If they ramp the power back up then, I'll know it was all bullshit. If not . . ."

"If not," Nasha says, "people start dying."

Right. That.

"I know where the fuel is. It would take me a couple of hours, tops, to get it back. I don't have to do it now. I really could wait until the weather turns."

"And what if bringing the fuel back doesn't solve the problem?"

I shrug. "If that doesn't solve the problem, then I'd say we're boned."

"Maybe," she says. "Find that out now, though, and we might have time to come up with a plan B. Find out when the snow has started flying, and this colony dies."

That hangs in the air between us for a solid ten seconds.

"You want me to go," I say finally.

She props herself up on one elbow to look down at me.

"No, babe, I don't want you to go. I don't want you throwing yourself on Marshall's mercy any more than you do. But Mickey, we've sacrificed so much for this colony. *You've* sacrificed so much for this colony. What Four went through, and Five, and Six, and Eight . . . if this place goes down, if everybody dies, that was all for nothing. *That's* what I don't want. I don't want to have watched you lay your head on the block so many times, and then find out that it didn't mean anything at all." She leans down to kiss me. "Also, I don't want to starve to death in the dark."

Yeah, that's a fair point.

"Look," she says, rolls away, and folds her hands behind her head. "If you bring back that bomb, I will make sure it's known that you did it, and that you doing it saved our asses. If Marshall takes you out after that, he'll have a rebellion on his hands.

You've said it before, babe—he's an asshole, but he's not an idiot. However much he may want to kill you, if you do this, I don't think he'll have the juice to do it."

I sigh. "You're willing to bet my life on that, huh?"

She turns her head to look at me. "I'm willing to bet *our* lives on it. If Security comes for you, they'll have to go through me first."

And that's the sort of thing that people say, of course. Most of the time, it's just empty words when the shit comes down. Somehow, though, with Nasha I don't think that's the case, and I feel a sudden stab of shame for thinking that she might be just as happy to watch me go down the corpse hole and then start over with Mickey11. I mean, I'm not under any illusion that she could actually protect me. Despite all appearances and attitude, she's not actually some kind of warrior goddess.

I'm not sure *she* knows that, though. She might not be able to stop Marshall's people from taking me, but I have a deep suspicion that she'd be willing to die trying. I snake one arm under her shoulders and pull her closer.

"Okay," I whisper. "I'll do it."

She strokes my cheek with one hand. "You're a good guy, Mickey. That bastard won't lay a hand on you."

I close my eyes and breathe in, breathe out. I guess we're about to see.

WE WAKE TO a beautiful morning. Looks like it rained while we were sleeping, but by the time Nasha and I step out of the main lock the sun is halfway up in a pastel-pink sky. I look over at her. Hard to read her expression behind the rebreather, but from the way she keeps touching me I'm starting to feel like she's afraid I'm going to just disappear.

"You don't have to come," I say.

Her eyes narrow. "Don't be an ass."

Okay, then.

I haven't been to visit the bomb since that day two years ago when I showed Nasha its hiding place. I wanted to. More than once I've woken up from dreams where one of our people stumbled across it and triggered it somehow, and the last thing I see is a flash of white light as the colony disappears. I didn't, though, because I was afraid Marshall might be tracking my movements.

Which leads me to wonder: What if he's tracking me right now? What would he do if he found out that the creepers never had the bomb, that it's been hidden under a rock pile all this time?

I don't have to wonder that much. Seems pretty clear that he'd kill me.

There's not much to be done about it, of course—but still, I try. We head up into the hills north of the dome first, mostly toward the cliff Berto showed me rather than toward the bomb. The ferns are knee-high on the hillsides, and little eight-legged lizard things are everywhere, scuttling away from our feet and leaping up onto the rocky outcrops to watch us. Once we're past the first crest and out of sight of the dome, I turn back across the slope and start working my way toward the bomb's hiding place. I'm feeling pretty proud of my spycraft when Nasha says, "You know we've got drones, right?"

I turn to look at her. "What?"

"We've got drones," she says. "If Marshall wants to know what you're up to, he doesn't have to stand on top of the dome with a pair of binoculars. He just needs to put a drone on you. He could be tracking us right now. Hell, he could be listening to this conversation if he wanted to."

I look up and turn a full circle. There's nothing overhead but a few wispy white clouds. Nasha sighs. "You're looking for a drone."

"Yeah. The sky is crystal clear. I'd be able to see it if one were up there, right?"

Nasha pulls the burner from her hip holster and sights off into the distance. "You see that hilltop?"

I squint in the direction she's pointing. It's a little hazy, but I'm pretty sure I can make out the one she means. "Yeah. So?"

"Push the mag on your ocular to maximum and then pick out a rock on that hillside—one maybe a meter across or less. Point it out to me."

Oh. I see where she's going here.

"That hillside," she says, "is, according to the range finder on my weapon, about three klicks off."

"Right. Which I assume is also roughly the altitude at which the drone that Marshall may or may not have following us would be flying."

Nasha taps her temple with one finger. "A standard surveillance drone is less than a meter across, and their underside mimics what the sky would look like from below. There could be a dozen of them up there right now, and we'd never know it."

"Oh." We walk a little farther. "Do you think there are?"

Nasha shrugs. "Probably not. I honestly don't think Marshall cares where you're going, as long as you come back with the bomb."

Yeah, she's probably right about that. We keep walking.

The place where I hid the bomb hasn't changed much. It's an ice-carved gully near the base of a massive granite outcropping. We pick our way down the rocky slope. There's the boulder I used as my landmark. Twenty meters upslope from there . . .

Twenty meters upslope from there is an empty hollow under a rock overhang.

Suddenly I'm very conscious of my heartbeat.

"Mickey?" Nasha says.

I don't respond.

She nudges me.

"Mickey? Where is it?"

I shake my head. "Doesn't matter."

She pulls me around to face her. Her eyes widen when she sees my expression.

"Doesn't matter where it is," I say. "The important point here is where it's *not*."

WE HAVE A long, silent walk back to the dome, Nasha and I. We're almost there, just a few hundred meters out from the perimeter, when she says, "I told you it was a stupid idea."

I stop. She walks on for a few more paces, then turns to face me.

"What?" I say. "Going to find the bomb?"

She closes her eyes and sighs behind her rebreather. "No, Mickey. Not going to find the bomb. Hiding it the way you did in the first place. I told you two years ago, when you first showed it to me. For shit's sake, that was a doomsday weapon! You buried it under some rocks like a goddamned pirate's treasure. There was no way this was ever going to end well."

"No," I say. "No, no, no. I remember that day, Nasha. Yeah, you said it was a dumb idea. *I* said it was a dumb idea. I just didn't have a better one, and neither did you."

She starts to reply, then stops and shakes her head. "I don't understand what happened. If a human had found that thing, they would have turned it over to Marshall. That, or accidentally set it off, I guess. Is it possible Marshall really has just been playing with you this whole time?"

I have to think about that for a minute.

"Maybe? Why, though? This seems like a lot of effort to go to just to make me squirm."

"I don't know," Nasha says. "I don't—"

"Does it help him to catch me in a lie?"

"Huh." She digs a finger under the rebreather strap at the crown of her head, scratches, and then resets her seals. "Depends, I guess."

"On what?"

"On what he's planning on doing to you now. If the idea is to shove you down the corpse hole, it might be helpful from a PR standpoint to prove that you've been jerking us around about this thing for the last two years. Traitor to the Union and all that, right?"

I shrug. "I guess. If he's got the bomb, though, doesn't he know that already?"

"Right. Right." A half dozen long, spiny legs poke up out of the soil between us. Before whatever it is has a chance to fully emerge, Nasha has drawn her burner and vaporized it. "Look, though. Marshall's pulled two copies of you out of the tank in the last week, right? What did he do with them?"

I stare at her as she holsters her weapon. That might have been the fastest that I've ever seen someone move, and it's not even clear to me that she noticed what her right hand was doing.

"That's, uh . . . that's what we were trying to find out with the download thing, right?"

"Yeah," she says. "But that didn't work, so we have to speculate. What's the last thing he asked you to do before you resigned?"

Oh. Right.

"He asked me to return the fuel from my bomb to the reactor."

Nasha taps one finger to her temple, then turns and starts walking again. After a moment's hesitation, I follow.

*   *   *

BERTO DROPS INTO my desk chair and runs his hands back through his hair. "You're kidding."

Nasha shakes her head. "He is not."

"You hid it."

"Yeah," I say. I'm pacing, which is pretty unsatisfying in a three-by-four space that's ninety percent full of stuff. "I hid it."

"Under a rock pile. You hid the most dangerous object on this planet under a rock pile."

Nasha sighs, pulls her feet up onto the bed, and leans back against the wall. "Yes."

"And you left it there. For two . . . goddamned . . . years."

"Fine," I say. "I get it. Not my finest moment, but I didn't have a lot of good options."

"And now it's gone."

Nasha sighs again, louder this time. "Get past it, Berto. We didn't bring you in on this so that you could tell Mickey how stupid he is."

He rounds on her now. "How stupid *he* is? What about you, Nasha? You were in on this from the start, right? If I'm understanding this correctly, he showed you where he buried that thing two years ago. What the absolute hell were you thinking?"

"I was thinking I wanted Mickey to stay alive," she says, voice ice-cold now. "I guess that's where you and I are not on the same page."

Berto's eyes narrow and he starts to reply, but I cut him off before he can start something that he's not going to be able to finish. "Look, Berto, we can all agree that this hasn't turned out the way I hoped it would. Mistakes were made, okay? But Nasha's right. We need to decide what to do now, not what we should have done two years ago."

He looks like he has something more to say on the topic, but after a moment's hesitation he pulls in a deep breath, holds it, and then lets it back out. "Fine. Fine. You're right. This isn't the time to worry about how your dumbassery has doomed us all to freezing to death in the dark. Let's try to figure out if there's any possible way we can get un-doomed."

"Right," Nasha says. "If Marshall has the bomb—"

"Marshall doesn't have it," Berto says.

"You don't know that."

"Yeah," Berto says. "I do. Mickey's still alive. If Marshall had the bomb, Mickey would be seventy kilos of slurry right now."

"But—"

"No," Berto says. "You two are overthinking this. Marshall isn't some kind of super-villain from an adventure vid. I know you think he's a monster, Mickey, and from your perspective I guess he probably is, but he's also a down-the-line administrator who is very focused on keeping this colony alive. If he had the bomb, he would have ordered you to feed the fuel elements back into the reactor. If you refused, he would have shoved you into the cycler, pulled a new you out of the tank, and ordered him to feed the fuel elements back into the reactor. What he would definitely not have done was wasted valuable time playing some kind of fucked-up mind game with you. So, the fact that you're still alive tells me that Marshall definitely does not have the bomb."

"We thought about all that," Nasha says. "Remember, though: Marshall pulled two copies of Mickey out of the tank this week."

Berto shrugs. "So Mickey says, based on one unconfirmed sighting. I've known cryptids with a better evidence base."

"No," Nasha says. "We've got confirmation on that part, at least. Quinn Brock admitted that he pulled two copies within a few hours of each other five days ago."

"Huh." Berto leans back in his chair and scratches his chin. "That's interesting. Does it change anything, though? I mean, did Quinn tell you what Marshall did with them?"

I shake my head. "He didn't know. He did say Maggie Ling was with Marshall, though. If Marshall told me the truth about that whole spoiling business, I guess they might have been dealing with whatever damage was done to the reactor itself by that mess. I don't have a ton of confidence in Marshall to tell me the truth right now, though."

"Maybe," Berto says. He sits silent for a moment, then shakes his head. "No. No, I'm not buying it. If Marshall has the bomb and he's already used copies of Mickey to feed the fuel back into the reactor, what possible reason would he have to keep you around? I think I'm back to my original position. The fact that Mickey is alive is proof positive that Marshall doesn't have the bomb."

Nasha looks at Berto, then at me. I shrug. He makes some good points.

"Fine," Nasha says. "Marshall doesn't have it. Who does?"

"Well," Berto says, "I guess there's an off chance one of our people might have found it and then not turned it over."

"Why?" Nasha says. "Why would anyone do that?"

Berto shrugs. "Didn't know what it was? Wanted to keep it for themselves? Planning to strong-arm Marshall into tuning the cycler to make whiskey instead of slurry? I don't know, Nasha. I'm just throwing out the possibility."

"No," Nasha says. "I'm not buying that one at all. If one of our people had found the bomb, they would have either turned it over to Marshall or accidentally killed us all by now."

"Okay," I say. "Marshall doesn't have it. Nobody else has it. Where . . ."

I trail off. Berto is grinning now, hands folded behind his head.

"What have you been telling Marshall for the past two years, Mickey? The creepers have the bomb, right? Congratulations, buddy. Looks like those little fuckers finally made you an honest man."

<Mickey7>: Hello?

<Mickey7>: Are you still listening?

<Mickey7>: I know it's been a while, but . . .

<Mickey7>: Please.

<Mickey7>: We need to talk.

"I'M COMING WITH you."

I pull my head out of the gear locker I'd been rooting through. Nasha is standing there, arms folded across her chest.

"I'm not going anywhere," I say. "I was just—"

Nasha rolls her eyes. "You've got an overloaded pack and two rebreathers laid out on the floor, Mickey. What am I supposed to think you're doing here?"

I sigh. "Marshall called me in after breakfast. He wanted an update on the negotiations."

"Okay. What does that have to do with the fact that you're packing up for some kind of expedition?"

"I told him things were at a delicate point."

"And?"

"And he told me negotiations of this magnitude are best concluded face-to-face."

Nasha breaks into a grin. "Do creepers even have faces?"

I dig back into the locker, pull out a box of protein bars, and stuff it into the pack. "Not the point. The point is, I'm going into the labyrinth, and you're not invited."

Nasha shakes her head, pops the locker next to mine and pulls out a rebreather, then walks over to the weapons rack and pulls down a linear accelerator.

"Seriously," I say. "You can't come with me, Nasha."

She straps the accelerator across her back and picks up a burner. "Yeah. I heard you."

"I haven't talked to them in two years. For all I know, they're just gonna tear me to pieces as soon as they see me."

"Seems totally possible. What's with all the gear?"

That stops me.

"It can't be more than a half-day's walk to get where you're going," she says. "Why are you packing like you're going on a journey?"

"Oh. Well. If they don't immediately tear me to pieces, I'm thinking this might actually take some negotiation, and I doubt they'll have anything for me to eat."

"Huh," she says. "Fair point."

She pulls a pack from her locker, digs around a bit, then pulls out a half dozen tubes of slurry and stows them away.

"Nasha. Stop." She turns to look at me. Her eyes are slitted and her mouth is a thin, hard line. "Look, there is a very good chance that this is going to end badly, okay? You can't come with me. You're not an Expendable."

"Neither are you," she says. "Remember?"

And the hell of it is, I actually hadn't remembered, not until she said it. I haven't uploaded in over two years now. Even if Marshall winds up pulling another Mickey Barnes out of the tank when I'm dead, it won't be me.

Nasha's face softens. She takes a half step toward me and touches my shoulder with one hand. "You're not an Expendable, babe. You're just Mickey Barnes now. That means you don't have to die for me anymore." She puts one hand behind my neck and pulls me to her until our foreheads touch. "That means you don't *get* to die for me anymore." She kisses me softly, and then brings her mouth close to my ear. "I'm coming with you," she whispers, "and if you give me one more word of shit about it, I'll break both of your legs, and then neither one of us will go."

* * *

THERE ARE TWO entrances to the creepers' labyrinth that I know of. The closer of the two is the one I came out of on the night two years ago when Berto left me to die. It's only a couple of klicks south of the dome, and not too far from the place where the bomb was hidden. The other is the hole that got me lost down there in the first place. If we had air transport, I'd probably go for that one. I definitely got the impression, just based on the layout of the place, that that one is more of a central hub. We don't, though. Our lifters are grounded until further notice, and after making a few discreet inquiries Nasha tells me that they're not making exceptions for colony-saving expeditions.

So we head out through the main lock, and we start walking.

The temperature has dropped at least fifteen degrees since yesterday, and the sun is a wan yellow smudge behind a high, thin layer of clouds. I'm carrying a pack stuffed with twenty kilos of food, water, and basic survival gear. Nasha is carrying two handheld burners, a long-barreled linear accelerator, and a wider range of ammunition types than I'd known existed. I'm not sure what good she thinks all of that is likely to do if the creepers decide to take us, but it makes her feel better to have it.

It makes me feel better to have her.

We're through the perimeter and just topping the first rise beyond when Nasha says, "So I know it's a little late to be asking, but what, exactly, is the plan?"

I glance back at her. "Go down into the labyrinth. Find one of the big creepers. Ask it for the bomb back."

We walk in silence for a half dozen steps.

"Okay. That's an outline, I guess. Don't suppose you've got any more detail?"

"Nope."

"Have you always been like this?"

I stop walking and turn to look at her. "Like what?"

"Like this," she says, and waves her arm at me. "Just drifting through life like a jellyfish, hoping everything's gonna work out."

I shrug. "Yeah, kinda."

"And it always just does, huh?"

"Well," I say. "Not always. Drifting through life is what got me onto this expedition, remember? So far it's gotten me irradiated twice, killed by lung worms, gut worms, and brain worms once each, and, as a capper, slowly vivisected." I grin behind my rebreather. "On the other hand, though, it also got me you—so I guess I'm calling it a win."

We keep walking. The dome is out of sight behind us when she says, "You really can talk to them, right? That part wasn't bullshit?"

"I could. I'm honestly not sure if I still can. I tried to ping them last night. They didn't answer me."

"Huh. And if it turns out you can't?"

"I don't know," I say. "Sign language? Hand puppets? How are you with interpretive dance?"

She shoves me, hard enough to make me stumble under the weight of my pack. "You're gonna get me killed today, aren't you?"

I sigh. "I hope not, Nasha. I really, really hope not." I don't add that there's a reason I told her to stay home. I don't *think* she was serious about breaking my legs, but I'm not inclined to put her to the test.

After an hour or so of walking, we reach the head of the gully that leads down to the bomb's old hiding spot. I have to stop here to get my bearings. We're on a steep, rocky slope dotted with clumps of greenery here and there. It's not a trail I'm looking for, exactly, but there should be a route that's a bit more walkable . . .

Yeah, there it is. It looks very different without two meters of snowpack smoothing it over, but there's definitely what almost looks like an old logging road winding its way through the scrub above us. All we have to do is follow that for another half kilometer or so, and we should find a hole cut into the hillside.

"We're almost there," I say. "Last chance to turn around."

"Oh no," she says. "Don't start up with that shit again."

Okay, then.

The entrance is closer than I remember, so much so that I almost miss it. It's Nasha who spots it, twenty meters upslope from us as we're trudging by. It's smaller than I remember too—only a meter or so across at the widest point.

"That's it?" Nasha says.

"Yeah," I say. "I think so, anyway."

She crouches down to peer inside. "You sure this is a good idea?"

"I don't know how many other ways there are for me to tell you that it's not."

She pulls a light from a pouch at her belt, clips it over her right shoulder, and turns it on.

"I should go first," I say.

She shakes her head. "You're the diplomat, remember? The muscle goes first." She draws one of her burners and points the targeting laser down into the hole.

I take a half step back and shrug. "Fine. It's not like they're gonna fill up on one of us and let the other one go. After you."

She turns to me and winks, then gives me a mock salute with her burner and goes.

THE HISTORY OF humanity's interactions with alien intelligences is depressingly thin. The Union occupies forty-eight worlds at this point, spread over a volume of space roughly sixty lights across. Almost all of those planets were at least marginally habitable before we showed up. You'd think at least a few of them would have had technologically advanced locals there waiting for us, right?

Not really.

There are intelligent natives on Long Shot, but so far as I know we've never really interacted with them in any meaningful way. They're basically arboreal squids, and their range is strictly limited to a single impenetrable jungle in the mountains at the heart of the planet's only continent. We made landfall on the coast, and as humans tend to do, we've pretty much stayed near the ocean ever since. There have been a few efforts to make contact, but the natives haven't shown much interest in the project, so it's never really gone anywhere.

There were intelligent natives on Roanoke. We never interacted with them because by the time we figured out they were there, they'd killed us all dead.

As far as confirmed advanced intelligences in Union space, that's pretty much it. There's one other probable, but we don't talk about that one much, mostly because we like to be able to get to sleep at night. Twelve lights spinward of Eden there's a main-sequence yellow star with a mass almost exactly that of Earth's sun. Orbiting that star, dead center in its Goldilocks zone, is a rocky little planet that observations from Eden showed to have an oxygen-nitrogen atmosphere with a healthy dose of water vapor. It's probably the best target we've identified in the thousand years of the Diaspora, and the good folks of Eden made it the goal of the first colony expedition they attempted, just over a hundred years after their own landfall.

Twelve lights is a long jump, but not a crazy-long one. By all reports, the trip went as well as it could have. Unlike us, for example, they didn't hit any rocks at relativistic speed, didn't need to send any of their people out onto the skin of the ship to get fatally irradiated, didn't have to sacrifice anybody at all to any of the various gods of deep space, in fact. They made turnaround right on time, were well into the deceleration phase of the journey, were most of the way through their new home's Oort cloud when they just . . .

Vanished.

We don't know exactly what happened to them. They were transmitting continuously, though, so we know they weren't aware that anything was amiss right up until the moment that they died. We're pretty confident that they didn't suffer any sort of catastrophic violence, because if they had, their remaining fuel stores would almost certainly have gone up, and that kind of blast would have been observable even from twelve lights away.

We do know that four hundred years later, Eden's daughter world Acadia mounted their own expedition to the same target.

Their ship disappeared in exactly the same way, at exactly the same point in their journey.

Colonization attempts fail. Colony ships, though, don't just vanish—not by themselves, anyway. It's hard not to conclude that somebody's at home in that system, and they don't want visitors.

If you accept that, it's also hard not to conclude that whoever they are, they have capabilities that are as far beyond ours as ours are beyond those of your average anthill.

There was some loose talk after the second loss about sending them a *Bullet*. They were sitting there, right in the middle of Union space, and they clearly had the capacity to do us harm. Fortunately, though, cooler heads prevailed. I'd like to say we left them in peace because we realized that we were the interlopers, that they had no reason to think that our incoming ships were in any way benign, and that they had every right to defend their home system. I'd like to say it was a moral decision.

It wasn't, though. We left them alone because we had no idea how they'd done what they'd done to those ships, and they scared the shit out of us.

My point, I guess, is that I don't have a lot of history or experience to draw on here. As far as I know, I'm humanity's first serious emissary to an alien intelligence.

I really hope I don't fuck this up.

I REMEMBER BEING hot the last time I was down here.

"You could have warned me about this," Nasha says, as a fine mist of condensation forms around her rebreather. "I could have packed a thermal."

The last time I was here, of course, it was below zero outside, and I was dressed accordingly. It's probably the exact same temperature down here now that it was then, but it feels distinctly chilly in nothing but a jumper and a single-layer skin suit.

"Sorry. I'm not any better dressed for this than you are, you know."

We've been underground for most of an hour by now, working our way gradually deeper through a mix of clean-cut tunnels and what appear to be natural seams in the rock. We haven't yet seen any signs of habitation. We've just reached a crossroads, with a smaller, rough-cut tunnel slanting upward, and two larger ones forking off to our right and left. Nasha leans back and plays the light clipped to her shoulder up the smaller one.

"Think that runs to the surface?"

I shrug. "Probably? It's too small for the big creepers to fit into, so I'd guess it's either a quick exit for the little ones, or maybe an air shaft."

"Huh." She turns to face the two larger tunnels. "Which way?"

I shine my light down one tunnel, then the other. "No idea. They both look pretty ominous to me."

"Are they talking to you yet?"

"Not yet. Maybe not ever. It's been two years. The comm gear they took out of Six might have failed by now."

She sighs. "Interpretive dancing aside, this is gonna be a really short negotiation if we can't speak to them." She steps closer to the wall, reaches up, and runs one finger along a shallow groove that spirals down through the stone before petering out a meter or so above the floor. "You think they used machines to cut these tunnels?"

I move over to stand beside her. "I'm not sure they make a distinction between themselves and their machines. The little ones are definitely hybrids. Wouldn't surprise me if the bigger ones are as well."

She slides her arm around my waist. "Seriously, Mickey—what happens if they can't talk to us? Or if they won't?"

"In that case, I'd imagine we die. That's kind of why I didn't want you with me down here, you know?"

She leans the side of her head against mine. "If that's the way it plays out, we're all finished, aren't we? If not now, then whenever the weather turns."

I sigh. "Yeah, it seems likely. Probably not by freezing, though. If we can't get the bomb back by asking nicely, Marshall will have to try to get it back by force. No way he just squats in the dome and waits for death."

"No," Nasha says. "Waiting for stuff to happen isn't his thing, is it? You think he could pull it off?"

"You'd know better than me. Our biggest advantage is our lifters, but they're no use if the creepers stay in their tunnels. We'd need to draw them out into the open, and I don't know how we'd manage it. As far as fighting down here goes, we've got plenty of accelerators, and we can make more, I guess. How many people could we pull together who know how to use them?"

She turns to look at me. "You know how to use an accelerator, babe."

"Yeah, but . . ."

And then I see where she's going.

"He wouldn't."

She tilts her head to one side. "You don't think so?"

"Leaving aside Marshall's religious objections to multiples, which I'm guessing he'd forget about pretty quickly if the colony's survival was on the line, every copy of me that he pulls out of the tank takes seventy thousand kcal out of our energy budget. That's not even considering the calcium and phosphorus and trace minerals. How many of me could he make without bleeding our stores completely dry?"

"He wouldn't care about bleeding our stores dry," Nasha says. "If he gets the bomb back, he's got plenty of power again, right? That means he can run the cycler all day for a month if he wants."

Which means that all those Mickeys, after saving the colony, would be rewarded by immediately getting converted back into nutrients and trace elements.

"That's dark," I say. "You really think Marshall would go down that road?"

"If he thought it would work? Hell, yes."

"And would it?"

"No idea," Nasha says. "How many creepers are there down here?"

I think back to the still image Eight sent me just before he died. "Lots. Enough that I don't think it matters how many Mickeys Marshall could pull out to fight them."

"He'll probably try anyway, you know."

"Yeah," I say. "Probably."

She leans into me. "If it comes to that, I guess I'd just as soon go down today with you. Not sure I'd want to live in a colony that would be willing to go that far."

I take her hand where it rests on my hip and give it a squeeze. She sighs again, straightens, and steps back from the wall.

"I've got a good feeling about this one," she says, and gestures to the tunnel on the right. She pats my shoulder, turns, and goes. After one last glance at that cut in the rock, I follow her down.

      \<Mickey7\>: Hello?
      \<Mickey7\>: I hope you're reading this. We've come to talk.
      \<Mickey7\>: We're in the tunnels now, hoping to make contact.
      \<Mickey7\>: This is important, for both of us.
      \<Mickey7\>: Hello?
      \<Mickey7\>: Can you hear me?

IT'S MAYBE TWENTY minutes later when we run across our first creeper. We're in a gradually upsloping tunnel and I'm thinking about maybe turning around and heading back to the last crossroads when it shows up in the wash of Nasha's shoulder light, maybe twenty meters ahead of us. It's one of the small ones, milky-white and a meter or so long, with a dozen legs and a pair of wickedly sharp-looking mandibles on its front segment. Nasha curses under her breath and reaches over her shoulder for the linear accelerator, but I cover her hand with mine and whisper, "Wait."

The creeper rises up until it's balanced on its last three segments. Its head weaves slowly back and forth, like a cobra preparing to strike.

"You said they don't care about these things, right?" Nasha whispers, and eases the accelerator over her shoulder until she has it in both hands.

"I said they aren't independently intelligent," I say. No point in whispering when the thing plainly knows we're here. "That doesn't mean blowing this one to bits wouldn't be interpreted as hostile, though. Imagine someone coming into your house, walking up to you, and cutting off the tip of your pinkie finger. You wouldn't call him a murderer, but you'd still be pretty pissed."

"Okay," she says. "Fair point." She lets the accelerator slide back until it hangs from the strap over her shoulder again and lowers her hands to her sides. "So what now?"

"Not sure," I say. I take a deep breath in, hold it for a moment, then let it back out. The creeper's head falls still.

I take a slow step forward.

"Mickey?" Nasha says. "What are you doing?"

"This is what we're here for. I'm making contact."

I take another step. The creeper stands frozen. Nasha steps up beside me.

"If it comes at us," she says, "I will end it, diplomacy or no."

"Fair," I say, and take two more slow steps.

The creeper drops back onto its legs. I can hear Nasha's intake of breath, and the clatter of the accelerator coming to bear. It doesn't come for us, though. Instead it wheels around and starts back up the tunnel. After it's gone a few meters, its head lifts and twists back to face us.

"I think it wants us to follow," I say. Without waiting for Nasha's response, I walk toward it at a slow, steady pace. After I've closed the distance between us to six or seven meters, the creeper turns and starts forward again.

"Okay," Nasha says from behind me. "I guess this is happening now."

I don't take my eyes from the creeper, but I can hear her stowing her weapon again. A few seconds later, she's walking beside me.

"If they decide they don't want to talk to us," I say, "we're not likely to be able to shoot our way out of here. You know that, right?"

Nasha bumps against my shoulder. "You'd be surprised what I can shoot my way out of. I hear you, though. As long as they're not actually trying to rip you apart, I promise to be good."

I take her hand. "Thanks, Nasha. I think this is a good sign, right?"

"Maybe," she says. "Or maybe they just like it better when their meat carries itself to the kitchen."

WHEREVER IT IS the creeper is taking us, it's a hell of a long way away. We slog through the darkness for what feels like days, although my ocular tells me it's actually more like a couple of hours. We run into other creepers here and there. Mostly they act as if we aren't there. At one point we reach a tunnel crossing where a stream of them—hundreds at least—is flowing past, blocking our path. The one leading us scuttles up the side of the tunnel and onto the ceiling to pass over them, then drops back to the floor and continues on. I look over at Nasha.

"Sorry," she says. "I can't do that."

Our guide isn't moving any faster than before, but it isn't waiting either.

"We're gonna lose him."

"Maybe," she says. "What do you want to do about it?"

I take a step forward, to the edge of the stream.

"Mickey?" Nasha says. "What are you doing?"

"Testing a hypothesis." I take another step, put my foot right in the path of an onrushing creeper.

It scoots around me and continues on.

"Come on," I say. "They won't hurt us."

I take a second step, then a third. They're all around me now, brushing against my boots occasionally but otherwise leaving me alone. Two more steps, and I'm clear. Our guide is barely visible in the wash of my shoulder light now, probably fifty meters ahead. I turn back. Nasha hasn't moved.

"Nasha? Come on. It's okay."

She shakes her head. I hold out my hand.

"Just walk through them. They won't touch you."

"Not gonna happen," she says. "I've seen what those things can do to a body."

I look behind me. Our guide is out of sight now.

"Nasha, please. We have to go."

She shakes her head again. Her voice is still level, but her eyes are big as dinner plates.

"You go, Mickey. I'll catch up with you."

God help me, I actually think about it for an instant.

Only an instant, though.

"No," I say. "It's okay. There can't be too many more of these things."

That turns out to be less than one hundred percent accurate. It's another two minutes or more before the flow of creepers slows to a trickle, and then disappears. When the last one is gone, Nasha crosses over to me.

"I'm sorry, Mickey," she says. "I just . . ."

Her voice cracks, and it occurs to me that this might be the first time I've ever seen Nasha afraid.

"It's fine," I say, and reach for her hand. She lets me take it, then pulls me into a hug.

"I don't actually want to die down here," she whispers, close to my ear.

"Good call," I say. "Let's not do that."

She squeezes me tighter, then lets go and steps back. "Think our friend is waiting for us?"

I shrug. "Only one way to find out."

She touches my hand, and we go.

HE'S NOT, AS it turns out.

After about five minutes of walking, we come to a three-way branching.

"What if that little bastard wasn't guiding us at all?" Nasha says as she shines her light down each of the tunnels in turn. "What if it was really some random creeper doing random creeper shit, and we just followed it around for a few hours?"

"In that case, I'd guess we're boned."

"Truth." She gestures toward the right-hand branching. "If I were the boss creeper, I think I'd be down this one."

Her guess is as good as any. A hundred meters or so down that tunnel, we come to another crossing. A creeper sits there, waiting for us. We walk toward it slowly, then stop when we're maybe three meters away.

"Is that our guy?" Nasha asks.

I look at her, then back at the creeper. "How should I know?"

She starts to answer, then shakes her head. The creeper crouches there, motionless. "Think it's dead?"

"No idea," I take a step forward, then two. Its mandibles are only a meter or so from my boots now. "Should I give it a nudge?"

"Please don't," she says. "I like you better with all of your parts attached."

I crouch down in front of the creeper. It's completely still.

"Huh. I think it actually might be dead," I say. I reach out slowly toward it. It doesn't react.

"Mickey?" Nasha says.

I touch its mandible with one finger. It rears up then and lunges toward me. I'm pulling my hand away, already falling backward, suddenly sure I'm about to die, when something zings past my ear and the creeper's front three segments explode in a hail of shrapnel. I land hard on my backside and scramble back a meter or two, then turn my head to see Nasha standing behind me with the accelerator in her hands.

"Nice," I begin, then have to stop to swallow back a surge of bile. "Nice shot. Holy shitstorms, Nasha. You could have killed me."

"Could have," she says. "Didn't. Pretty sure it definitely would have, though. Guess I just cut their pinkie finger off, huh? Think we're at war now?"

I get to my feet. I'm happy to see that I've managed not to wet myself. "Dunno. I hope not. We're in pretty deep here. Like I said before—I don't think shooting our way out is an option."

"Maybe not," she says. "Doesn't mean I can't try."

My ocular pings.

<Speaker1>: Contact established.

<Speaker1>: Do not destroy any more ancillaries, please.

"Mickey?" Nasha says. "You okay?"

I hold up one hand. "Maybe? I think they're talking to me."

    <Mickey7>: Where are you?

    <Speaker1>: Continue forward, twenty <untranslatable>.

"This way," I say. "I think, anyway."

We step over the dead creeper and continue down the tunnel. After two hundred meters or so it takes a sharp left-hand turn and then opens up into a wider space, almost an amphitheater. In the center of it, a creeper the size of a heavy-lift shuttle is curled around itself. Nasha plays her light across it.

"Oh shit," she says. "That's—"

"That's the boss creeper," I say.

    <Mickey7>: We're here. You are Speaker1?

The giant creeper stirs, and a smaller one, maybe three meters long and standing a meter or so off the floor, crawls out from its folds.

"Not exactly," it says aloud. Behind its double mandibles I can see complex mouth parts rather than the usual circular maw.

It speaks in Berto's voice.

"You've got to be kidding me," Nasha says.

"Not kidding," it says, and scuttles over until it's squatting in front of us. "Formally this construct is Speaker to the Creatures Who Have Recently Encroached Upon Our Nest, but Speaker will do. It is a pleasure to finally meet you, Mickey."

"THIS MAKES SENSE," I say. "In a nonsensical kind of way, anyway."

"No," Nasha says. "No, it does not. Why does this thing sound exactly like Gomez?"

"They've been tapping my feed. That's the only contact they've had with us, and Berto is pretty much the only person I talk to over comm."

"Accurate," Speaker says. "The vocabulary, tone, and inflection of my speech made up ninety-three percent of the variation seen in your incoming signals. We inferred that this was standard diction."

"No," Nasha says, and rubs her forehead both hands. "It's not. Mickey just needs more friends."

I shoot her a sour look, then turn back to the creeper. "You're the one we saw, aren't you? Two days ago, on the hill overlooking the dome."

"Also accurate," Speaker says. "We were observing your nest. We had assumed previously that your people would eventually either leave or die out, but both of those possibilities have begun to seem less likely as time has worn on. Consequently, we have been considering ways to open a dialogue."

"You could have said something to me then. It would have saved me a lot of trouble."

A ripple runs the length of its body. Was that a shrug? "You did not seem happy to see me. Understand—we put a great deal of work into this construct. Your vocal apparatus in particular is absurdly complicated. We did not wish to risk having to start over due to a misunderstanding."

"Fair point," Nasha says. "After what happened last winter, we're a little touchy about creepers close to the dome."

Speaker rears up until its head is level with ours, mandibles spread wide. Nasha takes a quick half step back and her hands go to her burners. I quickly step between them.

"No!" I say. "No. None of that. We're here to talk, right?"

"Apologies," Speaker says, and sinks back down to the floor. "I thought that this was the appropriate time for us to engage in dominance displays. Did I misunderstand?"

I glare at Nasha until she takes her hands away from her weapons, then turn back to Speaker.

"Yes," I say. "You definitely misunderstood. We're not here for dominance displays. Right, Nasha?"

"Right," she says, and folds her arms across her chest.

"Oh," Speaker says. "This is a 'Nasha'?"

"This is *the* Nasha," Nasha says. "Mickey? Why does it know who I am?"

"'Nasha' is a frequent topic of discussion in the communications we used to build our language model," Speaker says. "We have to say, you are not what we expected."

"Really," Nasha says. "What, exactly, did you expect?"

"I think this is getting off topic—" I begin, but Speaker cuts me off.

"Based on your conversations, we assumed 'Nasha' was some type of combat ancillary. You may remember that when you first arrived here, our ancillaries destroyed several of yours. The majority of them had weaponry of various sorts, and metallic exoskeletons. We thought 'Nasha' was likely of that type, only perhaps larger and more dangerous."

"Well," Nasha says, "you're at least half-right there."

"Not helpful," I say. "Really not helpful."

"You have no idea," Nasha says. "We're gonna talk about this later."

I need to redirect this conversation.

"Speaker," I say, "you know I've been here before, don't you?"

"Unclear," Speaker says. "Ancillaries of your type have been here several times. Two of these, we disassembled. The other two we permitted to leave. Are you saying you are one of those two?"

"First, those weren't ancillaries. I tried to explain this the last time I was here. Our kind doesn't have ancillaries. Each of us is an independent intelligence. We're all what you would call Prime."

"You misspeak," Speaker says. "Or I misunderstand. The ones we took were ancillaries."

I shake my head. "I did not misspeak. Our kind does not have ancillaries. Each of us is Prime. I'm not sure how many ways I can say this."

"No," Speaker says. "This is not true. We do not accept this."

"Why?" Nasha asks. "What's so hard to understand?"

A shudder runs the length of Speaker's body. "What you say cannot be true. If it were, this would mean that we have killed. You would not come here to talk if we had killed. We have seen your weapons. You would have brought them here, and you would have tried to kill us in return."

I consider mentioning that that is, in fact, precisely what we tried to do.

Probably best to keep that to myself, though.

"Apparently," Nasha says, "we're a very forgiving people."

Speaker rises and turns to face her. "We do not believe you."

"Look," I say. "Not the point. The point is that yes, I'm one of the ones who was here before. In fact, both of the ones you allowed to leave were me." I unbuckle the chest and belly straps on my pack, slide it off my shoulders, and swing it around to rest on the floor between us. "The last time I was here, I carried a pack that looked a bit like this one. Do you remember?"

Speaker settles back to the floor.

"There were two of you. One we disassembled. One we let go. The one we disassembled was an ancillary. You told us this."

I bite back the urge to snap at him. We need to stay on topic here. "Not important. The pack is what's important. Do you remember?"

"Do you deny telling us that the other was ancillary?"

"Please," I say. "Can we focus? These packs—they're important to us."

"You said the other was ancillary. It was identical in every way to the first one we disassembled. How could you have multiple identical Primes? This is nonsense."

"We're not like you," Nasha says. "Look at us. Isn't that pretty obvious? Why would we have the same social structure?"

"No," Speaker says. "We did not kill."

"You did kill," Nasha says. "You killed Six. You killed Eight. You killed Gabe Torricelli and Brett Dugan and Tom Gallaher and Rob Jacks and Gillian Carden. We're not here to call you to account for any of that, but these are facts."

I turn to Nasha. Her hands are back on her burners. Speaker's mandibles are opening and closing rhythmically.

"The packs," I say.

"No," Speaker says. "We cannot speak now. We need time to consider."

It curls around on itself then, and scuttles back to the giant still filling the center of the chamber. A coil lifts to admit it, and it disappears.

"THINK HE'S COMING back?"

I shrug. We're sitting on the cold stone floor now, against the wall near the opening where we entered the chamber. I'm leaning against my pack. Nasha's leaning back against me. She lifts her rebreather long enough to take a bite of a protein bar, then holds it up to me over her left shoulder. I bite off half of what's left, chew and swallow. It's been over an hour now since the big creeper has stirred.

"What do we do if he doesn't?"

"I don't know," I say. "I guess I could try to ping them. Seemed like we were in contact that way before Speaker showed up."

"Try."

"What, now?"

"Yeah," Nasha says. "I don't want to spend the night down here."

"Unless they're willing to help us out, I'm pretty sure the ship has sailed on that one. It's a hell of a long way back to the surface from here if we go back the way we came—and even if we could find a shorter route, it's already dark topside, and depending on where we come out, we have to be at least a couple of hours' walk from the dome."

She leans her head back until her cheek rests against mine.

"Ping them," she says. "Please?"

Fine. I blink to a text window.

    <Mickey7>: Hello?
    <Mickey7>: Are you there?

<Mickey7>: We really need to discuss those packs.

<Mickey7>: Hello?

I'm about to tell Nasha that they've apparently gone radio-silent when I get a ping-back.

<Speaker1>: We hear you.

<Speaker1>: We are not ready to speak.

"Sorry," I say. "I guess they're still thinking."

She groans, leans forward, and presses her fists against her forehead.

"This was a bad idea, Mickey. We shouldn't have come down here."

I wrap my arms around her and pull her back against me. "Maybe. We're here, though. Nothing to do now but wait and see what happens."

We've spent a surprising amount of time like this, Nasha and I—hanging around some shitty place, wrapped around one another, waiting for something awful to happen. Usually the thing we were waiting for was for me to die in some horrible way, but there have been a few times when it's been Nasha anticipating the call.

When that rock hit our forward shield during transit, while the original Mickey Barnes was getting absolutely fried while repairing the damage, Nasha was stuck in the carousel. It wasn't the worst place she could have been. A quarter of the internal volume of the *Drakkar* was exposed to dangerous-to-lethal radiation levels, and a half dozen people unlucky enough to be in the right parts of the forward compartments wound up dying in more or less the same way I did, only slower and more painfully. The carousel girdled the waist of the ship about midway between the nose cone and the engines, and roughly a quarter of its volume was exposed as well. *Which* quarter of its volume was exposed was constantly changing with the carousel's rotation, though, and Nasha was swept through the unshielded zone twice in the forty-five seconds that it took her to evacuate. Best guess is that she wound up absorbing about a hundred and fifty millisieverts all told—enough to throw off your digestion and thin out your hair a bit, but not enough to kill you.

Not right away, anyway.

Four years later, give or take, she started getting headaches.

I may not have mentioned this before, but Nasha is fierce. She wouldn't even take an NSAID until the pain was blinding, let alone report to medical. By the time I finally dragged her down to talk to someone, she was having balance problems and could barely tolerate normal shipboard lighting. The tech on duty took a look at her, asked a few questions, and stuck her head in a scanner. Ten minutes later, he was using a tablet and stylus to show us the extent of the mass in her left temporal lobe.

Union medical science is pretty amazing in a lot of ways. We can bio-print new, genetically matched organs at will. Nobody dies from liver failure or atherosclerosis or pulmonary disease or any of a hundred other things that used to mow humans down back in the pre-Diaspora dark ages. It's not magic, though—and the one organ we can't just replace is the brain.

They took her away then, and stuck her into another, bigger scanner for what they called a digital biopsy. The question, apparently, was whether the mass was a benign glioma, which they could cure with nanosurgery, or a malignant glioblastoma, which despite well over a thousand years of head-banging-against-the-wall frustration in medical research facilities from Earth to Eden to Midgard, they could not.

I hung in a harness with her for two hours in the medical bay while we waited to find out if Nasha was going to live or die. We

didn't talk. We just drifted there with my arms around her waist
and her head on my shoulder. When the tech came back out, tablet in hand, she lifted her mouth to my ear and whispered, "If it's
bad news, you don't have to stay with me."

She couldn't see the tech's face. I could. He was smiling.

"It's not bad news," I said, and kissed her. "But it wouldn't
have mattered if it was."

I said it. Was it true?

Nasha's stayed with me through far worse.

I guess I'm glad that I never got the chance to find out.

NASHA IS SLEEPING when I hear the giant creeper moving. I flip
my shoulder light on to see it lift its lowest coil and allow Speaker
to come scuttling out. I blink to my chronometer. It's 02:00. I
try to shift a bit under Nasha, and have to stifle a groan as new
blood flows into my legs. My lower back is killing me, the frame
of my pack feels like it's dug permanent divots into my shoulder
blades, and my ass has soaked up every bit of the chill from the
damp stone floor. Nasha stirs, mutters something unintelligible,
and nuzzles her head deeper into the soft spot where my neck
meets my shoulder. I sigh, and pull her a little closer.

> <Mickey7>: Can we communicate this way, please? Nasha is
>   sleeping.
> <Speaker1>: You do not wish to speak?
> <Mickey7>: If you don't mind.
> <Speaker1>: But . . .
> <Speaker1>: My name is Speaker.
> <Speaker1>: Also, did I mention how complicated your vocal
>   apparatus is?
> <Speaker1>: And how much work we put into replicating it?
> <Mickey7>: I know. It's just—

Nasha stirs again, shifts her weight against me, and lifts her head.

"Mickey?" she says. "What time is it?"

"Ah," Speaker says. "The Nasha is no longer sleeping now. We can speak, yes?"

Nasha sits up and focuses on Speaker.

"Oh," she says. "You again."

"Yes," Speaker says. "Who did you expect?"

Nasha stretches and yawns, then leans back against me.

"Did it tell you where the bomb is yet?"

Oh shit.

"Bomb?" Speaker says.

"Pack," I say. "We're looking for a pack."

"No," Speaker says. "Bomb and pack are not the same. We know bomb. This word appears in your communications frequently. It is a kind of weapon, no?"

"Oh," Nasha says, and presses her fists against her forehead. "Sorry."

Speaker's first three segments rise up from the floor, mandibles gnashing. I'm thinking about getting out from under Nasha and getting to my feet, thinking maybe it's fight-or-flight time, when it says, "Mickey? Please tell me—are we allies?"

That was not what I was expecting.

"We, uh," I begin, then have to pause to consider. "We could be allies. We would like to be."

"Your people were vulnerable when you arrived here, before you had finished constructing your nest. We did not attack you, despite the danger you clearly posed. You were vulnerable when you came down into our tunnels. We did not kill you. We set you free. We have proved our goodwill, have we not?"

"Yes," I say. "I suppose you have."

"Then we should be allies, should we not?"

"Yes," I say. "We can be allies."

"And allies are honest with one another, yes?" Speaker says.

"They should be," I say, with a small mental sigh.

"Agreed," Speaker says. "So, please be honest with us."

"It's a bomb," Nasha says. "The thing we're looking for is a bomb. It is an incredibly powerful bomb, in fact—powerful enough at a minimum to kill everything for a dozen klicks in every direction, even if you set it off underground. We need to have it back because we're afraid that you'll accidentally trigger it, and maybe kill us in the process of killing yourselves. Apologies for everything, but that's the truth."

Speaker's head weaves back and forth, and its mandibles clatter against one another for a long five seconds.

"Thank you," it says finally. "We appreciate the honesty." It drops back to the floor, turns, and scuttles back toward the giant creeper. "Please wait here. We need to consider."

The creeper's coil lifts, and Speaker disappears.

"Huh," Nasha says. "That could have gone worse."

"It could have gone better. What the hell, Nasha?"

She shrugs. "I said I was sorry. I was still half asleep and my brain wasn't turning over yet, you know? I'm actually not sure I am, though. We needed to get to the point. They're not stupid, Mickey. They weren't going to believe we came down here looking for a bag full of snacks. Everybody's cards are on the table now."

"Yeah," I say. "I guess so. Our cards are that we came down here two years ago with a giant bomb. I'm guessing that's what they're considering right now. How do you expect that to work out?"

"Don't know," Nasha says. "If it works out badly, though, my current plan is to put two explosive rounds into Speaker and then empty the magazine into the big one. Hopefully it doesn't come to that, right?"

I WAKE INTO coal-black darkness. Everything hurts. I blink to my chronometer: 07:30. Hard to believe I slept that long, but I guess when you're tired enough your body quits caring about things like circulation. Nasha sits up, and a few seconds later her shoulder light snaps on and I see her rummaging around in her pack.

"What do you think?" she says. "Slurry, protein bars, or both?"

My stomach gives a warning rumble. It's been over twenty hours since I've had real food.

"Let's start with the slurry. If that works out, I'll give the protein bars a shot."

"Suit yourself," she says, and tosses me a tube. I catch it, twist open the seal, and squeeze a bolus of goo into my mouth. I do my best to swallow, then pull a water bottle from my pack to get the grit out of my mouth and wash it down.

"It's been over five hours," I say around another mouthful of slurry. "You'd think they would have decided whether to kill us or not by now, wouldn't you?"

"Maybe," Nasha says. "Do they sleep?"

I shrug. "Toss me a bar, huh?"

These things are almost as bad as the slurry, but I feel like I should probably get something solid into my stomach before I get ripped to shreds and/or have to walk all the hell way back to the dome. Nasha drains a water bottle, stuffs the empty back into her pack, and then gets to her feet.

"Be back in a minute," she says. "I gotta pee."

I watch as her light bobs away along the chamber wall, then look away when it stops moving. She's still gone when the big creeper stirs, and Speaker emerges. It rises up, swings its head back and forth between me and Nasha, and then starts toward the spot where she's still crouched against the wall. It's halfway to her when she barks, "Hey! I'm busy here, pervert! Go talk to Mickey." It hesitates, then scuttles over to me.

"Greetings," it says when it reaches me. "What is *pervert*? We do not have this word."

That surprises me a little, considering that they've been monitoring my conversations with Berto for two years, but okay.

"It's a term of affection," I say. "Have you reached a decision about our request?"

"A difficult question. If we understand correctly now, you and your ancillary brought extremely dangerous weapons into our home."

"Eight was not an ancillary," Nasha says from across the chamber, "and *pervert* is not a term of affection."

"Regardless," Speaker says. "You and your . . ."

"Friend," Nasha says.

"Yes," Speaker says. "You and your friend brought death into our home."

"This is true," I say. "However, when we did that, you had already killed six of us. You killed my friend as well. Despite that, *I did not trigger my bomb.* I could have killed you, but I chose not to. That should count for something, shouldn't it?"

"We recognize this," Speaker says. "We must ask, however, why after so long you want this bomb back now. Have you changed your mind? Do you now intend to kill us? We reluctantly acknowledge a blood debt, but we did not understand what we did then. We will not submit to be killed."

Nasha comes back now to stand beside me.

"We don't want to kill you," she says. "If we did, we could do it. That wasn't our only weapon, you know. We want the bomb back to make sure that it *doesn't* get used."

"Ah," Speaker says. "This is good. Thank you. Very reassuring."

We wait for it to go on. Nasha looks at me. I shrug. She turns back to Speaker. "And?"

Its head bobs back and forth between us. "And what?"

I can hear the eye roll in Nasha's voice.

"*And* will you give us the bomb?"

"Oh," Speaker says. "Yes. We certainly would."

"*Would?*" I say. "Don't you mean *will*?"

"Apologies," Speaker says. "My usage may be incorrect. Your grammar is surprisingly complex. I was proposing a hypothetical. We *would* return the bomb to you *if* we had it—but we do not have it, so we cannot. Is that more clear?"

010

Have you ever had one of those days when it becomes painfully apparent that the universe is deliberately screwing with you?

I get to my feet. Nasha's eyes cut to me. It's impossible to read her expression behind her rebreather, but I'd put a week's worth of rations on "murderous."

"You don't have it," she says, her voice low and even. I notice her hands have drifted to the grips of her burners.

"We do not," Speaker says. "But if we did, we would give it to you. This has been decided."

"You don't have it," Nasha says. "We don't have it. So tell me, Speaker . . . who *does* have it?"

"Our friends to the south have it," Speaker says.

"Your . . ." Nasha begins, then shakes her head and says, "How do you know that?"

"We know that because we gave it to them."

Nasha's hands tighten around the burners.

"You gave our bomb to your *friends*?"

Speaker's head wavers. "*Friends* is not the right word, exactly. We have a name for them, but I do not know how to translate it."

Nasha turns to look at me. I sigh, and dig my knuckles into my eyes.

"You gave them our bomb," I say. "You . . . why would you do that?"

"They demanded something of yours," Speaker says, "as a tribute of sorts. As I told you, *friends* is probably not the correct word for them. *Assholes* might be more accurate, if I understand that term correctly. Our relationship with them has always been uneasy, and has often been hostile. Since your arrival they have become increasingly agitated about our access to you. They fear that you may provide us some advantage that we can use against them. Ancillaries have been taken. Threats have been made. When we examined your bomb, we found it to be filled with something we could not understand. It seemed interestingly mysterious, but the contents did not appear to interact with normal matter, so we judged it to be harmless. It seemed that it might make a useful offering."

"A useful offering?" Nasha says. "Fine, you didn't know exactly what it was, but you said yourself that it had something inside it that you didn't understand. Did it really not occur to you that it might be dangerous?"

Speaker lifts another segment off the floor and spreads its mandibles in what I now recognize as a threat posture.

"Why should this have occurred to us? We had no way to know what this thing was. *You* did. *You* knew exactly what it was. You knew this thing was a deadly dangerous weapon, and you left it sitting in a hole. Not a deep hole, not a safe hole where it would never hurt anyone. You left it on our doorstep under a pile of rocks where anyone could find it. Only a stupid, stupid person would do this with a deadly dangerous weapon, no? We know you have technology that we do not understand, we know you can do things that we cannot do, so we foolishly assume you are not stupid, stupid creatures. So yes, we assume it must be harmless. Is this our fault?"

"Okay," Nasha says. "Well. Now you know that it's not harmless. So. Get it back."

"We, get it back? Why would we do this? We do not want it. Now that we know what this thing is, we are glad to have it gone, glad that it is as far away from us as it can be. We do not understand why you would want such a thing back—but if you do, you should get it for yourselves."

Nasha folds her arms across her chest and tilts her head to one side. "So much for allies, huh?"

"We may have misunderstood this word *allies*. You speak as if you are Prime, and we are ancillaries. Is this what *allies* is?"

Nasha takes a step toward him. Her jaw is set in a way that I recognize from a hundred arguments over the past eight years. "Look," she says. "We need that device back. We don't necessarily want to resort to force, but if you won't cooperate with us, I promise you that we'll do whatever we need to do to make that happen."

Speaker rears up until only its last two segments grip the floor and its head looms over us. Nasha's eyes narrow and for an instant I'm certain she's about to fire on him, and that shortly after that we're both going to die. She doesn't, though, and Speaker doesn't attack her either. Instead, it settles back until its head is only a meter or so off the floor, and its mandibles click together in a staccato rhythm.

"Wait," it says. "Before we fight, consider this, please. Our friends are far away, much farther than we are now from your nest. If they accidentally trigger your bomb, neither you nor we will be hurt. Also, our friends will be killed, which would not bother us in the least. Perhaps . . . perhaps we should leave things as they are?"

I look over at Nasha. She seems to consider, then shakes her head.

"That's an interesting thought, but let me be a bit more clear. We *need* that bomb. We need you to get it back from your friends, and we need for this to happen before the cold comes back."

Speaker rises up again.

"Twice now, you demand that we follow your instructions. You should not do this. Allies do not demand. Assholes demand."

"Look," I say before Nasha can respond. "This may be a language issue. Nasha does not mean to make demands, only to express how important this is to us. We don't mean to threaten and we don't mean to demand, but we do mean to get that bomb back, one way or another. We would like to work together with you to do that. If that's not possible, we will not hold it against you. We will not attack you, but we will be forced to seek your friends out ourselves, and we can't guarantee that what happens then won't spill over onto you."

"Oh," Speaker says. "No. No, I would not advise that. Our friends to the south are not as friendly as we are. When you first arrived, and for long thereafter, they advised us very strongly to kill you all. If you go to find them now, they will not welcome you. They will very likely disassemble you. Before we gave them your bomb, they requested that we provide them one of your ancillaries. They were very eager to learn of your inner workings. Again, let me suggest leaving the bomb with them. Their accidentally triggering it seems to us to be the best possible outcome."

"No," I say. "Unfortunately, that's not an option. Nasha is right. That device is our responsibility. We need to get it back."

Speaker's head bobs back and forth between Nasha and me, mandibles clicking. Nasha's hands rest on her burners.

"Wait here," Speaker says finally. "We must consider."

Once again, he drops to the floor, turns, and scuttles away.

"Okay," Nasha says when he's gone. "I'm starting to get really sick of this."

I lift my rebreather long enough to rub my face with both hands. "He's negotiating with an invading alien species with unknown advanced technological capabilities—one which has already proved itself to be at least genocide-curious, if not actually genocidal. You can't blame him for being cautious."

I put my back to the wall, then slide down until I'm sitting again. Nasha lowers herself down to the floor beside me, settles back against the wall, and then leans the side of her head against mine. "Yeah, maybe not. Still, we've been down here for a long-ass time, and we're not any closer to having our hands on the bomb than we were when we left the dome."

"Maybe," I say. "Maybe not. Let's see what he comes back with."

"Yeah. By the way, are we calling that thing a 'he' now?"

"I guess so? Seems to fit with the voice, anyway. Unrelated: that was some solid good-cop-bad-cop you pulled there, with the hands constantly stroking the burners and all."

She nudges me with her elbow, and I can hear the grin in her voice. "Glad you liked it. I wasn't doing a bit, though. I was seriously considering opening up on his ass at one point there."

"You know burners just annoy those things, right?"

"I don't know," she says. "I'd bet two military-grade burners focused on one spot on his underside at point-blank range would do some real damage. If not, there's always the accelerator."

She may be right, I guess, but I kind of doubt it. Nasha didn't see what happened when Rob and Gillian turned their burners on the creepers that were dissecting Dugan two years ago, and those ones were tiny next to Speaker. Hopefully we don't have to find out, because I'm pretty sure the cannons on the pylons surrounding the dome wouldn't make a dent in the giant's carapace, let alone the popguns Nasha is carrying, and having killed Speaker would be cold comfort while that thing was tearing us into tiny, bloody bits.

"When he comes back," Nasha says, "what do we do if he says they won't help? All we know right now is that the bomb is somewhere to the south, right? Ninety percent of the planet is south of here. If they live in holes like these guys, it might not be super-easy to find them."

"That's an understatement. Also, unless they've shared a lot more with these guys than Speaker is letting on, we won't be able to talk to them."

"Ooooh, right. So we go in shooting?"

I lift my head away from hers and turn to look at her. "Is there any situation where your first solution *isn't* 'we go in shooting'?"

She laughs. "Is there any situation where that's not the absolute best approach?"

I sigh, slide my arm around her shoulder, and pull her against me.

"This is why I love you," I say. "You've got a real talent for boiling things down to their essence."

She slides her hand across my belly and rests it on my hip.

"You're goddamned right I do."

IT'S AN HOUR later, and we've gone through two more tubes of slurry, another pack of protein bars, and most of the rest of our water when Speaker returns. We didn't pack for a days-long expedition. If this doesn't end soon, things are going to start getting even more uncomfortable down here than they already are.

"We have come to a decision," he says when he reaches us.

I wait a beat for him to go on, then shoot Nasha a quick look and say, "And?"

"And," Speaker says, "we do not accept responsibility for your bomb falling into our friends' possession. You left it in a hole.

This was a very stupid thing to do. The fact that we were the ones to find it was only chance. Our friends could conceivably have found it themselves. Anyone could have. So, your current situation is entirely your own fault."

Nasha's eyes narrow and her shoulders tense under my arm. I put my hand over hers, mostly to keep her from reaching for a weapon, as he continues.

"We do not accept responsibility for the loss of your bomb. However, we do accept blood-debt for the killing of your not-ancillaries. We gave this great consideration, as we had no reasonable way of knowing that your kind are structured so strangely, but in the final analysis, we acknowledge that we did kill several of you. Because of this, we have determined that we are obligated to provide you what help we can in recovering your bomb from our friends, despite our feeling that this is not a wise course."

Nasha had already taken a breath to say something awful. She lets it out now, and I can feel her relax.

"Okay," she says. "Okay. Thank you. That's what we wanted to hear. You go talk to your friends, let them know we need that thing back immediately, and bring it to the dome. We'll take it from there, right?"

Speaker's head bobs, and his mandibles clatter together.

"Bring it to you? No. No, that is not what we meant. That is not on offer. We will give what help we can, but only within reason. We will offer advice. We will offer guidance. We will not go to war for you."

I glance over at Nasha. Her eyes have narrowed again.

"Right," she says. "Advice. Guidance. That sounds very helpful."

"Yes," Speaker says. "It will be."

"Two years of eavesdropping on Mickey and Berto, and you didn't pick up sarcasm, huh?"

Speaker's head swings over to me, then back to Nasha.

"Sarcasm?"

"Not important," I say. "The point is, we need more than advice and guidance, and I would think the fact that you killed six individuals would entitle us to more than that."

Speaker scoots back a meter or so, and his head dips almost to the floor.

"You wish to negotiate," he says. "This is fair. What do you feel you deserve from us?"

"More than advice," I say. "Material support."

I should have known what would happen now, but I still can't suppress a groan when Speaker says, "We need to consider," and scuttles away.

"So," Nasha says. "Have you given much thought to how smart these things are?"

I turn to look at her. She's sitting beside me now, back against the rough stone wall, draining the last of her water.

"The creepers, you mean?"

I can't see her expression, but I can hear the eye roll in her voice when she responds. "Yeah, Mickey. The creepers."

I shrug. "Hard to say, isn't it? They don't seem to have much of a material culture, do they? No cars or planes or houses, unless you count this place as a house. No weapons, so far as we've seen. No factories or obvious tech other than what's in their bodies."

"Right. On the other hand, they've been able to put together something that can speak our language at least as well as Gomez does in just a couple of years. What have we accomplished in the same amount of time? We don't even know if they have a language. Also, it took them, what, a couple of weeks to figure out how to use the comm gear they took out of Six to get inside your head? What did we learn from the creeper we took apart? Anything at all?"

"In all fairness, the creeper we took apart was already half-exploded when we got ahold of it. Six, on the other hand, was apparently one hundred percent intact and kicking when he got vivisected."

"Sure," she says. "Still, though—if we had captured a totally intact creeper, do you really think we could have done to them what they did to us? Do you think we would have been able to reverse engineer a totally alien communication system, decipher the signals it was producing, and figure out how to use it to manipulate the brains of the creepers on the other end?"

"When you put it that way, it seems pretty unlikely, huh?"

Nasha laughs. "Unlikely? Give us six weeks with a totally intact creeper and I'd be willing to bet Bio would still be trying to figure out which end eats and which end shits."

"Okay," I say. "Granted. They're better with electronics than we are, and maybe with biology too. What's your point?"

"Electronics? Biology? What about linguistics? Do you hear the way that thing talks? They're smarter than we are, Mickey. *Much* smarter."

I shake my head. "Lots of animals can do things we can't do. Bees can communicate the precise location of a food source two klicks away with a five-second dance. Doesn't mean they're smarter than we are. It just means they have a different skill set."

She turns to look at me. "Since when do you know so much about bees?"

I grin behind my rebreather. "You'd be surprised what I know. Anyway, it doesn't matter, does it? It's not like we're planning on playing chess with these things."

"I don't know," she says. "We're outnumbered on this planet by a whole hell of a lot. They can definitely outproduce us. If they can outthink us too . . ."

"We're screwed?"

"Maybe," Nasha says. "Or maybe we're just gonna really need to make some friends. I think I might try being a little nicer when Speaker comes back next time."

"Huh," Nasha says when the giant creeper's coils lift and Speaker emerges again. "That one was quick. Wonder what that means."

She's right. It's only been about ten minutes since he disappeared. We get to our feet as he approaches.

"So," Speaker says. "We have considered, and we agree to your request. We will not go to war for you, but we will provide material support."

"We're not asking for war," I say. "We don't want to fight your friends. We don't want to fight anyone. We just want our property back before it kills someone."

Speaker's head sways from side to side. "I can see that you do not know our friends."

"What kind of support?" Nasha asks. "What are you offering us?"

"Diplomatic and logistical support," Speaker says. "Not fighting support."

"Not enough," Nasha says. "It sounds like your friends are not actually your friends. Sounds like they're your enemies, in fact. If this comes to fighting, we want you to be with us."

"No," Speaker says. "Understand, please: This is a final offer. If it comes to fighting, we would rather fight you than our friends to the south. We only suspect that you have the ability to do us serious harm. We know from hard experience that they do."

"Clarify," I say. "What, exactly, is on offer?"

"I am," Speaker says. "I am on offer. When you go to face our friends to the south, I will go with you. This is the most we can give."

Nasha looks over at me. I shrug. "Better than nothing, right? At least we'll be able to talk to them."

"Sure we can't get the big guy?" Nasha says, and waves toward the giant creeper.

"Very sure," Speaker says. "Are we agreed?"

Nasha sighs. "Yeah, I guess we are. Welcome aboard."

<Black Hornet>: Mickey?

<Mickey7>: I'm right beside you, Nasha. Why are you texting?

<Black Hornet>: Can Speaker see this?

I GLANCE BEHIND us. Speaker trundles along a half dozen or so meters back, legs rippling in a viscerally disturbing way as he moves. We're crossing a steep, sunny, fern-covered hillside, still at least an hour's walk out from the perimeter.

<Mickey7>: I don't think so, but I guess I'm not sure. Depends on how thoroughly they've penetrated our communication protocols.

<Black Hornet>: Is there any way to find out?

<Mickey7>: Maybe. Let me try an old ComSec trick.

<Mickey7>: Hey, Speaker, are you seeing this?

<Speaker1>: Yes, I am.

<Mickey7>: There ya go.

Nasha bumps me with her shoulder. "Nobody likes a smart-ass, Mickey."

I grin behind my rebreather. "Found out what you needed to know, didn't I?"

She glances back. "Speaker? Any way you could give us a little privacy?"

"Privacy?" Speaker says. "I do not know this word."

"I need to say things to Mickey that I do not necessarily want you to overhear. Understand?"

"These things you wish to say—they are secrets?"

"Sure," Nasha says. "Private secrets."

"You wish to tell these secrets to Mickey, but not to me?"

"Yeah," Nasha says. "That's the gist of it."

His mandibles spread wide, then snap together. "Allies do not keep secrets from one another, Nasha."

She stops and turns to face him, arms folded across her chest. "Look, we're not talking about military intel here, okay? I just have some things that I need to discuss with Mickey before we get to the dome. These things do not involve you. That's what private means—things that involve us, but don't involve you."

Speaker stops just short of Nasha and rises up to head level. "What private things will you discuss?"

"If I told you," Nasha says slowly, "they wouldn't be private, would they?"

"No," Speaker says. "I suppose not."

Nasha glances over at me. I shrug. She sighs. "So?"

Speaker's mandibles clatter together rapidly in a way I'm starting to associate with confusion. "So, what?"

"So," Nasha says. "Will you please give us some privacy?"

"Oh," Speaker says. "Yes. Of course."

He drops to the ground, curls back on himself, and retreats down the hillside.

"I must say," he says as he goes, "this does not seem very friendly."

He stops when he's fifty meters or so off, turns, and looks back at us.

"Think that's far enough?" Nasha says, her voice now just above a whisper.

"I don't know," I say. "Want me to try an old ComSec trick to find out?"

Nasha's eyes narrow above her rebreather. "You're a funny guy, Mickey. It's gonna get you killed someday."

"It already has," I say. "Several times."

Nasha sighs. "Right. Look, what are we doing here? You're not planning on bringing that thing into the dome, are you?"

"I mean—"

"Let me stop you there, Mickey. We cannot bring a three-meter-long creeper into the dome. Totally aside from the fact that some Security goon would definitely kill him before we were through the perimeter, we can't give him the opportunity to gather intel on us."

I turn to face her fully and fold my arms across my chest. "Intel? Seriously? What do you expect him to learn, other than that a hundred and seventy humans crammed into a closed environment eventually start to smell like old socks no matter how many chem showers they take?"

"I don't know," she says. "We have no real idea of what his capabilities are, do we? I mean, doesn't it spook you at all, how easily these things have been able to learn how to manipulate our systems? Just as an example, how was he able to tap our text feed? Nobody in the dome could have done that other than Marshall and Amundsen. If we let him into the dome, would he be able to get into the general feed? Would he be able to pull specs for our weapons systems? For our life support? For the reactor? Come on, Mickey. Use your head."

I glance downslope toward Speaker. He raises two segments and waves a foreleg.

"Fine. You make some good points. So what do you suggest?"

Her eyes lose focus as her attention shifts from my face to her ocular's heads-up display. "Looks like we're three klicks out here, give or take, and we've got one more ridge that's blocking any line-of-sight transmissions. I'm not getting any comm signals from the dome at all right now. We should be safe to leave him here. We can pick him up again once we're ready to head south."

"That could take a while. A few days, maybe, depending on how much of a pain in the ass Marshall decides to be about this. You think he'll be okay just hanging around out here?"

"This is Speaker's planet," Nasha says. "His natural environment, right? I'm sure he'll be fine."

<Black Hornet>: Okay, Speaker. You can come back now.

<Speaker1>: You are finished telling secrets?

<Black Hornet>: For the moment, anyway.

We wait as he scuttles back up the slope.

"So," he says when he reaches us. "We can continue now?"

"Not exactly," Nasha says. "Mickey and I can continue now. You can wait here. We'll come back for you once we've gathered what we need."

"But . . ." Speaker says, his mandibles clattering. "But I wish to see your nest."

"I'm sure you do," Nasha says. "Wait here. We'll be back in a day or two."

"This seems unfair. You have seen our nest. You have seen it several times."

"And you've killed six of us, when all we did was roast a few ancillaries," Nasha says. "Life isn't fair. Two days max. Maybe three." She turns and starts walking. "Four at the outside."

Speaker turns to me. "You agree with this?"

"Sorry," I say. "We'll be back as quickly as possible. You'll be okay here?"

"I wish to see your nest."

"You will," I say. "Eventually. Right now, things are a little tense—because of all the killing, you know? If we brought you into the dome right now, things might not go well. Once we recover the bomb, everyone will be happier. You can come for a visit then, okay?"

He rises up to head-height, wavers, then drops back to the ground. "Fine. I will wait here. Try not to be too long. I do not like the outside."

I start to reach out, to give his carapace a farewell pat, but at the last second I remember what those mandibles can do. "Okay, then. See you soon."

Nasha's already cresting the hill. I give Speaker one last backward glance, then hurry to catch up.

I DON'T KNOW why, but I expected some kind of reception. We don't get one, though. Cat is leaning against a burner pylon when we come over the hill and start down toward the main lock. She's in standard black Security togs, no armor or helmet. The only thing that indicates she's on sentry duty is the accelerator slung across her back.

"Hey," she says when we're close enough for talking. "Where are you two coming from?"

"Just out for a stroll," Nasha says. "Marshall didn't tell you to be on the lookout for us?"

Cat laughs. "Marshall doesn't tell me shit. He knows I'm tight with you two. Apparently that makes me a security risk." She gives Nasha a once-over. "So what's with the arsenal? You guys doing secret missions or something?"

"Yeah," Nasha says. "Something. Okay if we head in?"

"Go for it," Cat says. As we walk past, she nudges me. "You can tell me about the secret mission later, right?"

Nasha shoots her a look. Cat winks and turns away.

"Swear to God," Nasha says as we're waiting for the lock to cycle. "If I ever find out that the two of you—"

"You won't," I say, "because we're not."

"Damn right," she says. The light above the inner door turns green, and Nasha strips off her rebreather as it slides open. There's another goon, a guy named Drake, on duty in the ready room. He's slouched in a chair against the far wall, wearing that glassy-eyed expression that says he's streaming media through his ocular. He glances up as we step out of the lock.

"Barnes," he says. "Marshall wants to see you."

I cross the room to the row of lockers on the far side, slide my pack to the floor, and start stowing gear.

"Did you hear me?" Drake says. "Marshall wants to see you. Now."

Nasha racks her weapons, then comes over to help me with the pack. I'm just pulling the last empty slurry tubes out of the side pockets when Drake gets to his feet.

"Look," he says, "I don't know who the—"

He stops there because Nasha has swung around and taken two steps toward him. He's got ten centimeters and probably thirty kilos on her, but he still takes a half step back.

"He heard you," Nasha says. "Now sit your ass back down and go back to watching porn or whatever else you were doing instead of your job, Drake. We've had a long couple of days, and we're not here for your shit."

Drake's mouth hangs open for a moment, then snaps closed as his face twists into a scowl. "Whatever. Just make sure you get to the commander's office in the next ten minutes. Your entry time has been logged."

He drops back into his chair and folds his arms across his chest as his eyes lose focus. I stow the empty pack, take a quick look around to make sure I haven't forgotten anything, and then start toward the door. We're into the corridor with the door sliding shut behind us when Drake mutters one word, *Bitch,* just loud enough to be heard.

"Don't," I say, and grab Nasha's arm as she spins back toward the door.

"Oh *hell* no," she says, and tries to pull free.

"Come on," I say, get my other arm around her, and pull her into something halfway between a fighter's clinch and a hug. "This isn't the time."

She growls, low and angry, right next to my ear, then shakes free of me and stalks away down the corridor.

"Fine," she says without looking back, "but I'm not forgetting that one."

I glance back at the closed door, shake my head, and follow her in toward the hub.

"BARNES," MARSHALL SAYS. "Adjaya. Come in. Sit down. Where's the bomb?"

I pull a chair away from his desk and sit as the door closes behind me. Nasha folds her arms across her chest and leans back against the wall.

"Hello, Commander," I say. "No preliminaries, huh?"

Marshall clasps his hands in front of him and leans across the desk.

"No," he says. "No preliminaries. You are about to tell me whether this colony is going to survive the coming winter or not. I'm not interested in dancing around the topic."

"Okay," I say. "Well, I have good news and bad news, sir."

"Barnes," Marshall says through gritted teeth. "This is not a joke."

"No, sir," I say. "You're right. Apologies."

"We don't have the bomb," Nasha says.

Marshall's eyes snap to her, then back to me. "You don't have it."

"No, sir," I say. "We don't. That's the bad news."

"And?"

"Sir?"

Marshall closes his eyes and takes a deep breath, in and out.

"The good news," he says when he opens them again. "Tell me the good news, please."

"Oh. Right. The good news is that we know where it is."

"You do."

"Yes, sir. We do."

"Then please explain why you're still here."

"We need gear," Nasha says. "We need people, and we need a lifter."

Marshall's eyes stay on me.

"Barnes," he says. "I need for you to explain to me, clearly and concisely, exactly what is happening with that bomb, or as God is my witness, I will murder you both."

I shoot Nasha a quick *Shut up* look. She shrugs and stares straight ahead. I turn back to Marshall.

"Well, sir, as you know, since Eight's death, the bomb he carried has been in the creepers' possession."

"I am aware," he says. "If you'll recall, that is the situation you were supposed to be remedying."

"Yes, sir. At your direction, Nasha and I went down into the creepers' labyrinth yesterday to retrieve it. Turns out, though, that the bomb is no longer in their possession."

"It's not."

"No, sir. Apparently they traded it away."

"They didn't trade it," Nasha says. "They gave it away. There's another, stronger bunch of them somewhere south of here. Our creepers gave up the bomb to them as tribute. That's why we need people, and that's why we need gear. We're going down there to get it back."

Marshall leans back in his chair and turns to face Nasha.

"Are you planning a diplomatic mission, or a raid?"

Nasha shrugs. "Plan for one, prepare for the other."

Marshall grins. "Yes. Yes, that's exactly right. I like the way you think, Adjaya."

"So. Gear, goons, and a lifter."

"Well," Marshall says. "Weapons and Security officers we can give you. A lifter, though? No. We've pulled the gravitics from our lifters and drained them back into the primary grid. I can give you a rover."

Nasha rolls her eyes. "A rover? Seriously?"

"Or," Marshall says, "I suppose you can walk?"

"A rover works," I say, before Nasha can talk us into crawling, probably with weights strapped to our ankles.

"Excellent," Marshall says. "Now, how many people do you anticipate needing?"

"Ten," Nasha says before I can answer. "All Security, obviously, and they'll all need armor, accelerators, and a full kit of ammo."

Marshall laughs, but there's no humor in it. "Ten? All from Security? Are you sure you don't need all twelve of our remaining officers? I'm sure we don't need anyone here to protect the colony."

"Look—" Nasha says, but Marshall cuts her off with a slash of one hand.

"No. Out of the question. We are not in a position to mount an invasion here, Adjaya. Diplomacy first. If that doesn't work, I'll give you enough of a team to attempt a forced extraction, but we're going to need to be a bit more protective of our essential resources than that."

"Fine," Nasha says. "Give us six from Security. We can pull the rest from somewhere else. Gomez knows how to handle a weapon. I'm sure I can find five or six others."

Marshall shakes his head. "This is not a negotiation, and I am not interested in you attempting to recruit colonists for this mission. Please remember that the issues we are having with our power supply are not general knowledge, and I do not wish for them to become so. As I said, I will provide you with an appropriate team. I'll work out the details with Mr. Amundsen while you two get yourselves cleaned up and fed and rested. Expect to assemble at the main lock at oh-eight-hundred tomorrow."

I look over at Nasha. She's clearly not happy. I give my head a short, sharp shake when she opens her mouth to argue. Her eyes narrow, but she closes her mouth again and nods.

"Thank you, sir," I say. "We appreciate the assistance."

"Yes," Marshall says. "I'm sure you do. Now go. I'll be there tomorrow to see you off."

"GOD, I HATE that prick."

Nasha stabs a hunk of sweet potato with her fork, brings it to her mouth, and chews. Ordinarily I'm jealous of Nasha's dinners. Tonight, though, I had a premonition that I might not need my ration card moving forward. For once, I splurged on the rabbit haunch.

I hope it wasn't one of the ones I liked.

"It could be worse," I say. "We've got a rover."

She stabs another hunk of potato, hard enough that it falls off the end of the fork in pieces.

"How far are we going? Do you have any idea?"

I shrug. "You were there with me in the labyrinth, right? You heard as much as I did."

"Their 'friends to the south' could be on the other side of the equator, for all we know."

"Yeah," I say. "Or they could be over the next hill. Given that the creepers don't seem to have air travel and their friends to the south are apparently close enough to give Speaker's group grief over us, that seems more likely, doesn't it?"

"Maybe," Nasha says. "Doesn't matter, though, if we don't show up with enough juice to do what we need to do."

I sigh. "Yeah, that's a valid point. You didn't really think he was about to give us the entire Security section, though, did you?"

She rolls her eyes. "Why not? I mean, what are they actually doing around here? Hanging around outside the main lock with their thumbs up their asses?"

"Maybe not much now," I say, "but if we don't wind up bringing that bomb back, Security's likely to be pretty important, no? Starving people aren't happy people, and someone's going to need to keep them in line and working until they're dead."

"Ugh," Nasha says. "That's dark."

"Maybe—but tell me Marshall isn't thinking about it."

Nasha's eyes narrow, and she scrapes up the last of her food.

"Anyway," I say, "two goons or twelve goons, it's not likely to make a difference, is it? If the creepers won't give us the bomb, what are the odds that we'll be able to take it from them?"

"I don't know," Nasha says. "Better with twelve goons than two, though."

I sigh, toss the last of the picked-clean rabbit bones onto my tray, and push it aside. "Look, I told you yesterday what I saw in the labyrinth two years ago. There are thousands of creepers down there, and their friends to the south are apparently stronger than they are, which I'm pretty sure means there are even more of them. How many creepers do you think twelve goons armed with accelerators firing one round per second could take out before getting swarmed and taken apart? That's not even considering the fact that we'd presumably be somewhere a half klick underground with no good way to find our way back out."

"Not likely," Nasha says. "If we knew we were conducting a raid, we'd drop tracers on our way in. We'd have no trouble figuring out how to get back out."

"Really? We didn't do anything like that yesterday."

She smiles. "When we left the dome yesterday, I thought you actually knew where the hell we were going. If I'd known how clueless you were, I'd have made sure to bring some along."

I sigh. "Fine. We could find our way out. That doesn't solve the original problem, which is that we'd be finding our way back out through a mass of ten thousand seriously pissed-off creepers."

"Those tunnels are narrow. They wouldn't be able to come at us all at once. With any luck, we could manage a fighting withdrawal."

"Until we got out into the open, where they could totally surround us."

She shrugs. "Hopefully by then we've killed enough of them that they decide to let us go."

"Look, let's hope it doesn't come to that, huh? Best case, maybe we can trade them something for the bomb. They don't know what it is. They don't know what to do with it. They know what metal is, though, and if they're anything like Speaker's creepers, they value it."

"So do we," Nasha says. "I didn't hear Marshall offering to give us a pile of titanium to barter with."

I lean across the table, take her hands, and give her a grin. "He didn't. He gave us a rover, though."

Nasha stares me down for a long five seconds. "A rover."

"Yeah," I say. "Four thousand kilos of rolling trade goods."

Nasha pulls her hands away and shakes her head. "You are not trading our rover away, Mickey."

I push back from the table, get to my feet, and pick up my tray. "It's not the first option—but if it comes to it, yeah, I am."

"And if it's too far to walk? How do you expect to get back to the dome?"

I give her the grin again as I pick up her tray, but there's a little less humor in it this time. "Come on, Nasha. Anywhere is walking distance if you've got the time."

WE DON'T SLEEP much once we get back to our room. It's not spoken, but I think we both have a strong feeling that this might be the last time we share a bed. Even when we're done, she doesn't roll away from me. Her legs twine around mine and her weight settles onto my chest, and as I start to drift I can almost imagine that she's slipping through me, that I can feel her fingers brush past skin and muscle and ribs to curl lightly around my heart. I close my eyes, breathe her in, and wait for morning.

"JAMIE?" I SAY. "What the hell are you doing here?"

Jamie looks up from adjusting the straps on his rebreather. He doesn't look any happier to see me than I am to see him. "You tell me," he says. "This is your show, right?"

I glance around the ready room. Cat is across the way pulling boxes of accelerator slugs out of a locker, and Lucas Morrow is filling the front pockets of a pack with protein bars. If we're only getting two goons, they're the ones I'd want, so that's good news, I guess.

"Did I miss something?" Nasha asks. "Are we bringing the rabbits with us?"

Jamie's face twists into a scowl. "Screw off, Adjaya. That's not all I do around here."

"Okay," Nasha says. "Enlighten me, because that is for sure the only thing I have seen you do since we made landfall. What is it that you do that qualifies you for this trip?"

"Well," he says, "for starters, I'm the only person who survived transit who's rated to pilot the rover. If you'd rather walk, though, I'm totally happy to go back to bed. Just say the word."

"No," I say, and shoot Nasha a quick glare. "Definitely not. We're happy to have you, Jamie. Thanks for volunteering."

Jamie barks out a humorless laugh. "Volunteering? Right."

"I volunteered," Cat says from across the room.

"I didn't," Lucas says. "I lost a coin toss."

The door slides open behind me, and Berto walks in. He's already carrying a full pack.

"Morning," Nasha says. "What've you got there?"

Berto grins. "Wouldn't you like to know?"

"It's an ultralight," I say. "Kinda like a hang glider, but he's got some kind of motors attached to the frame. It's his new favorite toy."

He shrugs out of the pack and drops onto a bench. "You suck, Mickey."

"You're not bringing that," Nasha says.

Berto looks up at her, his face set halfway between confusion and annoyance. "What?"

"You're not bringing a portable ultralight on this trip," Nasha says. "The only reason you'd want to is so that you can bail on us if things go sideways, and I'm not having that."

"First," Berto says, "bite me, Nasha. Second, there are a million useful things I can do with this thing other than bailing on you."

"Okay," Nasha says, and folds her arms across her chest. "Name them."

Berto holds up one finger. "For one thing, aerial reconnaissance."

"Don't see why we'd need that, but okay. What's two?"

Berto holds up a second finger, opens his mouth, hesitates, and then closes it again. "Well," he says finally, "I guess that's it, really. Doesn't matter, though. I'm bringing it."

I can see Nasha wants to press the issue, so I step between them and say, "Look, there's room in the rover, and it might be useful. He can bring it, okay?"

Nasha gives me a quick look that says, *You're gonna regret that,* but then shakes her head and says, "Fine. But if he does try to cut and run on us, I'm using him for target practice. It'll be fun to see what a burner does to an ultralight." Berto glares up at her, but doesn't respond.

"Well," Jamie says, "this trip's off to a solid start. I can see why Marshall put you in charge, Mickey."

I'm trying to come up with a better response than *Shut up* when the door at the far end of the room opens and Hieronymus Marshall enters. Marshall never looks particularly happy, but the expression on his face this morning is grimmer than usual.

"Well," he says. "It seems we're all here."

"What?" Nasha says. "This is the team?"

"This is the team," Marshall says. "Is there a problem?"

"Of course this is the team," Jamie says. "We're the expendables."

Marshall turns to look at him. "This colony no longer has an Expendable, Mr. Harrison. You can thank Mr. Barnes for that."

"No," Jamie says. "I don't mean like Mickey. I mean, we're the people you don't think you'll miss if this shit show falls apart and we all wind up dead. I'm the rabbit guy, right? Who cares what happens to me? Mickey's not even that. He's the assistant rabbit guy. Adjaya and Gomez are grounded indefinitely, so they don't have any kind of jobs at all."

"I've got a job," Lucas says. "So does Cat."

"Look, Jamie—" Berto begins, but Marshall cuts him off before he can get going.

"Enough! Let me be clear about this, Mr. Harrison: *There are no expendables in this colony*. Between those lost to the collision in transit and those lost two years ago, our population is alarmingly close to the limits of viability. We do not have a single body to spare. Moreover, the success of this mission is absolutely vital to our continued survival. The six of you were selected because, in both my and Mr. Amundsen's judgment, you give us optimal odds of success. Is that understood?"

Jamie looks like he wants to say something, but in the end he thinks better of it and nods.

"Good," Marshall says. "Is that clear to the rest of you as well?"

"Yes, sir," we mumble, more or less in unison.

"I should hope so. Now. Barnes and Adjaya are the only ones of you who have a complete understanding of what's at stake here, but I assume that will no longer be the case five minutes after you've boarded the rover, so I won't waste your time with a pep talk. It should suffice to say that failure, as they say, is not an option." He pauses to glance around the room. "Questions?"

For some reason, everyone turns to look at me.

"No, sir," I say. "No questions."

"Very well," he says. "Godspeed, Barnes. Please try not to fuck this up."

THE ROVER WAITS for us outside the main lock, looking like nothing so much as a giant creeper with six fat, deep-treaded wheels and a burner turret on the roof.

"Nice," Nasha says. "Does it have a door?"

Jamie knocks on the hull, and a moment later a clamshell hatch swings open at the vehicle's rear, the door forming a stepped ramp into the cabin. Nasha turns to look at him.

"Are there keys?"

"Nope. It's keyed to my ocular."

"So what happens if you get eaten?"

He shrugs. "Unless one of you wants to clear enough space to download the rover's operating system, you're walking home." He climbs the three steps up, then ducks to step through the hatch. "So I guess you'd better make sure that doesn't happen, huh?"

"So," NASHA SAYS. "Are you gonna tell them, or am I?"

"Tell us what?" Jamie asks from the cockpit.

I sigh. "You're gonna want to stop just past the crest of this hill."

"Really?" Cat says, and reaches for her rebreather. "Are we there already?"

"Not quite. We're just stopping to pick up a passenger."

"It's a creeper," Nasha says. "We're picking up a creeper."

Lucas leans forward and turns to look back at her. "What?"

"We're picking up a creeper," Nasha says again. "It's a kind of . . . liaison, I guess? They made it just for us, so try not to be a total ass about it."

"Uh-huh," Lucas says. "And where, exactly, are you expecting this thing to ride?"

"Curled up in your lap," Nasha says. "This is happening, Lucas. Get over it."

We should be in comm range by now. I blink to a chat window.

> <Mickey7>: Speaker? You still out here?
>
> <Mickey7>: Hello?
>
> <Mickey7>: We're ready to go now. Please respond.
>
> <Speaker1>: Hello, Mickey.
>
> <Speaker1>: Where are you? I have been very unhappy waiting here.
>
> <Mickey7>: Should be near your position now.
>
> <Speaker1>: A large metal thing is moving toward me. Should I be alarmed?
>
> <Mickey7>: Nope. That's us. I'll be out in a minute.

"Jamie," I say. "Hold here."

The rover slows, then comes to a gentle stop. I pull on my rebreather and get to my feet. The passenger compartment is a tube maybe six meters long, with benches running along both sides, storage lockers above, and just enough headroom in the center for me to stand. It doesn't have a proper air lock, but it does have an atmospheric trap at the rear, just in front of the hatch. I move to the back, wait for the trap to close behind me, and then punch the exit button. The hatch opens, and I climb out into knee-high ferns at the crest of the hill.

<Mickey7>: Where are you?

The ground erupts a dozen or so meters down the slope, and Speaker's head emerges from the hole.

"Hello," he says. "Thank you for coming back for me. Is that a weapon?"

I look back. The turret on the top of the rover has come to life. As I watch, it rotates around to orient on Speaker, and the focusing crystal at its tip goes from flat black to a dull, angry red.

"Hey!" I wave my arms over my head and step between Speaker and the rover. "Stand down!"

Jamie's voice comes from a spot just below the turret. "Move aside, Mickey! You said we were picking up a creeper. What the hell is that thing?"

Right. They've only ever seen the little ones. Should have been a bit more clear on this, I guess. "This is what we came here for, Jamie. Stand down."

"No," Jamie says. "For shit's sake, Mickey. That thing's the size of a—Ow! What the hell, Nasha?"

I don't hear Nasha's answer, but after a brief delay the turret rotates back to its original position.

"Great," Jamie says. "Why not? Bring it aboard if you want. I'm sealing the cockpit."

"Come on," I say as Speaker pulls the rest of his body out of the ground. "Let me introduce you to your new allies."

"CAN I PUT my feet on it?" Berto asks.

"No," I say. "You can't put your feet on *him*, jackass."

Honestly, though, I can see why he'd want to. Speaker fills most of the center of the rover's passenger compartment, and Berto's tall enough that he's practically chewing on his knees right now.

"Chen," Berto says. "Switch spots?"

Cat and Lucas are back by the hatch, where there's plenty of leg room. Cat gives Berto the finger without looking up from her tablet. Berto shoots her a poisonous glare, then turns to me. "This is the one we saw up on the ridge the other day, right?"

I nod. "Speaker's been watching the dome for a while, apparently."

"This is true," Speaker says. "I was awaiting an opportunity to make contact."

Berto starts to answer, but Cat cuts him off with a giggle. He turns to look at her. "Something funny?"

"Yeah," Cat says. "That thing sounds exactly like you."

Berto's eyebrows come together over the bridge of his nose. "No, it doesn't."

"In fact, I do," Speaker says. "That was one of my design parameters."

Berto looks to me. I shrug.

"No," he says. "I don't sound like that."

"You do," Lucas says. "Eyes closed, I couldn't tell who was talking."

Berto opens his mouth, hesitates, then closes it again.

"It's not so bad," I say. "Think of it as an homage."

Berto looks like he's got something obnoxious to say to that, but then he shakes his head and says, "Whatever. Anyway, it would have been nice if you'd warned us beforehand that we'd be traveling with a creeper, Mickey. Any other surprises we should know about?"

"No," I say. "Not that I'm aware of, anyway. Speaker hasn't told us much about where we're going, though."

"South," Speaker says. "We are going south."

"South is a big place," Jamie says over the intercom from the sealed cockpit. "Can you be more specific?"

"No," Speaker says.

That gets us ten seconds of silence.

"Mickey?" Jamie says finally. "Can *you* be more specific?"

"Head south," I say. "I guess we'll know when we get there."

WE'VE ACTUALLY GOT decent survey maps of the entire northern hemisphere at this point, so we're not exactly heading out into the unknown here. The terrain south of the dome rises up pretty quickly into a series of sharp ridges a hundred or so klicks wide with deep, glacier-carved cuts in between. Some of the deeper ones are still packed with ice. We'll want to avoid those, because they're probably undermined by runoff and terminally unstable after two years of warming, and if we wind up breaking through the surface somewhere it's gonna be a long walk home.

Farther on, the terrain flattens out for a while before running into a mountain range that peaks out at almost fifteen thousand meters. Hopefully where we're going isn't farther than that, because there's no way we're getting through that range in this vehicle.

We've packed supplies for a couple of weeks. That should get us to the foothills and back with plenty to spare. If that's not enough, I guess we're going to need to reconsider.

"So, SPEAKER," CAT says without looking up from her tablet. "Just out of curiosity, what did you wind up doing with the people you took from us two years ago?"

Speaker's head lifts enough for him to turn half-around toward the back of the compartment.

"I have already discussed this with Mickey and the Nasha," he says. "I would rather not do so again."

Berto grins. "Mickey and the Nasha? Are you two starting a band?"

Cat shoots Berto a sour look before turning back to Speaker. "Is that so? One of the people you grabbed during the winter was my bunkmate and another was my friend, and I'd really like to know what happened to them. So, I would rather you did do so again."

"They killed them," Nasha says. "Not much more to say, is there?"

"This is true," Speaker says, "but to be clear, it was not our intent. We meant only to exchange ancillaries."

Cat's face twists into a scowl. "Exchange ancillaries? What the hell is that supposed to mean?"

"It's a whole thing," Nasha says. "They don't have much of a concept of individual life."

"Untrue," Speaker says. "This was a misconception. We understand our mistake now."

"It was understandable," I say. "The creepers are a hive mind."

Speaker rounds on me. "Also untrue."

"It is, as we understand it. Your ancillaries are not individually intelligent."

Speaker's mandibles clatter together. "Untrue. Untrue. Am I not intelligent?"

"Sure, I guess so—but you're not an ancillary."

A ripple runs the length of his body. "I am. This should be obvious. Do you imagine we would trust you to carry away our Prime?"

"So the smaller ones," I say, "the ones that we destroyed . . . they're intelligent?"

"No," Speaker says. "Obviously not."

"You're avoiding," Cat says. "What did you do with my friends?"

"I am not avoiding," Speaker says. "I am clarifying."

Nasha nudges him with her boot. "Answer the question."

Speaker twists toward her, waves one foreleg in an opaque gesture, then turns back to Cat. "We disassembled them," he says. "We hoped to find more useful innovations to assimilate, as we did when we disassembled the first of the Mickeys that we captured, but unfortunately they were all quite badly damaged during retrieval. We were able to learn some things regarding your biology, however. It was particularly useful to see examples of both of your basic forms. We have no such differences in body function, so this was an interesting discovery." After a few seconds of silence, he goes on. "Understand—for us, these are ordinary interactions between two unfamiliar Primes. Exchange of ancillaries is mutual and voluntary if the meeting is friendly, forced and sometimes one-sided if not, but it always occurs."

"Huh," Nasha says. "Always?"

"Yes," Speaker says. "More or less."

She leans forward with her elbows on her knees. "Your friends to the south—they feel the same way?"

Again, a ripple runs the length of Speaker's body. "Of course. Is this not why we have brought so many of you?"

We ride in silence for a long while after that.

"I'M BORED," LUCAS says.

Cat shakes her head without looking up. "Of course you are. Why didn't you bring a tablet?"

"I thought this would be exciting. Didn't realize it was actually going to be sitting on a bench and staring at the wall for the rest of my life." He shifts in his seat uncomfortably, then leans his head back and sighs again. "Who wants to tell me a story?"

"A story?" Nasha says. "What are you, four?"

"I can tell you a story," Speaker says.

Lucas barks out a short, sharp laugh. "Wasn't really talking to you, Wormy."

"My name is not Wormy," Speaker says. "Please call me Speaker."

"Whatever," Lucas says. "Point is, I don't want to hear a story from you."

Nasha breaks into a grin. "I don't know, Lucas. I'm kind of interested."

"As you should be," Speaker says. "I am an excellent story-teller."

Lucas looks back and forth between them, then closes his eyes and slumps a little deeper on the bench. "Fine. Make it a good one."

"Very well," Speaker says. "This story begins one hundred and seventy days ago. The sun was hot in a clear sky after two days of rain. A soft breeze moved through the fern fields, which were a-swarm with a million tiny hunters. Just past midday, Berto opened a dialogue with Mickey, initially related to whether Mickey would like to join him for lunch. However, the topic very quickly turned to Mickey's relationship with the Nasha. It seems that there had been an issue with their sexual—"

"Hey!" Nasha says, as I drop my head into my hands and the rest of the cabin bursts out laughing.

"I am sorry," Speaker says. "Have I misspoken?"

"No," Cat says around a giggle. "Not at all. I, for one, would very much like to hear the rest of that story—but I think every-one else was kind of hoping you might have a story about *you*."

"Oh," Speaker says. "Why? My life has been both brief and dull. I was sure you would find the intimate relations of Mickey and the Nasha much more interesting."

"Well—" Cat begins, before Nasha cuts her off.

"No," she says. "Nobody wants to hear that." She shoots me a look that tells me very clearly how much I'm going to regret having that chat with Berto, then turns back to Speaker. "Chen is right. We want to hear something about you. Not you in particular, maybe, but your people. You got a creation myth or something? Gods and spirits and all that mess? Those are always fun."

"Creation myth?" Speaker says. "I do not believe I understand."

"You know," Cat says. "Like, where did you come from?"

Speaker twists around to face her. "Oh. I thought this was clear. We come from here. We have never been elsewhere. Your people are the ones who have come here from somewhere else. In truth, it would probably be more useful if you told me where you come from. This has been a point of some speculation for us."

"That's an interesting question," Nasha says. "What have you speculated?"

Speaker hesitates. "I would rather not say."

"Wormy doesn't want to give away information," Lucas says without opening his eyes. "He's trying to learn as much as he possibly can about us while giving us the least possible information about him. It's exactly what I'd do in his situation, but that doesn't make it any less annoying."

"Again," Speaker says, "my name is not Wormy."

"It's a nickname," Lucas says. "A sign of affection."

"How about we trade?" Nasha says. "A story for a story?"

"Yes," Speaker says. "This seems fair. Will you begin?"

Nasha turns to me, one eyebrow raised.

"Nope," I say. "This was your idea."

She sighs. "Fine. Here's a story for you. These people? They're all from a place called Midgard. I am too, I guess, but my parents came from another place. They called it New Hope. Sounds nice, right? Very hopeful. It wasn't, though. I never saw New Hope, but my parents told me stories. It wasn't as god-awful as this place—no offense—but it was close. They needed CO_2 filters to breathe, it rained pretty much every minute of every day, and there were things there—not as spooky as you, maybe, but bad enough.

"Anyway, once they'd made planetfall, they made it work, because just like us, they didn't have any other choice. They planted crops, built out the colony, started raising babies. Things were going okay until some of the younger ones—the bottle babies, like my parents—figured out that one of the local species was maybe probably intelligent. Problem was, that species was one of the only things native to New Hope that humans could actually eat, and the colony had been capturing them for slaughter almost since the day they made planetfall.

"My father was nineteen then. He joined a liberation group and started writing articles and dumping them into the colony feed, trying to convince the old guard that they needed to respect the local life. My mother went further. The group she was with launched an attack on one of the facilities where the natives were being held. She told me that they didn't intend to kill the workers there, but . . . well, mistakes were made all around, I guess. After that, Command rounded up some of her friends and stuffed them down the corpse hole while they were still kicking. The next day, the sister of one of the ones who'd been killed went after the commander with a burner. She didn't kill him, but apparently she really pissed him off, because he tried to have Security detain every single planet-born colonist. The first officers who tried to carry out the order got ambushed, hit by hijacked military burners, and roasted in their armor.

"After that, things got bad. When it was over, the old guard was gone. They should have known that they'd never really had a chance. They were old, after all, and they were outnumbered two-to-one or more. Most of the colony's infrastructure was gone too, though, and the planet-born survivors didn't have the knowledge base or the resources to rebuild it. Also, a lot of them had come to the conclusion that they should never have come to an inhabited world in the first place. So, they boosted back up to orbit, did the best they could to retrofit the shell of the colony ship that had brought them there, and abandoned the planet. Five years later, eighty-two of them made orbit around Midgard, where they've been getting shit on ever since.

"The end."

The cabin is silent once Nasha stops speaking.

"Wow," Cat says finally. "That's not exactly the story we got in school."

"Yeah," Nasha says. "No shit."

"I am confused," Speaker says. "Was this story intended to reassure me of your good intentions toward us?"

Nasha shrugs. "Maybe. Did it?"

"No," Speaker says. "Not at all."

"No kidding," Cat says. "That story really didn't show humanity in the best light, did it, Nasha? Maybe you could have started him off with something a little less genocidal?"

"Sure," Lucas says. "You could have told him about Gault."

"Or the Bubble War," Berto says.

"The Bubble War?" Speaker says.

"Not relevant," I say. "Anybody have something a bit more appropriate to talk about?"

"I think it's Wormy's turn," Lucas says. "A story for a story, right?"

"These other places," Speaker says. "New Hope and Midgard—they are other worlds?"

"Maybe," Nasha says. "What do you know about other worlds?"

"We know many things. For example, we know there are six

other worlds orbiting our sun. I do not believe you come from any of these, however. Two are airless and very hot, and the other four are more like failed stars than planets. Nothing like you could exist on any of their surfaces. There are moons as well, some large enough to be worlds in their own rights, but none we know of that could harbor life. We do not know of any worlds orbiting other stars, but it seems reasonable that they might exist. Perhaps you would know the truth of this better than we."

I wouldn't have thought the creepers would know any of that. I need to file that away for future reference, in the same folder with the conversations I've had with Nasha on the topic. She's right. The creepers are not primitives. I'm still not sure I buy that they're really that much smarter than we are, but in any case it seems pretty clear that they're not significantly dumber, and underestimating them is probably a good way to get us all killed.

"So that's where you think we come from?" Nasha says. "Other stars?"

A ripple runs the length of Speaker's body. "The possibility has occurred to us, but this is a point of great contention. On one side, it seems clear that you are unlike any other creature on this world, and in fact you appear to be unable to survive here without significant augmentation. This argues that you come from elsewhere, and as I said, it seems impossible that your home could be another world orbiting our sun. On the other side, we have concluded that travel across the distances that separate us from even the nearest stars should be impossible. However, you are clearly here, so . . ." He trails off, and his mandibles clatter together. "The amount of energy required to cross the gulf between stars would be . . ." He falls silent, and stays that way for a long while. I glance over at Nasha. She shrugs. I'm about to say something when he speaks again. "I think," he says, "that it is possible that you may be a great deal more dangerous than we had thought."

"SO IS WORMY gonna tell us a story?"

I open my eyes. I'd been dozing, half dreaming about being down in the labyrinth with Eight again. Nasha had been resting her head on my shoulder, but she sits up now and squints across the cabin at Lucas. "Are you back on that again?"

"I told you," Lucas says. "I'm *bored*."

"You're a child," Nasha says. "I'm going to war with a god-damned child."

"We are not going to war," Speaker says. "I thought I was very clear about that."

"Yes, you were," Nasha says. "I guess we'll see, huh?"

We've been rolling for about six hours at this point, and for the last two we've been picking our way along high ridges, charting a path to avoid the worst of the remaining glaciers, barely moving faster than a walking pace most of the time. Lucas is right. It's really boring.

"I did agree to tell a story in exchange for the one the Nasha told," Speaker says. "Is this an appropriate time?"

"Depends," Nasha says. "This isn't more excerpts from Mickey's comm, right?"

"No," Speaker says. "Instead, I can tell a story explaining why our world is sometimes warm, as now, and sometimes cold, as when you first arrived here. Would that suffice?"

"Sure," Lucas says. "Go nuts, Wormy. Entertain me."

"Very well," Speaker says. "This story involves our sun, and also the world whose orbit is just outside ours. It can usually be seen clearly in the southern sky. Do you know it?"

"We're aware of it," Nasha says. "Massive gas giant. Twelve

moons, some of them almost big enough to be habitable if they weren't frozen solid and buried in the planet's radiation belts."

"Yes," Speaker says. "For the purposes of this story, I will refer to the sun as Fire, and the planet as Ice. Is this acceptable?"

"Those are terrible names," Lucas says.

Speaker twists around to face him. "What?"

"Those names," Lucas says. "They're terrible. Is that really what you call them?"

"No," Speaker says. "We do not communicate using atmospheric compression waves. Would you rather I tell this story in our language?"

"No," Lucas says. "Just pick better names."

"Mutt and Jeff," Berto says.

Speaker turns to him. "Mutt and Jeff?"

"Yeah," Berto says. "Those are good names. Use those."

He turns back to Lucas. "Is this acceptable?"

Lucas grins. "Sure. That works."

"Very well. So, in the beginning, there was one Prime, which was Mutt. As time passed, she found she was lonely, and so birthed seven ancillaries to serve as companions. These are the seven worlds in our system."

"Wait," Cat says. "Why are you calling them *he* and *she*? Didn't you say before that you don't have sexes?"

Speaker twists to face her. "We do not, but you do, no? Please remember that this story is for you, not for me. You see?"

"Yeah," Lucas says. "We've got it."

"Good. So. All was well for many years. Over time, though, Jeff, who was the greatest of the ancillaries, began to chafe at his status. He thought himself nearly as great as Mutt, and wished himself to be Prime."

"Can you do that?" Nasha asks.

"Do what?"

"Can one of your ancillaries become Prime?"

"Of course," Speaker says. "Where do you suppose Primes come from?"

Nasha shrugs. "Honestly, I hadn't given it much thought. Keep going, please."

"Yes. As I said, Jeff wished to become Prime, but Mutt would not allow it—so Jeff gathered his own ancillaries from the outer darkness, and flung them in at Mutt and her followers, one after another, for all of an age. These had no effect on Mutt, of course, but they took a terrible toll on her ancillaries, striking them again and again until they were little more than molten rubble. Eventually, Mutt took pity on her children, and offered peace. Jeff would hold sway over the ancillaries of the outer darkness, while Mutt would maintain her hold on the three inner worlds.

"Jeff, however, would not agree. He insisted that the outermost of Mutt's ancillaries—our world, of course—should be his as well. He threatened to continue his war until all the inner worlds were destroyed. Mutt responded by launching a great column of fire as a warning to him. Though unhurt, Jeff was frightened then, and so he proposed a compromise. Our world would be shared between the two of them. After some further argument, Mutt agreed—and this is why our world is as it is today. When Mutt holds sway, we are warm and green. When Jeff takes his turn, however, the ice covers everything, and life must dig deep and await Mutt's return."

"Okay," Lucas says. "I see now why you wanted to go with Fire and Ice. Probably should have stuck to your guns there."

"So that's it?" Nasha says. "That's what you believe?"

"What?" Speaker says. "No. Of course not. That was just a story. We understand what planets are, and how our sun functions."

"Huh," Berto says. "That puts you one up on us."

"But this is what you used to believe, right?" Nasha says. "It's mythology—an ancient story passed down from before the time that you understood all that stuff."

"No," Speaker says. "This story was not passed down. I invented it today. You did not like my original story, so I made this one instead. Did you not like it?"

Nasha has just opened her mouth to say something more when Jamie cuts in over the intercom.

"I hate to interrupt story hour, but does someone want to tell me what's happening here?"

A viewscreen on the bulkhead between the cabin and the cockpit comes to life. It takes me a disoriented moment to realize that we're seeing the view from a side-facing camera. It takes another minute to see what Jamie's talking about. Off in the distance, just where the ridge drops away, things are coming up out of the ground. Lots of things. My first impression is that they look like the leggy creature Nasha burned when we were on our way back from finding out that the bomb was missing. These are bigger, though. Much, much bigger.

"Speaker?" I say. "Those wouldn't happen to be your friends to the south, would they?"

Speaker rises up and spreads his mandibles in a threat posture. "No," he says. "Our friends to the south are like me in appearance, more or less. These are likely . . . I do not know the correct word in your language, but . . . associated with our friends to the south?"

"Associated?" I say. "Like allies?"

A ripple runs the length of Speaker's body. "No, not allies. You and we are allies. Allies are equals. These are something less than that."

"Vassals?" Berto says.

"What does this word mean?"

"Sort of a mix between allies and slaves."

"Yes," Speaker says. "This sounds more correct than either allies or associates. These creatures are vassals."

"Is there a reason you didn't warn us about them?" Nasha asks.

"I did not warn because I did not know. Vassals of our friends to the south do not ordinarily venture so close to our home—certainly not in such numbers as these. They should fear provoking a response from us, but it seems something has overcome their caution. It may be that they have been lying in wait for you."

I really don't like the sound of that. I'm about to say so when Jamie says, "They're coming up all around us. We can't go much faster than we are over this terrain, and it looks like they're keeping pace with us. I guess it's possible I might be able to roll over them or burn them down, but I don't think we can outrun them."

I turn to Speaker. "Pretty sure I know the answer to this, but are they dangerous?"

A ripple runs the length of his body. "To me? Possibly not. They should still have enough respect for my nest to avoid damaging me. To you, though? Yes, I think very much so."

"Berto," I say. "Get airborne. Now."

He turns to stare at me.

"What?"

"You heard me. Unpack that ultralight you insisted on bringing, get it rigged, and get into the air."

"I can't," he says. "I need a cliff or something to launch from, remember?"

I turn to the viewscreen. "Jamie—how fast can you get this thing going?"

"Over this terrain? I don't think more than twenty meters per second, and I won't be able to hold that if I'm smacking into monsters along the way."

"Berto, is that enough to get you up?"

He scratches his head. "Maybe? If I go to full thrust with the drive units right from the jump, I guess it's possible. It'll be close, anyway."

I nod. "Good enough. Get geared up and go."

Berto pulls on his rebreather, grabs his pack, and starts toward the back of the cabin.

"I told you," Nasha mutters as he passes her.

"What?"

"I told you," she says. "I knew you'd wind up using that thing to bug out on us as soon as things got hairy."

He rounds on her. "Fuck you, Nasha. Did you hear what I just said about getting off the ground? It's probably at least fifty-fifty that I'm about to go nose-down into the turf out there and get ripped apart by those things on the viewscreen while you're sitting safe and snug in here. Fuck. You."

"No arguing," I snap. "No time. Berto, go."

"I'm gonna need help," Berto says. "Two people, probably, to hold me down until I'm ready to fly."

I get to my feet, then turn and offer Nasha my hand. She rolls her eyes, but she lets me pull her up.

"Sure," she says. "Why not?"

We grab our rebreathers, and we go.

"THIS IS BAD," Berto mutters as he snaps the last spar in place. "This is seriously bad."

"No shit," Nasha says. "So why don't you hurry up and get out of here while you've still got the chance?"

We're clinging to the top of the rover as it bounces along the crest of a rocky ridge at what feels like breakneck speed, but is actually probably barely faster than I could run. As Berto works, I'm having trouble not picturing him trying to take off, then smacking straight into the ground and getting crushed under our wheels.

"I'm not talking about those things," Berto says. "I'm talking about my prospects of actually getting airborne. You feel that? We're slowing down. Think we could get Jamie to turn into the wind?"

"I don't think there's much of a breeze going right now," Nasha says. "Hard to say which way he should turn."

"I'm screwed," Berto says. "Screwed, screwed, screwed." He's got the fabric out of the pack now. As he lays it across the skeletal frame, a sudden gust from the side billows it up until it almost covers him. "Help me," he says as he presses it back down and starts stretching fabric over the frame. "This thing is gonna start pulling."

Nasha grabs a wingtip in one hand and the rim of the burner turret with the other. I take the other wing and anchor myself to the open hatch at the rear.

"This isn't gonna work," Berto says. "There's no fucking headwind. We're not going fast enough. Those things are gonna tear me apart." He doesn't stop working, though. Thirty seconds more, and he's finished with the last connections. The glider really is bucking now, catching the air and trying to haul itself out of our hands. Berto steps through the harness and grasps the control bar. "I'm serious," he says. "This is suicide. You know that, don't you?"

"Yeah," I say. "I know a bit about suicide, Berto."

I glance around. There must be at least a hundred of the things out there now. They look like six-legged spiders with the creeper's cutting mandibles jutting from their faces. They range from a meter or so across the legs to a few that could be half the size of the rover. They're mostly scattered along our flanks maybe fifty meters off to either side, running with us, holding pace as others move to surround us in front and behind.

"Okay," Berto says. "This isn't getting any better, is it? If we're gonna do it, now's the time."

Nasha and I move in closer to him, hand over hand along the wings, until we can rotate the frame around to face the front of the rover. The wind kicks up again, from the direction we're traveling this time, and the glider nearly pulls itself out of my hands.

"Shit," Nasha says. "There's the headwind you were looking for. You gotta go, Berto. I don't think I can hold this thing much longer."

"Just a sec," Berto says, and runs a finger along his control bar. The thrusters under the wings begin to hum. "Okay. Ready?" He takes a deep breath, holds it, then lets it out slowly. "Let go."

As soon as he's free of us, Berto runs for his life. In three strides he's barely touching the rover. He leaps, kicks hard off of the burner turret, and takes flight.

Well, "takes flight" might be a bit generous.

As soon as he's past the nose of the rover, Berto begins a slow, steady descent. He's pulling away from us, so he must be accelerating, but over the course of five seconds or so he goes from an altitude of three meters, to two, to barely avoiding dragging his toes in the turf.

"He's not gonna make it," Nasha says.

"He will," I say. "He has to."

I've given him enough shit over the past two years for killing me. I really don't want our friendship to end with me killing him in turn.

As he accelerates away from us, Berto's gaining ground on the things ahead. He's not sinking anymore, but he's not rising either, and the distance between him and them is dropping precipitously. Thirty meters. Twenty meters. Ten. At that point, they seem to notice him. The two running directly in front of him peel off to either side as he sweeps toward them, seemingly confused as to whether he represents a threat or an opportunity.

That's all the opening Berto needs. He cuts through their line, wingtips nearly brushing the spiders on either side. After a moment's hesitation the things give chase, but it's too late. Apparently he's managed to build up enough speed now, because he abruptly leaps away from the ground in a steep, sweeping climb.

"Holy shit," he says over the comm. "Holy goddamn fucking shit. Did you see that? Did you see how close that was?"

"We saw," I say. "I'm glad you made it."

"Yeah," he says. "Thanks. Me too. So what now?"

"Now?" I say. "Now you stay up there and watch what happens to us. If we get through this, we'll pick you up again when we're clear. If not, you haul ass back to the dome and let them know what happened. They'll need to put together another expedition. Maybe this time Marshall will authorize a lifter, huh?"

"Maybe," Berto says. "Hopefully it doesn't come to that, though. You gonna fire up the burner now?"

"No," I say. "I don't think so. I'm pretty sure there are too many of them to fight. I'm hoping they eventually give up the chase."

"I don't know, buddy. They look pretty determined from up here. They're closing the noose on you, you know."

I glance around. He's right. They're closer on the sides now, and the ranks in front of us are filling in.

"We'll see what happens," I say. "Whatever it is, though, make sure you stay out of it, right? I need you to make it home safe."

"You got it," he says. "Good luck, Mickey."

"Yeah," I say. "Thanks."

Nasha's already swinging herself back through the hatch. I give one more look around, then follow her down.

"HELP US, SPEAKER. What do we do here?"

Speaker rises from the floor of the cabin until his mandibles are at my eye level. "I am unsure. As I said, this behavior is uncharacteristic of our friends, so my experience may be a poor predictor of what they intend. Can you destroy them?"

"Maybe. If the burner does more damage to them than it does to your people, or if they hold their distance long enough for Nasha and Cat and Lucas to pick them off one by one with their LAs. What do you think?"

He seems to consider. "I do not know what your burner can do, or how well armored these creatures are. I know they will not stay back and allow you to hunt them, however. As soon as you initiate hostilities, they will certainly attack."

"Do you think the rover's armor will hold them off?"

"Again," Speaker says, "I do not know what this machine's properties are. If it is similar to the armor your fighters wear, or the substance of your nest, though, I think not."

"Lucas? Cat? What do you think?"

Lucas is running a diagnostic on his accelerator while Cat stuffs ammunition into every pocket of her jumper.

"We're the muscle here," Lucas says without looking up. "You're the brains, remember?"

"I vote we start shooting and see how they like it," Nasha says. "They've never seen anything like what we can do to them. Maybe they'll spook."

"These are most likely all ancillaries," Speaker says. "They will not be frightened, even if you manage to kill them all. I am sure they see this machine as a miraculous source of rare metals. They will not let it go."

"They're getting close," Jamie says from the cockpit. "If I'm going to use the burner on them, I need to do it soon."

I close my eyes. The rate of fire for the linear accelerators is about one round per second. Assuming Nasha, Cat, and Lucas don't miss a shot, they can kill three of those things per second among them. What can the burner do? If they're anything like the creepers, it'll need a dwell time of a few seconds at least to take one down. There looked to be a hundred or so of them out there, all told. That means we'd need probably thirty seconds to take them all out at an absolute, optimistic-beyond-all-reason minimum. Thirty seconds with Nasha, Cat, and Lucas exposed on the roof of the rover . . .

If I had three random goons with me, I might risk it. If one of them was Drake, I almost definitely would. With Nasha, though, or Cat?

"We can't fight them. Speaker, what are our options?"

"Well," he says, "if fighting is not an option, I suppose that only leaves surrender."

"No," Nasha says. "Hell, no. I'm going back up top."

She pulls her rebreather down over her face and starts for the hatch, but I catch her arm.

"Speaker, can we negotiate? I get that they want the metal in the rover, but surely they don't actually want to lose half their ancillaries or more to get it, right?"

"I would not be so sure," Speaker says. "You may be under-estimating the value of rare metals to us. Half of their ancillaries for the opportunity to scavenge this machine would be more than a fair trade."

"They don't know how many of them we can kill," Lucas says. "They don't know anything at all about our capabilities. Can we bluff them?"

"Bluff?" Speaker says.

"Lie," I say. "Convince them we're more dangerous than we actually are."

"This is possible," Speaker says. "Would you like for me to try?"

"Hey," Jamie says, "it's kind of do-or-die time here, Mickey. One of them just tried to get a grip on our flank."

"Slow down," I say. "Speaker's getting off."

"You sure about that? Once they're on top of us, I'm not sure we'll be able to get moving again."

"We'll cross that bridge if we come to it. Right now I think we're out of options."

"To be clear, I am not certain they will speak to me," Speaker says. "They may simply disassemble me."

"If they do," Nasha says, "then I guess we've got our answer, right?"

With a shudder, we roll to a stop.

"Rebreathers on," I say. "Jamie—pop the hatch."

We're all on our feet now. Speaker waits at the back hatch, forelegs tapping against the decking. Cat and Lucas stand to either side of him, explosive rounds locked and loaded, accelerators trained on the first crack of daylight that's just appeared at the top edge of the hatch. I'm standing behind Speaker with Nasha beside me. She's holding her weapon across her chest, her finger nervously stroking the safety. I'm staring straight ahead, jaw set, one of Nasha's burners held at the ready.

I'm desperately trying not to wet myself.

The hatch swings open.

The plain behind us is swarmed with spiders.

With a final glance back at us, Speaker descends.

"NOT FOR NOTHING," Cat says, "but I'm really liking Take Charge Mickey. I don't think I've seen this side of you before."

"It's always been in there," Nasha says. "It only comes out for special occasions, though."

"Yeah," Lucas says. "I bet."

Nasha rolls her eyes and mutters, "A child. An actual goddamned child."

I'd love to jump into this discussion, but I'm apparently the only one in the cabin who's still focused on the fact that Speaker is negotiating for our lives right now.

"Berto," I say over the comm. "What's going on out there?"

"Well," he says, "they haven't eaten him yet. That's gotta be a plus, right?"

"Okay, yeah. That's good, I guess—but what are they actually doing?"

"Dancing."

"Dancing?"

"Yeah, pretty much. Speaker is up on his rear segments, prancing around and waving his legs in the air. One of the spiders is circling around him, basically doing the same."

"Are they fighting? Is this some kind of ritual combat thing?"

"No," he says. "I don't think so, anyway. They're not touching each other."

"Huh. Maybe this is how they talk? Speaker said they don't communicate using sound waves. Maybe they have a visual language?"

"Maybe. Not sure how long you were expecting this to go on, but if it doesn't wrap up soon we're gonna need to make a decision about what I'm doing. These drive units have a limited charge, you know. I can't stay up here much longer if you want me to make it back to the dome in one piece."

"Understood. If it comes to that, just go. Come back with an armed lifter if you can. If not, I guess you need to assume we're dead."

"And?"

"See if Marshall can pull together another expedition."

"Right. To go where, exactly? Without Speaker, we have no idea where these 'friends to the south' are, let alone any idea of how to communicate with them."

"Go back to the creepers. Maybe they'll give you another Speaker?"

"Tell you what," Berto says. "How about you guys just don't get killed here, okay? Seems like that's our best option all around."

"Duly noted," I say. "I'll see what we can do."

THE HATCH SWINGS open. Speaker returns.

"Well?" I say. "What's the story?"

"Negotiations have not concluded," Speaker says. "They ask for a demonstration."

I glance around the cabin. All eyes are on me. "A demonstration? Of what?"

A ripple runs the length of Speaker's body. "I have argued that they should not simply dismantle this rover, and you with it, because you are extraordinarily dangerous. As Lucas suggested, I have tried to *bluff* them. They do not entirely believe me. They require a demonstration."

"Okay, but what kind? What do they want us to do?"

"They did not specify," Speaker says, and settles back down onto the deck. "However, it needs to happen now, before any further discussions. If it cannot be provided, they intend to begin the dismantling."

Nasha drops her rebreather over her face. "Jamie," she says. "Open the hatch."

"Mickey?" Jamie says.

After a few seconds of silence, I sigh and say, "Do it, Jamie."

"You got it," he says.

The hatch swings open.

Nasha strides out onto the ramp, takes aim, and fires. The nearest spider—a big one, probably three meters across the legs—bursts like an overripe melon. The rest scuttle madly, some toward the rover, some away. Nasha turns and ducks back through the hatch.

"Okay," she says. "Seal it up."

A spider charges her from behind. The hatch slams. The spider clangs off the armor with a sound like a hammer blow.

"There's your demonstration," Nasha says. "Now get back out there and tell them to leave us alone."

"MICKEY," BERTO SAYS. "Time's up. I'm counting on a tailwind if I leave now. If I wait any longer, there's no way I'm making it back to the dome."

"Okay. Good luck, I guess—and don't worry. I'll tell Nasha you were under strict orders to get the hell out of here."

"Tell him I knew it," Nasha says from across the cabin. "Tell him if we die out here I'm one hundred percent gonna haunt his ass."

"Nasha says—"

"Yeah," Berto says. "I heard. Thanks."

"I guess it's up to you to make sure the next expedition is less stupid than this one. See if you can get more Security, or at least heavier weapons. See if you can get a lifter. And hey—if Marshall pulls a new me out of the tank, he should be able to communicate with the creepers every bit as well as I could. Go see them. See if they'll give us another Speaker."

"Oh no," he says. "Don't start with that shit. I gave you up for dead once, remember? It didn't work out. This time, I'm assuming you're gonna find a way to weasel out of this right up until I actually see your mangled corpse—and even then, I'm checking for a pulse."

"Thanks, Berto. Hey, how's it going out there?"

"Still dancing," he says. "They haven't killed him yet."

"I guess that's all we can ask at this point."

"Guess so. Anyway, I'm going. Good luck, buddy."

"Thanks, Berto. You too."

"You know," Nasha says, "we're putting a hell of a lot of trust in Wormy."

I roll my eyes. "Please don't call him Wormy. It's bad enough coming from Lucas. I don't need that crap from you too."

"Sorry," she says. "Seriously, though—he's been gone for over an hour now. What the hell is taking so long?"

I shrug. "You remember how they negotiated with us in the labyrinth. Apparently creepers don't rush this kind of thing."

"For all we know, he's out there telling them how to cook us."

"You're right," I say. "He might be—but what's our other option?"

"Three of us up on the roof with explosive rounds, and Jamie going hard with the burner. That's our other option."

I shake my head. "I thought about that before Speaker went out the first time. The math doesn't work. There are too many of them."

"Disagree," Cat says. "We've got three LAs and two handheld burners, plus the turret. That's a hell of a lot of firepower when the things we're fighting don't even have crossbows. You really think our odds are better sitting here waiting for Speaker to talk our way out of this?"

I lean forward and rest my forehead on the heels of my hands. "Look, it's not like the fact that we're trying the diplomatic route means that we don't have the option to go fire-and-fury later, but if we start shooting now, that's it. No going back from that. Let Speaker do what he can. If nothing else, it buys us time."

Lucas barks out a harsh laugh. "Time? Time for what, Mickey? Squatting in this B.O.-smelling can waiting to find out if Wormy can convince those things to just kill us instead of eating us alive? If we're gonna do this, I'd just as soon do it now. There's no cavalry to come for us, and the only thing waiting's doing as far as I can see is giving them time to bring in more reinforcements."

I look up. He's staring at me, one hand resting on his accelerator. "If I thought we could shoot our way out of this," I say, slowly and clearly, "I'd do it, Lucas. There are at least a hundred spiders out there, and we can kill a max of three per second. I don't know how many ways I can say this: the math does not work."

"The math doesn't work if we believe that they'll just keep coming once their friends start exploding," Nasha says. "I'm not sure I buy that, though. I'm betting that once the shrapnel starts piling up, the rest of them cut and run."

"I like the way Adjaya's thinking," Lucas says. "Get us up top, gun the engines, and see if they can catch us while they're tripping over their friends' bodies."

"I hear you," I say. "If what Speaker says about their concern for casualties is true, though, you're totally wrong. You heard him say they'd be more than willing to let us take down half of them or more to get a shot at the rover, right? Are you willing to bet all of our lives on the idea that you understand those things' psychology better than Speaker does?"

"It's not about understanding," Lucas says. "It's about trust, and I trust Wormy about as far as I could throw him."

"Be that as it may, I'm not going to risk our survival—and the colony's, remember—on the idea that we can shoot our way out of this. Not yet, anyway. If Marshall had given us the firepower that we asked for, it might be a different story. As it stands, though, I still think Speaker is our best bet."

"I guess we'll see," Lucas says. "Don't get me wrong—I hope you're right, Mickey. I've got a bad feeling, though. There's stuff Wormy's not telling us." He settles deeper into the bench and tucks his chin to his chest. "Hope it doesn't wind up getting us all killed, huh?"

ANOTHER HOUR PASSES before the hatch swings open and Speaker scuttles in.

"I have good news," he says as it slams shut behind him. "We have agreed to a compromise."

I glance around the cabin. Everyone is looking at me, not Speaker.

"Okay," I say. "What do they want?"

He hesitates, and I feel my stomach clench.

"Well," he says. "As we anticipated, they require us to surrender the rover. From their perspective, the metal in this machine is priceless."

"I bet," Lucas says. "Tell you what, though. Unless they know a lot more than you'd think about plasma physics, they're about to get a big surprise when they cut into the power system."

"What else do they want?" Nasha asks.

Speaker rises up to face her, but doesn't speak.

"What is it?" Nasha says. "We knew they wanted the rover. If that was *all* they wanted, you would have just said so."

"Yes," Speaker says. "Well."

She folds her arms across her chest. "Well?"

"In consideration of the one you destroyed, they require that you provide them an ancillary."

"Jamie?" Nasha says. "Fire up the burner and get ready to roll."

"No!" I say. "Wait! Just . . . just wait. I need to think."

Lucas is wide awake now, on his feet and reaching for his weapon. "Think, Mickey? What are you thinking about? Which one of us you're gonna hand over to those monsters? 'Cause I'll tell you right now—it's not gonna be me."

Cat's up too now, accelerator in hand and pulling her re-breather down over her face. "I'm with Lucas," she says. "Time to go down swinging."

"Please," Speaker says. "Please consider, friends. This is not the time for rash actions. It is better to lose one than all, no?"

"Fair enough to say that we don't understand their psychology," Nasha says. "They sure as shit don't understand ours." She pulls her burners from their holsters and hands them to me. "Here. Not sure if these will help out there, but they probably won't hurt. Jamie—how long until you're ready to open up?"

A moment of silence follows. Then, for the first time since we picked up Speaker, the cockpit door slides back into its recess, and Jamie ducks through and into the cabin.

"No," he says. "Speaker is right. So is Mickey. Those things are all around us. If you go out there and start shooting, they'll be on top of the rover and tearing you apart before we've gone twenty meters. I could try with the burner, but I can't target them with that if they're crawling over our skin. The time to fight was when we were moving and they were spread out. It's too late now."

Nasha stares at him, her jaw hanging open, for a long five seconds. It's Lucas who finally breaks the silence.

"Okay, rabbit man. What do you suggest, then? How do you plan on picking one of us to feed to the spiders? Because, just to reiterate, it's goddamn well not gonna be me."

Jamie closes his eyes. When he opens them again, his face has taken on a hard, angry set.

"No," he says. "It's not gonna be you, Lucas. You're muscle, and we need muscle. Same goes for Chen, right? And it can't be Mickey, can it? He's our creeper whisperer. Nasha? She's a fighter too, and Mickey would never let her go anyway. So, who does that leave, dumbass?" He looks at us each in turn, then shakes his head. "Don't look at me like that, you assholes. And if you make it back to the dome somehow, don't you fucking dare tell anybody that I volunteered for this. I am not fucking volunteering, understand? I'm just recognizing reality. I got pushed into this fiasco because I'm rated to pilot the rover. That's my function here. If we're giving up the rover, then what am I? Dead weight." He laughs. "Dead weight. Dead meat. Same thing." He turns to Speaker. "Should I take a rebreather, or will they just tear me to pieces as soon as I step through the hatch?"

"I cannot advise you on this," Speaker says. "They demanded

an ancillary. They gave me no indication of what they intended to do with it."

"It?" Lucas says. "Fuck you, Wormy."

"Jamie," Nasha says. "You don't have to do this. We can just go—just roll over them. We don't even know these things are capable of breaching our armor."

"They are," Speaker says. "After engaging with them, I can confirm this."

"Doesn't matter," Cat says. "Nasha's right. This isn't happening. We don't do human sacrifices."

"They do not request a sacrifice," Speaker says. "They request an ancillary. Please recall that you are the strangers here. This is customary for us."

"We don't give a shit what's customary for you," Nasha says.

"If you fight," Speaker says, "they will kill you all."

"Just so you know," Lucas says, "if we go down, you're going with us, Wormy. You're not squirming away. I'll put the round in you myself if it comes to that."

"No," Speaker says, "that will not be necessary. I told them that I could bargain in your place. If you try to fight them now, they will see this as a betrayal on my part. They will certainly disassemble me along with you, and they may attach the guilt for my deception to my nest. Please consider that what you do here may be the beginning of a broader war."

"Not our problem," Cat says.

I drop onto the bench and lean back against the wall. "It is our problem, Cat. If they wind up going to war, there's no way this doesn't spill over onto us. It's barely a klick from the perimeter to the nearest part of their labyrinth."

"Mickey is correct," Speaker says. "If it comes to open combat between my nest and theirs, the winner will turn to you next, if only to replace the materials lost in the fighting. I think you would be quickly overwhelmed."

"Maybe," Lucas says. "Maybe not. We've got weapons systems you haven't seen yet. You'd be surprised what we can do if we're pushed to it."

"Stop," I say. "Everybody, just . . . just stop, for one goddamn minute. Please. Jamie, sit down. Lucas, shut up. Speaker, how locked in are we with these things? I get that you may not have really understood how we'd react to being asked to give someone up. Can you go back out there and renegotiate? Tell them we don't have ancillaries? Maybe there's something else we can give them instead."

"I can try," Speaker says. "However, I should tell you that, from their perspective, an agreement has been reached. We take agreements very seriously. If I attempt to renege at this point, the most likely outcome is that they destroy me, and then destroy you."

"Sounds good to me," Lucas says. "Maybe we can get a jump on them while they're working on you."

"Lucas," I say. "Seriously. Shut up. You are not helping."

He opens his mouth to reply, but I guess something in my face convinces him to let it go.

"How much time do we have?" Nasha asks.

Speaker turns to her. "Time?"

"Yeah. How long can we stall before they start getting antsy?"

"I do not understand," Speaker says. "What good does stalling do? At best, it delays the inevitable. At worst, it may allow for more of them to arrive."

"Honestly," Jamie says, "if I'm going to do this, I think I'd rather get it over with. Sitting around thinking about it for another hour is not going to make me any happier."

"No," Nasha says. "You're not going out there until you absolutely have to. It's like the king and the thief, right?"

She looks around the cabin. All she gets back are four blank stares.

"The king and the thief," she says. "It's a parable. My mom must have told it to me a hundred times. None of you know what I'm talking about?"

"Maybe it's a New Hope thing," Cat says.

Nasha rolls her eyes. "Look. There's this thief, okay? And he gets caught, and they haul him in front of the king to be sentenced. I guess he stole something big, because the king sentences him to death. As they're hauling him away, the thief says, 'Wait, Your Highness! If you spare me, I'll teach your horse to speak!'

"Well, that gets the king's attention. 'How long would this take?' he says. 'A year,' the thief replies. 'Give me a year, and your horse will speak.' The king thinks it over, then shrugs and says, 'Fine. A year it is. If my horse doesn't speak before that time is out, you'll hang.' The thief bows, and the guards lead him away.

"Once they're out of the throne room, one of the guards says, 'What was the point of that? All you've done is postpone your hanging.' The thief smiles. 'A year is a long time,' he says. 'The king may die in that time. I may die in that time. Or who knows? Maybe the horse will learn to speak.'"

After a long, awkward silence, Speaker says, "What is a horse?"

"Doesn't matter," Nasha says. "The point is, we hold out for as long as we can. So, how long is that, Speaker?"

Speaker takes a moment to consider, mandibles gnashing together.

"This is not entirely clear," he says finally. "We did not specify a time frame."

"Okay, then," Nasha says. "We wait until they come knocking."

"So here's something I don't understand," Nasha says, breaking a silence that's lasted almost two hours but has felt more like a month. "This planet is kind of a shithole, right? No offense, Speaker, but this place isn't really super-friendly to life, is it?"

"I do not have a point of comparison," Speaker says. "It seems friendly enough to me."

"Take my word for it," Nasha says. "It's not. That's not my point, though. My point is that the Union has explored a whole lot of planets over the past thousand years, most of them more habitable than this one, and in all that time we've run across, what, one other intelligent species?"

"Two," I say. "Roanoke and Long Shot. Three, if you count the system that ate Eden's first colony ship."

"And Acadia's," Lucas says. "Did they ever figure out what was going on there?"

I shake my head. "Not really. All we know is that something makes ships vanish without a trace as soon as they hit the system's Oort cloud, and that anything that can pull that trick is probably not something we want to mess with."

"Didn't you say there were sentients on New Hope?" Cat says. "That's at least four, right?"

"Whatever," Nasha says. "Point is, most habitable planets don't host technological intelligence, right? What are the odds that there would be *two* of them here?"

"The universe is a weird place," I say. "It's a good question, though. I guess our base expectation is that the emergence of one intelligent species on a planet suppresses the emergence of any others. That's what happened on old Earth, anyway. There were a half dozen hominids that could have made the jump, but as soon as we crossed the Rubicon, the rest of them mysteriously disappeared. Who knows, though? Maybe this is just a kinder, gentler place?"

"How about it, Speaker?" Nasha asks. "Any insights here?"

"I'm sorry," Speaker says. "I do not think I understand. You believe there are two thinking species on this planet?"

That gets him a long moment of silence.

"You told us you've been negotiating with those things," Nasha says finally. "Are you telling us that they're not even sentient?"

"As I have tried to explain, this is a complicated question. The creatures outside are primarily ancillaries. By your definition, many of these may not be sentient. However, there seems to be at least one Prime present as well."

"I'm not talking about the individuals," Nasha says. "The species, though—they're sentient?"

"Again, I think I fail to understand. We have agreed that we are sentient, have we not? Do you not acknowledge that I am sentient?"

Nasha opens her mouth to reply, hesitates, then closes it again.

"So," I say. "Are you saying those things out there are creepers?"

"Please clarify: Am I a creeper?"

"Yeah," Lucas says. "You're a creeper."

"Then yes, the creatures outside now are also creepers. We are the same. I told you that they are vassals of our friends to the south, did I not?"

"But—" Nasha begins.

"You're a worm," Lucas says. "They're spiders. You're not the same."

"Apologies," Speaker says. "I thought we were clear on

this point. This shell is not biological. It is a construct. How else could we have mimicked your vocal apparatus in such a short time? This gives us great flexibility. We can take on many forms."

"Really?" Lucas says. "You're a mech?"

I shake my head. "Not really. Creepers aren't mechs, exactly. They're some kind of hybrid—or at least the specimen we captured was."

"Correct," Speaker says. "We are hybrid. Part biological, part mechanical. This is why we put such value on obtaining metal. Availability of various metallic elements is the most important limit on our reproduction."

"Huh," Nasha says. "I'm even less eager to hand over the rover now. How many of those things will they be able to make with what they scavenge from this?"

"Hundreds," Speaker says. "Depending on exactly what materials it is made of, possibly many hundreds. This machine is a great resource."

"Uh-huh," Lucas says. "I'm suddenly very curious about exactly what went down in those negotiations."

"Damn straight," Cat says.

"What are you thinking?" Nasha asks.

Lucas shrugs. "Pretty obvious, isn't it? Wormy just admitted that his bunch is just as desperate for metals as those things outside are, didn't he? It's logical to assume, then, that he wants a chunk of this rover just as badly as the spiders do. So, he goes out there and tells them that he can talk us into surrendering without a fight if his nest gets a share of the spoils. It's a pretty straightforward scam."

Speaker rises up from the deck and twists to face Lucas. "Scam? I do not know this word. Do you accuse me of betrayal?"

Lucas doesn't quite bring his accelerator to bear, but his

finger finds the trigger guard. "I'm not accusing you of anything, Wormy. I'm just calling it like I see it."

This is bad. I need to end it now. I get to my feet.

"No," I say. "We're not doing this. Lucas, stand down. Speaker, you too. We're all friends here, remember?"

"Speak for yourself," Lucas says. "Friends don't feed friends to spiders."

"They would not *eat* him," Speaker says. "We have no interest in you as a food source. Your proteins are not digestible."

"Really?" Lucas asks. "And how would you know that?"

"They know because they dissected me two years ago," I say. "They took Six, and they pulled him apart to see what made him tick."

"So is that what they're gonna do to me?" Jamie asks. "Take me apart?"

"Most likely, yes," Speaker says. "Your people are a new thing in this world. This alone makes you worthy of study. Moreover, you have proven to be dangerous. It is understandable that we feel a need to examine your inner workings, is it not?"

"I'm getting a serious urge to examine *your* inner workings, Wormy," Lucas growls.

"Hey!" I say. "I said that's enough, Lucas! Put a cork in it, would you? *We are not doing this*. We are not going to kill each other right now. We've got enough problems with those things outside. Speaker—tell me truly: Did you agree to take a share of the metal if we let those things pull the rover apart?"

"Yes," Speaker says. "I did."

"Oooooooh shit," Nasha says into the stunned silence.

"Speaker?" I say, careful to keep my tone neutral. "Did you sell us out?"

"No," he says. "I did not sell you out, if I understand the term correctly. I obtained the best bargain for all of us that I could.

Understand, please: They were adamant that they would take the rover. If they were to take all of it, they would be able to create hundreds more of themselves. They are already stronger than my nest by some measures. Perhaps this would allow them to create enough additional ancillaries to enable them to overwhelm and displace my Prime. I have told you that this is their goal."

"And we told you, that's not our problem," Cat says.

"Think, please. We are your allies. If we are displaced, your position is worsened, even if you do not believe that our friends would be able to destroy you. If we take a portion of the metal from this machine, we will be more likely to be able to keep our place. This benefits us both, no?"

"That's it," Lucas says. "Mickey, are you hearing this? You cannot seriously still be considering following through on this deal. I'm not gonna pop him now. I get that we need him to find the bomb, and we need the bomb to live. From here on out, though, he's got to be considered a hostile, and we cannot trust a goddamned word he's said about those things out there. I know the creepers can cut through man-portable armor, and I know they cut through the decking in the main hatch, but this rover is built to military specifications. It's designed to withstand a fusion blast at a thousand meters. If they can cut into it, then I guess we're screwed, but if we walk out of that hatch into the middle of those things, I will guarantee you that they don't let us walk away."

I look to Jamie. He won't meet my eyes. Cat is looking up at Lucas and nodding. I turn to Nasha. She shrugs. "The man's not wrong, Mickey."

It's then that we hear the *tick tick tick* of claws on the roof of the rover.

"Whatever you choose," Speaker says, "choose now. I believe that our friends have come knocking."

* * *

CONFESSION TIME: I have never been good at snap decisions. Once, when I was a kid back on Midgard, I spent so much time waffling back and forth over what flavor to pick in an ice-cream shop that my mom wound up dragging me out of the place bawling with no ice cream at all. I didn't ask anyone to my school's valedictory ball because I couldn't decide which of three girls I'd rather be rejected by. I wound up on this godforsaken planet because I couldn't decide whether this was better or worse than just killing myself to get away from Darius Blank.

It is entirely possible that I was not actually the ideal person to put in charge of this mission.

"JAMIE!" NASHA SAYS. "Get back in the cockpit. We're rolling."

"No," Speaker says. "Please, reconsider. If this rover moves, you are committed to fighting. There will be no more negotiations, and there will be no further delay. You may believe you can escape, but I tell you that you will not succeed. If you try, they will kill us all."

"And your folks won't get their share of the booty, right, Wormy?" Lucas says. He's already geared up and ready to roll. "Pop the hatch, Jamie. It's go time."

Jamie looks up at me. "Mickey? You're still running this show, right? You need to make the call."

I open my mouth, close it, and open it again. In the span of five seconds I go back and forth fifteen times between fighting and surrender. Nasha is watching me. The look on her face is unreadable.

I'm about to tell them to do whatever the hell they want to do when my ocular flashes.

<RedHawk>: Mickey? You guys still in there?
<Mickey7>: Berto??

<RedHawk>: They're all over you, buddy.

<Mickey7>: I know. I know. Where are you?

<RedHawk>: Hold tight, Mick. It's about to get bumpy.

"Down!" I say, and drop to the floor. "Grab on to something!"

Nobody moves. Nasha rolls her eyes, and Lucas has just opened his mouth to say something obnoxious when a deafening blow strikes the side of the rover and lifts it up until it balances precariously, just on the verge of rolling. Nasha stumbles, cracks her skull against the far bulkhead, and goes down in a loose heap. Lucas and Cat manage to catch themselves against the hatch as Jamie sprawls on the floor next to me. Only Speaker seems unbothered, crouching in the middle of the aisle as the rover drops back onto its wheels, only to be struck and lifted again from the opposite side.

"Mickey?" Lucas yells. "What the hell is happening?"

"It's Berto!" I yell back. "Jamie, get us moving!"

It takes a third explosion, this one a little farther off and not quite as catastrophic, to get everyone going. Jamie scrambles into the cockpit, and a few seconds later we're rolling. Lucas bangs on the hatch with one fist. As it swings open, two legs jam themselves through the space at the top. Cat fires, the spider disintegrates, and then she and Lucas scramble out and up. Nasha's down and not moving. I hesitate, but there's no time to help her now. I grab her accelerator, slap on a rebreather, and follow Cat and Lucas out onto the roof.

The scene outside is chaos. I'm expecting to see a heavy lifter overhead emptying out its missile tubes, but when I look up all I see is Berto and his goddamned glider. There are three massive craters behind us, and as I'm pulling myself up another explosion erupts maybe fifty meters off to the right side. The blast wave nearly throws me off the rover. The burner turret is hot, playing its beam back and forth over a twenty-degree arc in front of us. Cat and Lucas are crouched to either side of it, firing steadily, clearing our flanks. The spiders are scrambling in every direction. I drop to my belly, bring the accelerator to bear, and start picking off targets. After twenty seconds and one more explosion, there's nothing left moving in my field of fire. I hear two more shots behind me, then one more a few seconds later.

Then nothing but the steady crunch of tires on rocks.

"You're clear," Berto says over the comm. "Looks like the survivors have gone to ground."

Nasha.

I stow my accelerator and scramble inside.

THE FIRST THING I see when I swing through the hatch is Speaker. He's crouched over Nasha, mandibles working, feeding arms stroking her slack face.

"Hey!" I bark. "Get away from her!"

He lifts and twists to face me. "Mickey. The Nasha is injured."

"Back away," I say, and gesture with the barrel of Nasha's accelerator. "Back the fuck away."

He shuffles a meter or so back toward me, and I see the blood. So, so much blood.

It's puddled around her head and running in little rivulets across the deck.

I drop my weapon and scramble past Speaker to fall to my knees beside her. She's sprawled in the middle of the aisle between the benches, head turned to one side, one arm flung out to the side and the other thrown across her chest. I put two fingers to her throat. Her pulse is rapid and weak, but it's there. I'm trying to remember my medical training, but all I can see is the blood, and my brain is a roaring void.

"Mickey?" Cat says behind me. "Is she okay?"

"I don't know," I say. "I don't know. She's bleeding so much . . ."

"Let me see," she says, and gently pushes me aside. She puts her hands on either side of Nasha's neck and carefully runs her fingers up along her spine, bringing her head back to a neutral position. Her fingers continue up into Nasha's hairline for another few centimeters before she pauses. "Here's where the blood's coming from," she says. "It's not actually that bad. Feels like the wound is mostly superficial. Head wounds bleed a lot, but they tend to clot up pretty quickly."

"We're about to run out of ridgeline," Jamie says from the cockpit. "Any idea where I should be going?"

"South," Speaker says.

"Right," Jamie says. "Thanks. Super-fucking-helpful."

Lucas brushes past me, an already open first-aid kit in hand. He crouches beside Cat and hands her gauze, scissors, and a tube of disinfectant gel. Cat dresses the wound quickly, then pries each of Nasha's eyes open and peers into them.

"So?" I say. "Is she okay?"

"No," Cat says without looking up. "She's not dead, though, and I'm pretty sure her neck isn't broken. That's something."

"She's concussed," Lucas says. "Maybe a subdural hematoma. Maybe a brain bleed. Nothing we can do about any of that here. She'll either come out of it, or she won't."

> \<Mickey7\>: Berto—can you carry someone with that glider?
> \<RedHawk\>: What? No. This thing barely has enough lift to keep me up here. Why?

I blink away from the chat window. "Is that kit seriously the only medical gear we've got here? Don't we have any actual equipment?"

Lucas shakes his head. "We don't have a surgical suite, if that's what you're asking. If Nasha's got a brain bleed, that's the only thing that'd save her, and it would have to be quick. If she doesn't, then we just need to wait for her to come around. That's pretty much all they'd be doing back at the dome anyway."

My vision blurs, and it occurs to me that I'm hyperventilating. Lucas gets to his feet, takes me by the arm, and guides me down onto one of the benches.

"Get it together," he says. "You losing your shit isn't gonna help Nasha one way or the other."

I'd like to argue.

But the fact is, he's right.

I drop my head into my hands and slow my breathing. After a minute or so, the fuzz fades away from the edges of my vision and my brain starts to function again. I look up. Cat has Nasha laid out on her back with cushions strapped around her head to stabilize her neck. The cabin is nose-down now by probably twenty degrees as we pick our way down off the ridge.

"Speaker," I say, then take a deep breath and gather myself when I hear the quaver in my voice. "Speaker. You said that the spiders wouldn't give up, no matter how many of them we destroyed. They did give up. You misled us. Explain."

"I did not mislead you," Speaker says. "You are mistaken."

"I told you," Lucas says. "You're wasting your time talking to him about this, Mickey. He's not on our side."

"I *am* on your side," Speaker says, "although I must say that you are making it increasingly difficult for me to justify this position. I gave you the best counsel that I could provide. Nothing that I told you about our situation was untrue."

Lucas looks as if he'd like to spit. "Bullshit. You said they wouldn't break, remember? That was why we had to surrender. That was why we had to hand over this rover, which you admitted you were planning to keep a chunk of. We didn't do it, though, did we? We fought instead, and they did break, just like Nasha said they would. You lied, Wormy. You lied to try to get us to give up. You lied to try to get us to turn Jamie over to the spiders. That's not good counsel, friend."

Speaker twists to face Lucas. "I say again, *friend*. I did not lie."

Lucas starts to reply, but I hold up one hand to stop him. "This is semantics, Lucas. You're saying he lied. He's saying he misjudged the spiders. Neither of you can prove your point, so there's no use in arguing over it."

"No," Speaker says. "You are not listening to me. I did not lie, and I did not misjudge. I said that the spiders, as you call them, would not give up the chance to capture this rover. I said that they would not be deterred from this by casualties. These are both true statements."

"Speaker," I say. "They are not. They were deterred by casualties, and they did give up."

"No," Speaker says. "This is untrue. You brought some new weapon to bear against them. I did not know that this was a possibility. If you had shared this information with me, I may have given you better advice. The spiders were likewise not prepared for this, and they seem to have retreated to consider. I promise you, however, that they have not given up."

"So you're saying they'll be back?"

"Yes," Speaker says. "They will most certainly be back, and there will be no more negotiating. When they return, they will do what they can to breach the walls of the rover. If they succeed, they will kill all of us, and my nest will get none of the spoils. Our friends to the south will very likely then have the strength to displace us. When that has been accomplished, they will turn to dismantling your dome and removing what metal is to be had there. Is this the outcome you hoped for?"

The silence that follows stretches on for a long, long while.

* * *

WE CATCH UP to Berto just after sunset on a flat, open stretch of rocky ground in the hollow between two ridges. He's already got the glider broken down and packed when we roll to a stop beside him. Jamie pops the hatch, and I walk out to meet him.

"Hey," he says. "How's Nasha?"

I shake my head. "Not great. She's alive, but she's not responsive. She needs a real medical suite."

He grimaces. "Sorry, Mick. You want to turn back?"

I close my eyes and breathe in, breathe out. When I open them again, Berto's face is an even mix of pity and concern. "Yeah," I say. "I want to turn back. Of course I want to turn back. But we can't turn back, because if we don't recover that bomb we're all screwed anyway, including Nasha. So instead my plan is to do my best to keep it together until we do what we need to do here, and then to completely lose my shit unless and until she wakes up."

"Sounds like a solid plan," he says. "Think you'll be able to pull it off?"

I sigh. "I don't know. I'm not used to being on this end of things, you know? I'm supposed to be the one bleeding out, not her. Do you think . . . is this how it was for her? Do you think she felt like this every time I went down?"

"I don't have to think," Berto says. "I saw it."

I don't have any answer to that. We stand in silence for a moment, until finally Berto shoulders his pack and starts toward the rover. He stops, though, just as he reaches the ramp, and turns back to look at me.

"Hey," he says. "I'm sorry, Mickey. I didn't mean to drop that first round quite so close to you, and I should have given you more warning. It's just . . ." He runs his hand along a three-centimeter-deep gouge in the armor next to the hatch.

"Things looked pretty desperate down there, you know? I wanted to . . ."

"Yeah, I know," I say. "You're a hero, Berto. You wanted to save the day."

The words are already out of my mouth before I realize how bitter they sound. Berto's face looks like he's just been punched.

"And you did," I quickly add. "You got there in the nick of time, and you totally saved our asses. If you'd gotten there five minutes later—hell, probably thirty seconds later—we'd all be dead by now. You didn't have time to do anything more than what you did. I don't blame you for what happened to Nasha."

He looks down, one hand braced on the top of the hatch. "Thanks, Mickey." He ducks through and into the cabin. As he does, he mutters something else that I can't quite catch. It's not until I'm back in the cabin and the hatch is swinging down behind me that I realize it was "I do."

"So," I say. "What happened out there, Berto? I expected you to come back with a heavy lifter, or not at all."

"Yeah, well," he says. "I tried."

Cat and Lucas are both riding shotgun on the roof, so it's just the two of us in the cabin now, other than Speaker and Nasha. She's under a blanket, laid out on the bench next to me, strapped down to keep her from rolling. Speaker fills half the center aisle, stretched out flat. He hasn't spoken or moved since we started rolling again. Berto sits across from me, leaning forward with his elbows on his knees.

"How did you do it?" I ask. "I mean, you said those drive units had limited charge, right?"

"Well," he says, "first thing I did when I got within range of the dome was to get Marshall on the comm and try to convince him to give me a lifter. He pointed out to me that all of our lifters' gravitic grids have been removed and drained, and that even if he wanted to authorize me to take one, which he did not, it would take at least six hours to get them recharged and reinstalled. So that was a no-go. It would have taken almost as long to recharge the drive units on my glider, though, so I had to bust up a couple more drones and swap them out. That took me about forty-five minutes. Once that was done, all I had to do was secure some ordnance and get back in the air."

"Right. Speaking of which, what, exactly, did you drop on us? I didn't think that glider had enough lift to let you carry a missile launcher."

He laughs. "No, it doesn't, but you're closer than you think." He reaches into a side pocket of his pack and pulls out a shiny silver ovoid, about the size of two fists.

"Okay," I say. "What is that?"

"This," he says with a grin, "is the part of an air-to-ground missile that makes it go boom. I liberated a few of them from the armory." He pulls out another from a different pocket. "I've still got two of them left, just in case."

"Huh." I reach out, and he hands me one of the warheads. It's warm to the touch, and heavier than it looks. "How does it work?"

"You mean what makes it go boom?"

I roll my eyes. "Yes, Berto. What makes it go boom?"

"Well," he says, "currently, these are set to detonate on impact. Any deceleration greater than forty meters per second squared and they'll trigger. It's configurable, though. They're keyed to my ocular. I can put them on a timer, or make it an altitude trigger, or just set them off if I want to. It's a pretty slick system when they're in a missile and you're in a combat situation, being able to reconfigure your weapons on the fly. It didn't take much thinking to realize that I could take advantage of the system to turn them into grenades."

"So, what, you just dropped them on us?"

He shrugs. "Yeah, pretty much. I mean, threw more than dropped, but the effect was the same. It was a tricky optimization problem, actually, figuring out how to make sure I hit what I was aiming for. I had to get low enough to be accurate, but not so low that I got caught in the blast and killed myself."

"Huh. Well, I'm glad you worked it out."

"Yeah, me too. Incinerated in my own fireball was not the way I was planning on checking out." He leans back against the bulkhead and yawns. "So what's the plan going forward?"

"Same as it was, I guess. Find Speaker's friends. Get the bomb back somehow. Get it back to the dome without getting killed. Save the colony."

"Those are goals, Mickey. We kinda need an actual plan."

"I know," I say, then close my eyes and rub my face with both hands. "I'm working on it."

FUN FACT: IN addition to not being a terrific decision maker, I am also not exactly a wiz at forming effective plans. Case in point— why am I here on Niflheim, where I have been half-starved, deliberately infected by multiple fatal diseases, and dissected by creepers at least once and probably twice, rather than well-fed and safe in my crappy but totally nonfatal apartment back in Kiruna? There are a number of answers to that question, but they really all boil down to this: I had an extremely bad plan. I placed a number of wagers without really understanding either the odds or the stakes, and when, one after another, they all turned out poorly for me, I didn't have the slightest hint of a fallback position. Darius Blank and his torture machine might have been my motivation for signing on to this gig, but my own stupid brain was the root cause.

All that said, the dregs of an idea for how to get us out of this situation are beginning to seep into my head. Is it better than my plan to get rich by fleecing an extremely dangerous criminal? Unclear. One thing is clear, though.

Everything depends on Nasha waking up.

"WE NEED TO hole up somewhere," Jamie says from the cockpit. "I can't drive all night."

He makes a fair point. In a straight line we're only about eighty klicks south of the dome, but it's taken us fourteen hours to get here—and what time he hasn't spent in the cockpit, Jamie's spent waiting to get dissected by creepers, which I can say from experience is also pretty stressful. Cat and Lucas have been up on the roof for the past few hours, taking the occasional potshot at shadows in the distance, but mostly just hunkering down and staring at the horizon. They're probably pretty much done too.

"You're right," I say. "See if you can find a spot that's defensible, okay? High ground. Good sight lines. No tunnel openings nearby."

"Sure," he says. "I'll see what I can do."

"We should spell Cat and Lucas," Berto says. His eyes shift to Nasha. "You sitting here isn't gonna help her. They can watch her sleeping just as well as you can."

He's not wrong. I sigh, and stand, and pull on my rebreather.

"Pop the hatch," Berto says. "We're going up top."

We move to the back of the cabin. The atmospheric trap closes behind us, and the hatch swings open.

"Is Speaker dead?" Berto asks as we climb up onto the roof. "He hasn't moved a muscle since I got back."

"No," I say. "I don't think so, anyway. I think he's mad at us."

Cat and Lucas are up by the turret, sitting back-to-back with their weapons across their knees.

"Hey," Berto says. "You two want a break?"

Cat turns to see us, then rolls her neck in a long, slow circle, stretches, and stands.

"Thanks," she says as Lucas gets to his feet. "I really needed to pee."

"No problem," Berto says. He takes her weapon as she passes. Lucas hands his to me.

"Keep an eye on Nasha," I say. "Let me know if anything changes with her."

"Will do," Lucas says. He swings himself down and into the cabin, and the hatch closes behind him.

Berto settles down against the turret. I take my position on the other side. After five minutes or so, Berto says, "So. You think they'll really come back?"

I shrug. "Speaker seems to be pretty sure of it."

"Yeah," Berto says. "Speaker seems to be pretty sure of a lot of stuff. You really trust him?"

That's a good question. Do I?

"It's not a matter of trust," I say finally. "He's a source of information. He's the only source of information we have about what to expect from the spiders. He's the only source of information we have about where we're going, or what to expect when we get there. If we had some other source to compare him against, that would be one thing, but we don't. So I guess my feeling is that we take what he says with a grain of salt, but we can't totally discount it, because we don't have anything else to fall back on."

"We've got our own observations," Berto says. "He said they wouldn't run. They ran. Now he says they'll come back. What's to say he's right this time?"

"I mean, he makes a fair point, doesn't he? When he said they wouldn't run, he wasn't factoring in the idea of you swooping in and dive-bombing the shit out of them. If I'm understanding correctly, aerial assault is a completely new thing on this planet.

It's kind of understandable that they'd want to take a minute to think things over after that."

Berto shrugs. "Maybe. On the other hand, it would also be understandable if they saw what I just did to them and came to the conclusion that they're screwing with something that they'd be better off leaving alone. The folks on Eden really wanted to drop a colony in The System That Shall Not Be Named, didn't they? When they found out that whoever's living there now has a Magical Ship Eraser, though, they decided that it was in their best interests to leave them the hell alone."

"Not exactly. Acadia tried too, you know, and when their ship vanished they wanted to send them a *Bullet*. We're not nearly as smart as you're giving us credit for."

"Yeah, well," Berto says. "Nasha seems pretty convinced that the creepers are smarter than we are, right? Maybe they'll get the message quicker than we did."

I laugh. "I guess it's possible. If what Speaker says about their need for metals is true, though, I could imagine them being willing to take another run at us. He hasn't given us any details, but I get the impression these guys and Speaker's nest have been in a kind of cold war for a long time, and they both see us as something that might put their side over the top."

Berto's head tilts to one side. "Cold war?"

"Yeah," I say. "It's an old Earth thing. A couple hundred years before the breakout, there were two nation-states that pretty much dominated the planet. They both had fusion bombs and ballistic delivery systems, so direct warfare would have been suicidal for both of them, but they had networks of proxies, smaller countries who could—" Berto lets his head loll back and rips off a long, loud snore. I sigh. "Fine, you ignoramus. Don't worry about it. Point is, Speaker's nest and their friends to the south clearly don't like each other, and we've obviously got resources that could be game-changing here. You can see how that might motivate them to take risks that might seem crazy otherwise."

"Maybe," Berto says. "Or maybe Lucas is right, and Speaker is just trying to manipulate us."

"Okay. So what would we do differently if we thought that was true?"

After a long silence, Berto says, "Yeah. That's a good point."

It's a nice enough night, anyway. We're picking our way up along what I'm pretty sure is the last ridgeline before we hit the open plains, moving through what I would have called an alpine meadow back on Midgard, meter-high ferns swishing against our tires. The air is cool and dry and crisp, and the stars are hard, bright pinpricks in a jet-black sky.

"You know," Berto says, "nights like this, I could almost convince myself that we made a good call coming here."

I'm about to reply when a ghost flickers in my peripheral vision. I turn toward it, and close my left eye so that I can focus on what my ocular is showing me. It flips rapidly from enhanced visible to infrared and back, then presents me a pseudo-colored image of the two superimposed.

I brace myself against the turret and bring the accelerator to bear.

"Good news," I say. "Looks from here like Speaker was telling the truth after all."

"Stop," Berto says. "You're wasting rounds."

I lower my accelerator, take a deep breath in, hold it, and then let it out slowly. He's right. The spiders—if that's even what they are—are most of a thousand meters off, pacing along with us just like they did when they first found us, but outside of the effective range of our weapons now.

"I think Chen packed self-guided rounds," he says. "We should be able to hit them with those, I think. Not sure they carry enough punch to take them out, though. I know they're not rated to penetrate standard combat armor."

"Not sure it matters," I say. "Speaker was right. They're tracking us. At some point, they'll try to swarm us. I don't know that picking off one or two of them now makes any real difference."

Berto shrugs. "Maybe not. Can't hurt, though." His eyes unfocus as he blinks to a chat window. A minute or so later, the hatch swings open and Cat climbs onto the roof. She comes up to stand beside us, one hand on the turret for balance, closes one eye, and squints into the distance.

"Oh," she says after a few seconds. "Yeah, I see them out there."

Cat takes her weapon back from Berto, drops to one knee, and swaps out the magazine for a bulkier one that she pulls from a pouch at her waist. She braces herself and brings the accelerator to bear. "It would be nice if we could quit bouncing around for a goddamn minute," she mutters, then growls and pulls the trigger.

"I think you hit it," Berto says.

"I did," Cat says. "It went down, but I'm pretty sure it got back up."

"Maybe," Berto says. "That might have been another one taking its place."

I've got my ocular on infrared at maximum resolution at the moment. I saw the flare of the round's drive, but I couldn't see what happened when it hit. I flip over to enhanced visible spectrum, which gives me enough resolution to actually see individual spiders out there. Cat fires again, and an instant later one of them drops.

She's right, though. After a moment, it gets back to its feet and keeps running.

"Waste of time and ammunition," Cat says.

"Maybe," Berto says. "Maybe not. Looks like they're pulling back a bit farther, anyway. You may not be killing them, but those rounds can't feel good."

"I only packed two mags of self-guided," Cat says. "Forty rounds all told. I'm not about to empty them both just to annoy those things."

"Really?" Berto says. "What else were you planning to do with them? If we wind up getting vivisected, nobody's giving you a medal for being frugal with your ordnance, you know."

Cat gets to her feet and turns to face Berto. "If those things close to five hundred meters, I will be more than happy to empty my supply of explosives and kinetic energy rounds into them. In the meantime, though, I'm going to hang on to these ones, if that's okay with you. I don't plan on getting vivisected either way, and you never know when the ability to hit something from really far away might come in handy."

Berto looks like he's about to argue, but then he thinks better of it and shrugs. "Fine. You're probably right. I don't like just letting those things pace us like that, but if they're gonna keep their distance I guess there's not anything we can really do about it."

"At least we're in open terrain," Cat says. "If we were down in one of those cuts right now, they could be practically on top of us before we knew they were there."

Small blessings. If we're going to do what I think we need to do, we need to do it now. If we wait until they close the noose on us again, we're finished.

"Come on," I say. "We need to get back inside. We've got some choices to make."

WHEN I GET back into the cabin, Nasha is sitting up, leaning forward with her elbows on her knees and cradling her head in her hands. The relief that floods through me leaves me almost giddy. If she hadn't come around . . .

Best not to think about that.

"Hey," Lucas says. "What's the situation up there?"

"They're pacing us," Cat says. "Keeping their distance for the moment."

"For the moment," I say, "but that's not likely to last. Nasha—how do you feel?"

She looks up slowly, her eyes narrowed. "What? Are you fucking kidding me?"

"Sorry," I say. "I know. I know. You feel like shit. What I mean is, can you function? Can you stand? Can you walk?"

She sighs, then gets to her feet, one hand braced on the back of the bench. Once she's up, she takes her hand away. She wobbles a bit, then steadies.

"Well, I can stand," she says, then lifts first one foot, then the other. "I can probably walk, I guess. Don't think I'd want to try to run. Why?"

"You don't need to run," I say. "I don't think so, anyway. I just need you mobile. We're abandoning ship."

That gets me a solid five seconds of silence.

"What?" Lucas says finally.

"We're abandoning the rover. Speaker has made it pretty clear that the metal in this vehicle is what they really want. They asked for one of us too, but I'm betting that was a distant second on their priority list. If we leave the rover undefended, their choice is to get ninety-five percent of what they wanted with no risk, versus getting five percent of what they wanted and losing half their ancillaries in the process. Speaker says they're intelligent. I'm taking him at his word, and assuming they'll make the right call."

"And if they don't?" Cat says. "We killed a whole lot of them earlier today, you know. If the situation were reversed, I'd be pretty pissed off. They could track us down and kill us first, then come back for the rover."

"They could," I say, "but I don't think they will. We killed ancillaries. If what Speaker has told us is remotely true, they won't have the sort of reaction to that that we would if they'd killed half of us. They won't be thinking vengeance. They'll be thinking spoils. They'll prioritize the rover. Taking it apart will take them a fair amount of time. By the time they're done, we'll be long gone and not worth tracking."

The looks on the faces of the other people in the cabin range from dubious to borderline hostile. Lucas nudges Speaker with one boot. "What about it, Wormy? Is he right?"

Speaker doesn't react at first. When Lucas prods him again, though, he rises slowly to eye level and turns to face him. "Mickey is almost certainly correct that they will focus on the rover. Depending on how many ancillaries they have with them now, they may delegate some to pursue you. Then again, they may not. This is difficult to predict."

"You?" Lucas says. "Don't you mean *us*?"

"No," Speaker says. "I do not mean *us*. I will not be accompanying you."

That is not what I expected to hear. I open my mouth, realize I have no idea what to say, and close it again. I look to Nasha. Her face is twisted into a scowl, but I can't tell if it's meant for Speaker or for me.

"Yeah," Berto says finally. "You will be accompanying us, Speaker. You definitely will."

"I will not," Speaker says. "I apologize for leaving you in difficult circumstances, but if I abandon this machine, the others will take all of it, and my nest will get none. This cannot be permitted. If I stay with the rover after you have abandoned it, there is some small possibility that I may be able to enforce my claim to a portion of the spoils."

I stare at him, openmouthed. "You actually think that agreement you made still holds? We've killed a shit-ton of spiders in the meantime, remember? They may not be vengeful, but I'm betting they'll at a minimum consider any concessions they made earlier to be null and void."

"You may be correct," Speaker says. "It is very possible that if I do not flee with you, they will disassemble me along with the rover. However, I am obligated to try to convince them to abide by our agreement. As I told you previously, if they are able to make use of all the materials in this rover, there is a strong possibility that they will become strong enough to displace my nest. For both of our sakes, this cannot be allowed to happen."

I shake my head. "Sorry, Speaker, but this isn't negotiable. We need you. Without you, we have no way of even finding your friends to the south, let alone talking to them. You have to come with us."

"I appreciate your position," Speaker says. "Please, appreciate mine. You ask me to put my own nest in great danger in order to protect yours. If our positions were reversed, what would you do?"

"Just so we're clear," Berto says, "we're not actually asking you. We are telling you. You will come with us when we abandon the rover."

"You threaten me?"

Berto hefts his accelerator. It's not quite aimed at Speaker, but it's not entirely *not* aimed at him either.

"It's not a threat," Berto says. "It's just a statement of fact. We will not leave you behind—not in one piece, anyway."

Speaker rises to face Berto, mandibles spread wide. "I am not helpless."

"You're not," Berto says. "You are outnumbered, though, and you are outgunned. You might be able to take one of us down before we shot you, but definitely not two."

"Look," I say, far too late. "Back off, Berto. Nobody is shooting anybody. Speaker—we need you. We need you as an ally, not as a prisoner. We need your willing help. Berto is right that we can't afford to leave you behind, but I understand your concern about how what happens here might impact your people. We don't want your nest to be displaced by these things any more than you do. So . . ." I glance around the cabin. Everyone is watching me. I might be about to make the worst mistake yet in a life filled with some pretty awful ones, but I don't know what else to do at this point. "So, I will promise you now that if we succeed in recovering the bomb and then make it back home alive, we will not permit your nest to be displaced. You see the kinds of weapons we have. There are a lot more of them back at the dome, and others as well that make these ones look like toys. If we are able to recover the bomb and get home safely, we will commit to defending your people if you are attacked. That's what allies do, right?"

Speaker's mandibles close, and he gradually settles back down toward the deck.

"You have the authority to make this commitment?"

No, not remotely.

"Yes, I do. If I tell our people that we've made this agreement, I promise you that they will honor it."

"To say this is not a trivial matter, Mickey. I have told you how we view agreements."

"You have, and I understand that. We also take our agreements seriously. Now, do we have a bargain?"

After a long, strained silence, Speaker drops fully back to the deck and says, "Yes. Yes, under these conditions, we have a bargain. I will admit that I am relieved to not have to face the spiders alone. Understand, though, that if your people do not do as you say they will, there will be serious consequences. If we are attacked and you do not come to our aid, all prior understandings will be void. If we manage to defend ourselves, your dome will provide us the metals we need to recoup our losses, voluntarily or not—and if our nest falls, I promise you that yours will not be far behind."

Berto shoots me a hard look, but I'm not in a place to worry about what might happen six hours from now, let alone six months. For the moment, this is good enough.

"Thank you, Speaker." I look around the cabin. Cat and Lucas are back by the hatch. Neither of them will make eye contact. Nasha is sitting again, cradling her head in her hands. Berto raises one eyebrow. I nod. "Everybody else, pack up, but pack light. We're bailing soon, and I think we've probably got a long walk ahead of us."

ONE BY ONE, we jump down from the back of the moving rover. Nasha goes last. She hesitates, wavers a bit, then hops down, stumbles, and drops to her hands and knees. The rest of us are already on the ground, trying not to silhouette ourselves against the deep black sky within view of the spiders. The hatch swings closed as the rover bounces off along the narrow peak of the ridge, then turns to the west and begins to descend. Jamie has set it to roll to a stop after a klick or so, more or less at the bottom of the slope.

"So?" Berto says. "Are they coming for us?"

Lucas rises up to his knees and closes one eye.

"I don't think so," he says after a few seconds. "Looks like they're still tracking the rover. Should we get moving?"

"No," I say. "We'll stay here until they're clear. I don't want them to notice that we've bailed if they haven't already." I crawl over to Nasha. She's still on all fours, head hanging down, long braids just brushing the ground. "Hey," I say, more quietly now. "You okay?"

She looks up, her eyes narrowed with pain. "I'm alive. That's something, right?" She settles back into a sit, wraps her arms around her legs, and rests her forehead against her knees. "I'm sorry," she says after a moment. "I'm not sure I can do this, Mickey. I can barely stand. How many kilometers do we have ahead of us?"

I touch her shoulder. She flinches, and I pull away.

"Doesn't matter," I say. "However far it is, you'll get there. You're the strongest person I've ever met. You could walk back to Midgard if you had to."

"I don't know, Mickey," she says without looking up. "I don't think I've ever hurt like this before. I'm not bailing on you. Whatever we have to do, I'll try to do it. If it turns out that I can't, though, you're going to have to leave me. You know that, right?"

I open my mouth, hesitate, then close it again.

"I'm serious," Nasha says. "I know you don't want to think about this. I know more than most what it's like to watch someone you love die, you know? But every human being on the planet is depending on this mission. You can't let me slow you down."

I put my hands over hers and lean closer. "No. I don't want to hear this shit, Nasha. Every human being on the planet can rot, as far as I'm concerned. I'd trade every one of them for you."

She raises her head from her knees. The expression on her face isn't suffering now. It's anger. "Don't be stupid, Mickey. If I can't get where we're going, and then somehow get back to the dome, I'm already dead. Say you told these guys to fuck off and stayed with me. How long do you think the two of us would last out here, even if those things didn't come back for us?"

I shake my head. "Doesn't matter. Wherever you go, I go. If you're so concerned about saving the colony, I guess you're gonna have to pull your shit together and start walking."

She stares at me.

I stare at her.

"Lie down," I say.

Her eyes narrow. "What?"

"Lie down," I say again, almost whispering now. "Please. Lie down, and don't get up until I tell you to."

"Look—"

"Please," I say. "Please, just trust me."

"Hey," Lucas says. "The rover's stopping."

I turn away from Nasha and crawl twenty meters or so over to a spot where the land begins to drop away. At max magnification through my ocular I can see the rover as it rolls to a halt down in the valley.

"We should go," Lucas says. "We don't know how long it'll take those things to get through the demolition. We need to be long gone when they're done."

I glance back at Nasha. She's flat on her back, one arm half covering her face, the other resting on her stomach.

"No," I say. "Not yet. I need to see what they do now."

"Uh-huh," Lucas says. "And the fact that you're stalling has nothing to do with the fact that Adjaya's down again, right?"

I turn to look at him. He stares back, then shakes his head.

"I'm sorry, Mickey, but we need to move," he says. "We need to put distance between us and them, and we need to do it fast. If she can't move now, maybe Nasha can catch up with us once she's on her feet again."

Lucas stands and looks around. Nobody else moves.

"Get down," Berto says after a long, awkward moment. "You're making an ass of yourself, Lucas."

Lucas turns to Cat.

"Gomez is right," she says. "Shut up and get down."

He hesitates, starts to speak, then growls and drops to one knee.

"Don't worry," I say. "We'll be moving soon enough."

Down in the valley, the spiders are gathering. Over the course of ten minutes or so, they press in around the rover, forming a cordon maybe two hundred meters across. After another few minutes, one of them approaches. It circles the rover twice, then clambers up onto the hull. It moves slowly, stopping every step or two to tap at the metal with a foot. Eventually, it reaches the burner turret.

It bites through the barrel of the burner cleanly, shears it completely away.

"Well," Berto says, just at my shoulder, "I guess that answers our question about whether they can penetrate our armor or not."

"Yeah," I say. "Guess so."

"Okay," Lucas says. "We see what they're doing, right? Can we go now?"

"Relax, Lucas," Berto says without looking back. "We'll be moving in a minute."

"Relax?" Lucas says. "We need to—"

"You need to shut up," Berto says. "Seriously, Lucas. Things are happening here."

"Not to interfere," Speaker says, "but Lucas is correct. They are ignoring us now, but they have not forgotten about us. Once they have completed the dissection of the rover, they will come looking, and they are able to move much more quickly than we are on foot."

"I understand," I say. "We'll get moving very soon, I promise."

Below us, the ring of spiders has closed around the rover, and pieces are starting to come off. Twenty or so of them are climbing over and around it, gouging out hunks of armor and tossing them aside. Another thirty or more are in a tight cluster around the slowly disintegrating chassis, gathering the pieces the others are removing and sorting them into piles.

"What do you think?" Berto says. "Is that all of them?"

"Not sure," I say. "It has to be most of them, though. I thought there were a hundred or so originally. Between your bombardment and Cat and Lucas's sniping we must have killed half of those at least."

"That sounds right," Berto says. "Did they bring in reinforce-ments, though?"

I shrug. "Who knows?"

"I guess it really doesn't matter," he says. "It's as many as we're gonna get. Time?"

"Yeah," I say. "Time."

I close my eyes. Even through my tight-shut lids the flash half-blinds me. The heat comes an instant later, far more intense than I'd been prepared for, burning the exposed skin on my hands and forehead. After that comes the pressure wave, throwing me onto my back like a blow from a giant's fist, and last the sound, crash-ing over me, roaring, deafening, loud as the end of the world.

IT TAKES A minute or so for me to crawl over and make sure Nasha's okay, and then for the ringing in my ears to drop off enough to hear voices again. When it does, the first one I hear is Cat's.

"Sweet mother," she says. "What the shit was that?"

Lucas gets to his hands and knees, then rocks back onto his heels and shakes his head. "No idea. What the hell, Mickey? Think you could have warned us that was coming?"

I grin behind my rebreather. "I told you to get down."

"Get down? You think that's enough?"

"He couldn't say anything," Cat says.

Lucas turns to look at her. "Couldn't?"

Her eyes flick to Speaker, then back to Lucas. "Couldn't. Obviously. Drop it, Lucas."

He looks like he has more to say, but after a moment of consideration he thinks better of it.

"Anyway," Cat says, "what was that? That couldn't have just been those things cutting into the plasma chamber, could it? I mean, if the rover had that kind of power I would have expected it to move a little faster, right? Did somebody forget to tell me we were packing a pocket nuke?"

I shake my head. "You're right about the size of the blast, but no. I don't think so, anyway. Berto? Any idea what just happened?"

"Not sure," he says. "I wasn't carrying fusion devices, and I wasn't carrying antimatter, so that blast probably wasn't me. I mean, my warheads were definitely the catalyst, but you saw what I was packing last night. That explosion was a hell of a lot bigger than anything I was carrying could account for. If I had to guess, I'd say that the initial blast I set off breached the drive unit's plasma containment, and the interior of the cabin acted as a resonance chamber to amplify the burst." He touches one hand to the back of his head, checks his fingers for blood, and then scowls and wipes them on his shirt. "Now that I think of it, though, if that's what happened, then there might actually have been a bit of a fusion reaction going on in there, at least briefly. Anyway, we should probably all go through radiation protocols when we get home."

"Great," Jamie says. "This trip just gets better and better."

I climb unsteadily to my feet. "It does, actually. Speaker, you should be happy, anyway. Unless the spiders can build new ancillaries out of titanium vapor, your nest should be secure—even more so than before, really, because in addition to vaporizing the rover, we just vaporized another fifty or sixty spiders. We can get on with our mission together now, yes?"

Speaker rises slowly to look down into the valley. The mushroom cloud that rose over the explosion is beginning to dissipate, revealing a blackened crater at least a hundred meters across.

"This . . ." he says. "This is what your bomb can do?"

"Oh no," Berto says. "Not remotely. The bomb we're searching for makes that one look like a firecracker. If we were fifteen hundred meters away when that thing went off, we'd be just as dead as the spiders."

Speaker turns to look at him. "Why would you make such a thing?"

Berto shrugs. "Why? That's a good question. Because we can, I guess. You see why we need to recover it, anyway."

"What will you do with it?"

"Excuse me?"

"This bomb," Speaker says. "If we recover it from our friends to the south, what will you do with it?"

"Dismantle it," I say. "If we are able to recover the bomb and return it to the dome, we will render it harmless. We don't want this sort of destructive power loose in the world any more than you do."

"This is a promise?" Speaker says.

"Yes," I say. "A promise."

"Very well," he says, and settles back to the ground. "Our friends are not far now. We should go."

I get to my feet, then turn to help Nasha up. She wavers a little when I let go of her hand, then steadies.

"You okay?" I say.

She drops her chin to her chest, then rocks her head back with her eyes shut tight and her hands cradling the back of her neck.

"Close enough," she says. "I think I can walk, anyway."

I look around. They're all watching me.

"Okay," I say. "Let's go. Speaker? Lead the way."

Speaker rises and twists around to look at me for a long moment, then drops back to his feet and scuttles off along the ridge to the south. One by one, the rest of us turn to follow.

BACK ON MIDGARD, back when I was just Mickey Barnes and the worst thing I had to worry about was running out of credits in between subsidy payments, I loved backpacking. There was a trail that ran almost eight hundred kilometers along the crest of the Ullr Mountains just south of Kiruna, and over the course of five years I solo-hiked the length of it four times. I loved the solitude. I loved the feeling that my life was entirely self-contained. I loved the ache in my muscles after a thirty-klick day. I loved planting myself on an overlook somewhere and knowing that if I slipped and fell there was a fair chance that nobody would ever find my body.

I do not love what we're doing now.

Start with the rebreather. By any objective standard, it's fantastic tech. It allows us to survive more or less forever in an atmosphere that would kill us in under five minutes if we were unprotected. The way it does that, though, is by filtering out the components of the atmosphere that we don't want and concentrating the ones that we do. The upshot of that is that our lungs need to constantly pull twice as much gas through the mask as we're actually getting to breathe, which means that hiking with this thing on is like hiking underwater while breathing through a straw that smells like halitosis. Add in the fact that I've been awake for twenty hours and counting. Top it off with the understanding that we're probably being hunted, and that if we wind up getting run down it most likely means the death of every human on the planet.

Yeah, not loving it.

I haven't checked my chronometer in a while, partially because I'm too tired to bother but mostly because it makes me sad, but it must be close to dawn now. Over the past several hours we've made our way down off the last ridge and well out into the flatlands, all the while listening to Speaker tell us over and over again that it's just a little bit farther, a little bit farther. We're hiking toward the mountains in the distance through what seems like an endless field of knee-high ferns when Jamie falls in next to me.

"We have to rest," he says. "I know you guys caught some sleep on the ride yesterday, but I've been awake for almost a full day now." He glances back. When he speaks again, his voice is lower. "More to the point, Nasha is about to drop. She won't admit it, so just blame it on me, right? Call a halt."

I turn to look back at Nasha. She's at the rear of the line, ten meters or more back from Cat. Her eyes are half-closed, and as I watch she stumbles over nothing and nearly goes down before catching herself.

Jamie shouldn't have been the one to notice that.

"Speaker," I say. "How much farther?"

"Not far," he says without slowing. "Half the next day. Maybe more. Not far at all."

I need to have a talk with him about what "not far" means.

"Okay," I say, and stop walking. "We'll hold here. Six hours to rest and eat, and then we push on. That should get us there before sunset, right, Speaker?"

"Not wise," Speaker says. "Not wise to stop here. We are exposed. The spiders may yet be following."

"Sorry," I say. "Not wise to keep walking until we drop either. We'll hold here."

"Don't have to tell me twice," Lucas says, then shrugs out of his pack and starts stomping a circle of ferns flat to the ground.

"Don't get too comfortable," I say. "You've got first watch."

He scowls, but doesn't complain. I drop my pack as well, then go back to meet Nasha. When I'm close, she squints up at me and says, "If this is for me . . ."

"It's not," I say. "It's for everybody. It doesn't help us to get where we're going if we can't function when we get there. Jamie's been up since we left the dome, and the rest of us aren't doing much better."

"Fine." She walks into me, wraps her arms around my shoulders, and sags against me. "I'm dying, Mickey," she says, her voice barely more than a whisper now. "My head feels like there's a rat in there, gnawing at the inside of my skull, trying to get out. My vision is fading in and out, and I'm starting to hallucinate. I almost fell just now, because I thought for a second that there was a creeper coming up out of the ground in front of me. I might make it to where we're going, but there's no way in hell I'm walking all the way back to the dome."

"One step at a time," I say. "Rest now. You might feel better when we're ready to move again."

"Maybe," she says. I hold her arm as she drops to her knees, then settles back into a sit.

"Sit tight," I say. I go back to my pack, then return with my emergency blanket and a stuff sack that holds my change of clothes. I wrap the blanket around her shoulders, fluff the sack into a pillow as well as I can, and then ease her down on her side. The soil here is thick and black and soft, and the ferns form a bower around her. "Try to get some sleep, huh?"

She closes her eyes. "I'll see what I can do. If I don't wake up when it's time to move, just leave me."

I crouch down to kiss her forehead. "Right. Whatever you say, boss."

She catches my hand and squeezes, then lets me go. I get back to my feet. Looks like everyone else has pretty much dropped where they were standing. Lucas is sitting on his pack with his accelerator lying across his knees. Cat's on her knees, using her teeth to tear the wrapper off of a protein bar. Berto and Jamie both look like they're already asleep, sitting half-up with their packs still strapped to their shoulders.

"Mickey," Speaker says, and scuttles over to crouch next to me. "I say again, we should not stay here."

"I hear you," I say, "but as I said before, we don't have a choice. I don't know how your metabolism works, but we cannot function indefinitely without rest. If the spiders find us here, then we'll fight them. This is the best we can do."

He follows along beside me as I walk back to my pack. After a moment's consideration, I decide that I'm more tired than hungry. I kneel, then sit, then settle back against the pack and close my eyes.

"If we are caught here," Speaker says, "they will disassemble me."

"I'm sure they'll disassemble all of us if they can," I say. "We certainly disassembled plenty of them."

"I do not wish to be disassembled."

"Yeah," I say. "Join the club."

"It is not only the spiders," Speaker says, and presses one foreleg into the ground. "You see this soil? Soft and moist. Good for diggers. You understand?"

I'm not sure I do, but I'm not sure I care. "Diggers. Got it. We'll watch out for those too."

He keeps talking, but I'm not listening anymore. My chin sinks down to my chest, and my breathing slows. The last thing I hear is a rhythmic scratching sound, like razor-sharp claws being dragged across bone.

I WAKE TO bright, streaming sunlight and the sound of screaming.

I'm up and on my feet before my brain is fully engaged, and it takes me a long moment to process what I'm seeing. First, the screaming. It's coming from Lucas. He's on his knees beside his pack, eyes wild, hands twisting behind his back. Cat is on her feet behind him, backing slowly away, accelerator in hand. Jamie and Berto are just shaking themselves awake. Nasha hasn't moved.

As I watch, Lucas staggers to his feet and twists around to face Cat. His hands are wrapped around what looks like a white, naked tail protruding from the middle of his back. He's pulling at it, trying to yank it out, but whatever it is, it's burrowing deeper into him, slowly disappearing. Somehow, his screaming gets louder, and as he loses his grip and whatever it is slips fully inside him he drops back to his knees and his voice jumps an octave.

It's then that I see there's a bloody, ragged hole in the back of his thigh, and another writhing white tail protruding from just above his right kidney.

"Diggers!" Speaker says from behind me. I look back to see him dancing as if he's trying to get all of his feet off the ground at once. "You see? Diggers! We should not have stopped here!"

Cat's accelerator barks, and Lucas abruptly falls silent.

"The hell, Cat?" Jamie yells, upright and backing away now. "You killed him! You fucking killed him!"

"Goddamned right," Cat says. "He would have done the same for me."

Berto catches her by the shoulder and pulls her back. "Grab your shit. We've got to move."

Nasha is on her knees now, one hand on the ground for balance, eyes narrowed to slits against the sun. "Mickey? What's happening?"

I snatch my pack up, check it quickly for dangling white tails, pull the straps over my shoulders, then sprint over to Nasha and pull her to her feet. Berto edges almost close enough to Lucas's gear to grab his accelerator, then sees another white head pop up out of the ground less than a meter from his boots and backs away at a run.

"Go!" Speaker says. "We have to leave! Where there are three, there are a hundred! Quickly! Quickly!"

The fact that Speaker is clearly terrified borders on disorienting. I wasn't sure that he was even capable of fear. Nasha clutches at my hand. Speaker is already scuttling away, but I can't take my eyes off of Lucas. He's sprawled on his back now, a gaping hole in the center of his chest where Cat shot him. A narrow white head pokes out and turns to orient toward me. It has a mouth like a lamprey's, a round maw ringed with bone-white teeth.

"Come on," Nasha says. She tugs at my arm. The digger dives back into Lucas's torso. Nasha pulls me two steps backward. "Mickey," she says. "Come *on*." She cups my cheek in one hand and pulls my head around. "We have to go."

I look back. The soil around Lucas is writhing now. Nasha drops my hand and starts after Speaker. After another moment's hesitation, I follow.

WE COVER THE first panicked kilometer at something between a fast march and a slow run. It's Jamie who finally forces us to slow down when he sees that Nasha is falling off the pace.

"We're clear," he says. "Right, Speaker? We're clear?"

"Yes," Speaker says. "Yes, probably. The ground is harder here. We should be safe for the moment."

"That's twice," Cat says when she's caught her breath. "Twice now that we've been ambushed by something that you definitely knew was out there. Warn us next time, Speaker, or I swear—" She pauses to cough something up, then lifts her rebreather to spit it out. "I swear, I will end you."

"Warn you?" Speaker says, as his forelegs go through a rapid, agitated dance. "I did warn you. I told you many times that stopping there was unwise. I told Mickey that ground was ripe for diggers. It does not help to warn if you will not listen."

Cat turns to me. "Mickey? He told you about those things?"

"No," I say. "Well, maybe. He did say something about diggers, but what does that mean? He didn't say what diggers are or what they do. If he'd said that diggers are things that come up out of the ground and tear your guts out we would have kept walking."

"I warned!" Speaker says. "I warned! Why would I warn if diggers are harmless? Do I warn about ferns? No! Do I warn about rocks? No! You are strangers here. If I warn, you should listen!"

I open my mouth to respond, but . . .

But he's not wrong.

"What else is there?" Cat asks. "What else do we need to know about between here and wherever the fuck we're going?"

"What else?" Speaker says. "Who can say? The world is wide. There are many species in it, and your people are soft and fragile. Nearly anything here could kill you."

"Soft and fragile?" Cat says, her voice a flat monotone now.

Speaker rises up, seems to hesitate, and then drops back to the ground. Is he actually learning to read the room? "No," he says. "No. Apologies. That was not called for. You need not be soft for diggers to kill you. Diggers kill us. Diggers kill almost anything. This is why I wanted not to stop there."

"Fine," Cat says. "Apology accepted, I guess. So what else is there? What do we need to know?"

"Difficult to say," Speaker says, "but I promise to warn you. If anything bad comes along, I will warn you like I warned you of the diggers, but louder."

"Thanks," Cat says. "Warn us all next time, huh? No matter what you think, Mickey isn't actually our Prime."

We walk on. After another few minutes, Cat sidles up to me.

"Lucas was my friend," she says, her voice pitched too low for anyone else to hear. "He was my friend, and I killed him. I'm going to see the look on his face when I shot him for the rest of my life, however long that turns out to be. Is that on you, Mickey?"

"I . . ." I look around. Nobody else is paying any attention. Even Nasha has drifted away, shuffling along with her eyes fixed on the ground in front of her. "I don't know, Cat. Maybe. If it is, I'm sorry."

"Yeah," she says. "I'm sure."

I'd like to say something more then, but Cat is clearly done with the conversation. I sigh, and duck my head, and keep walking.

WE WALK.

The sun makes its way across the sky. The mountains in the distance never seem to get any closer.

Sometime after noon, I give Nasha the last of my water. She downs it without pausing. Her eyes are half-closed, and her face is a rictus of pain.

Cat and Berto have our remaining two accelerators strapped across their backs. I'm carrying one of Nasha's burners. Jamie has the other. None of us is paying the least attention to anything other than putting one foot in front of the other. It occurs to me that if the spiders find us now, we'll probably die without getting off a shot.

"How much farther?" Jamie asks, for what must be the twentieth time.

"Not far," Speaker says. "Almost there. Almost there. If we could move more quickly—"

"We can't," I say. "Stop asking."

Nasha takes my hand. The air has a chill to it now, but her palm is slick with sweat.

"We're gonna die out here," she says. "You know that, right?"

I sigh. "Maybe."

She stumbles, and has to use my arm for balance. "We're out of water, we're exhausted, and how much food are we still packing? A few protein bars and some slurry? It's a hundred klicks back to the dome, and getting farther every step. There's no maybe about it."

"The creepers must need water," I say, although Speaker hasn't yet shown any evidence of that. "Maybe our friends to the south will let us fill up a few bottles."

Nasha coughs out a short, sharp laugh.

"Right," she says. "We'll be lucky if our friends to the south don't just dissect us on the spot."

I sigh again, a little louder this time.

"You SEE?" SPEAKER says. "Almost there. Just a bit farther now."

I look up from my feet for the first time in hours. The sun is halfway down, poking wanly through high, thin pink clouds. The mountains, which had been steadily receding, are suddenly on top of us.

"There," Speaker says. "You see?"

What I see is a near-vertical granite cliff rising directly out of the plains, stretching across our path like a wall marking the end of the world and rising high enough that I have to crane my neck to see where it rolls off into an ordinary mountain slope.

"Please," I say. "Tell me we don't have to climb that."

"Climb?" Speaker says. "No. No climbing. This is our goal. You see? We have arrived here with no more dying."

I give a quick look around. That sounds like the sort of thing that you say right before doom rains down on your head. No spiders, though. No diggers. No monsters of any kind—just five half-dead humans and an overly chipper creeper.

"Just to be clear," Cat says from behind us. "The cliff is where we're going?"

"Inside the cliff," Speaker says. "In the cliff is the entrance."

We keep walking. After another ten minutes or so, Speaker says, "Very soon now. Almost there."

We keep walking. The cliff blocks out the sun now, and rises up high enough that it almost looks like it's looming over us. The ferns have died back here, probably from lack of light, and the ground has turned to packed earth and pebbles.

"There," Speaker says. "You see?"

And much to my surprise, I do. There at the base of the cliff, maybe two hundred meters distant, a black mouth gapes.

"Great," Nasha says. "Another labyrinth."

I shrug. "What did you expect?"

We slow our pace as we get closer, until finally, by mutual unspoken agreement, we come to a halt twenty meters or so from the entrance.

"What now?" Cat says after a long silence. "Do we just walk in?"

"No," Speaker says. "No, I would not recommend that. That would be unwise."

"So we wait?"

"Yes," he says. "We wait."

Those words are still hanging in the air between us when a wave of meter-long creepers comes boiling out of the entrance. We fall back, Cat and Berto scrambling for their weapons, while Speaker holds his ground, dancing. They ignore us and fall on him, latching on to his limbs with their mandibles and dragging him toward the cliff. He tries to keep dancing at first, then begins to struggle when they bite through one of his legs.

"Friends!" Speaker says. "Please! Defend me!"

I have one of Nasha's burners in hand now. I aim and fire, play the beam across the body of one of the creepers tugging at his rearmost segment. It ignores me for two or three seconds, then releases its grip on Speaker and turns toward me. Berto's accelerator barks, and the creeper shudders and drops, its first two segments now just broken wreckage. Cat picks off another that's moving around Speaker's body, but they're both using explosive rounds and they can't hit the ones that have hold of Speaker without hitting him as well. Speaker is thrashing now, rearing up and then being pulled back down, until one of them climbs up onto his back and sinks its mandibles into him, just below his first segment.

He falls limp.

The creepers swarm over him and drag him toward the hole.

"Mickey?" Berto says. "What do we do?"

I open my mouth, but nothing comes out. The fact is, I have no idea.

By the time I close it again, it's over, and Speaker is gone.

018

FOR A SOLID two minutes, none of us moves or speaks. Finally, Berto walks over to one of the dead creepers and rolls what's left of it onto its back with the toe of his boot.

"Look," he says, then crouches and pries a chunk of shattered carapace away. "You can actually see where the organics end and the mechanics begin."

Nasha drops to her knees, then sits, then flops onto her back and throws one arm across her eyes.

"Nasha?" Jamie says. "You okay?"

"Oh yeah," she says without moving. "I'm great."

Cat turns to look at me. "What now, Mickey? I mean, you're still in charge of this fiasco, right?"

"I . . ." I begin. The truth, though, is that I don't have any kind of reasonable answer.

"Don't just ask what now," Berto says after a long, painful silence. "He's the decision maker here, not the oracle. Give the man some options."

"Okay," Cat says. "Option one: go in shooting."

"Option two," Nasha says. "Lie here until we die."

219

"Option three," Jamie says. "Walk back to the dome and forget any of this bullshit ever happened."

"Okay," Berto says. "Those are all stupid. Mickey?"

I look up. "You think you can get to the top of that?"

Berto follows my gaze. "What? The cliff?"

"Yeah. Can you make it to the top with your pack on your back?"

"Huh." He takes a few steps back and scratches his chin. I can see his eyes moving across the face, already tracing out the first hint of a path. "Maybe? I'd want to do a walk-around, see if there's another route that's more climbable than what we're looking at here—but even if there's not, I guess it's possible. Why? What are you thinking?"

"Same thing that I was thinking with the spiders. If we go down here, I need someone to get back to the dome and let them know what happened."

"Okay," Berto says. "So you want me to free-climb a five-hundred-meter granite face with a fifteen-kilo pack on my back, then just hang around up there waiting to see if you get eaten?"

"Yeah, pretty much. Unless you think you can run fast enough to get airborne from the ground?"

He actually has to think about that one.

"No," he says finally. "I barely made it yesterday even with the speed boost from the rover and a jump-off point three meters off the ground. Pretty sure if I tried to get airborne from a flat start I'd just wind up busting up the glider and hurting myself."

"Fair enough," I say. "Anybody got any water at all left?"

Cat pulls a bottle from a side pocket on her pack. "Quarter-liter, maybe?"

"Give it to Berto."

She looks like she wants to argue, but after a moment's thought, she hands it over.

"Thanks," I say. "Jamie?"

He shakes his head. Nasha wasn't carrying anything, and I've been empty for hours now, so it looks like that's it.

I turn back to Berto. "Okay. Get climbing, I guess. Good luck. I'll keep you posted on what's happening down here if I can."

He hesitates, jaw working as if he has something to say. In the end, though, he just turns and walks away.

"HE'S GONNA DIE," Cat says. "He's gonna slip and fall, and then we're gonna have to watch him splatter right in front of us like a rotten tomato. You know that, don't you?"

We're standing shoulder to shoulder at the base of the cliff, heads tilted back, watching Berto climb. Nasha's still on her back, eyes covered, either sleeping or pretending to. Jamie's sitting cross-legged on the ground with one of Nasha's burners across his lap, staring at the mouth of the creepers' labyrinth.

"Maybe," I say. "I guess we all have to die eventually, right?"

"True," she says. "Berto's not going to die eventually, though. He's going to die soon. Like, in the next ten minutes."

I sigh. "The way things have been going, I wouldn't be surprised if we are too, Cat. The thing is, though, Berto is actually the least likely of any of us to die today. If and when the creepers decide to come back for us, we're finished. He'll watch them take us apart, then take off in his homemade flitter and be back at the dome in a couple of hours. Just like always, everything works out for Berto."

Cat shakes her head. "Not gonna happen. There's no way in hell he makes it to the top."

I turn to look at her. "Care to make a wager on that?"

She laughs. "Gamble over whether our friend lives or dies? Sure, why not? I guess that's who we are by now. What are the stakes?"

I have to think about that for a minute.

"Dinner when we get back to the dome? Not potatoes and slurry, either. This meal has to include at least one rabbit haunch and two tomatoes. Loser pays."

Cat squints up at me. "That's a pretty low-risk bet, considering that the odds of us ever making it back to the dome are probably even lower than the odds of Berto making it to the top of the cliff."

I shrug. "Take it or leave it."

She turns her attention back to Berto as he wedges one boot into a vertical crack and stretches up for a handhold. "You seem suspiciously confident. Why?"

I smile, though she can't see it behind my rebreather. "Did I ever tell you how I wound up on this mission?"

She tilts her head to one side. "I don't think so. We talked about it, didn't we? That night in the gym, right? You told me you weren't a prisoner, and that you weren't conscripted. I didn't believe you."

I laugh. "Well, it's true. I was not a prisoner, and I was not conscripted. I actually volunteered for this gig. It wasn't an entirely voluntary volunteering, though. I was in a shit-ton of trouble—and the reason I was in a shit-ton of trouble, aside from the general fact that I'm an idiot, was that I bet against Berto being able to do something that no human being should have been able to do, and then sat there and watched him do it. I promised myself then that I wouldn't ever make that mistake again."

We fall silent for a while then, and just watch. Berto is maybe a third of the way up the face at the moment. He moves like a spider, unhurried, hands moving from one hold to the next, toes finding near-invisible irregularities in the rock face.

"He looks like he knows what he's doing, anyway," Cat says. "Was he a pro climber or something back on Midgard?"

I shake my head. "Nope. Not so far as I know, anyway, and I'm pretty sure he would have let me know if there was yet another thing that he was great at."

"Okay. Dedicated amateur, then?"

"Don't think so."

"Dilettante?"

"Not really."

"So as far as you know, he's got no serious climbing experience of any kind."

I shrug. "Yeah, pretty much."

"And yet you knew he'd be able to pull this off because . . ."

"Two reasons. First, Berto is a physical savant. You know he was the top-ranked pog-ball player on Midgard, right?"

"I did not. Is that a big deal? I was never much into sports."

"Yeah," I say. "It's a big deal. He beat guys who had dedicated their lives to the sport, one after another, barely breaking a sweat, and he accomplished it basically as a goof. People were calling him the greatest natural talent the planet had ever seen, and then he walked away after three years because he was bored."

"Okay," she says. "And?"

I turn to look at her. "Huh?"

She rolls her eyes. "You said there were two reasons. That's only one."

I look up again. Berto is balanced on his toes on what looks like a two-centimeter ledge, one hand stretched above him and gripping a tiny nub, the other pressed flat against the rock beside him.

"Look at that," I say. "You see where he is now?"

"Yeah," she says. "About to fall."

"Your heart's racing just thinking about being up there right now, isn't it?"

She shrugs. "Maybe."

"Right. That's the other reason. I guarantee you that his is thumping away at a steady sixty beats per minute right now. The thing about Berto is that the part of our brains that makes most of us panic when, just for example, we realize that we're two hundred meters up a sheer rock face with nothing but two toes on a stray nub of rock between us and a quick and painful death—that part just isn't there for Berto. You remember that stunt he pulled with the flitter a couple of years ago, right?"

"Yeah," she says. "I remember. I put a hundred kcal into the pool that he took from us."

"Well, a guy who would do something like that for a couple of dinners isn't going to flinch at a little rock climbing."

"Maybe," she says. "Look, though. He's stuck."

I push my ocular to max magnification. She's right. He looks like he's in an okay place at the moment, with both feet on a narrow ledge a few meters higher than where he'd been before and his right hand wrapped around a gnarled knob of granite. His left hand, though, is about a half meter short of the next solid hold. As I watch, he stretches and leans, his right hand almost coming free of its grip, but unless he's got a limb extender in there it's not going to work.

"You're right," I say. "Doesn't matter, though. He's just gonna have to back down, try to find another—"

He jumps.

Two hundred meters up a sheer granite cliff face, with no safety equipment and a fifteen-kilo pack on his back, Berto Gomez gathers himself, and jumps.

Cat sucks in air and takes a half step back.

Needless to say, Berto makes the catch.

The new hold is a deep horizontal crack in the rock. Berto gets both hands into it, swings briefly, and then finds a hold with his right foot, steadies, and stands.

"Holy God," Cat says.

"Yeah," I say. "You see what I mean?"

After a brief pause to wipe the sweat from first one hand, then the other, Berto keeps climbing.

<RedHawk>: That was fun. Can I do it again?

<Mickey7>: You're the goddamned worst.

<RedHawk>: Did you see the jump?

<Mickey7>: Yeah, Berto. We saw the jump.

<RedHawk>: Pretty sweet, right?

<Mickey7>: The god. Damned. Worst.

<RedHawk>: Anyway, it's nice up here. The view is unbeliev-
able. I can see all the way back to the ridgeline.

<Mickey7>: Great. Let us know if anything is sneaking up on us,
huh?

<RedHawk>: Will do. Speaking of which, I'm kind of wishing I'd
brought a weapon with me. If anything catches me here, I'm
pretty much defenseless.

<Mickey7>: Yeah, well. We're all taking our chances at the
moment.

<RedHawk>: Truth. What's your plan down there, by the way?

<Mickey7>: Honestly? I don't really have one. I'm just kind of let-
ting events carry me, at this point. Hopefully Speaker comes
back, or the local creepers send a Prime up to talk to me.

<RedHawk>: And if neither of those things happens?

<Mickey7>: I don't know, man. My best guess would be that we
sit here until something kills us or we all die of thirst, but I'm
definitely open to suggestions.

<RedHawk>: I'll let you know if anything comes to me.

<Mickey7>: Unrelated, and I know I probably should have asked
you this before, but do you have enough charge in your
thrusters to get back to the dome from here?

<RedHawk>: An excellent question.

<Mickey7>: Thanks. Got an excellent answer?

<RedHawk>: I do not.

<Mickey7>: And if you don't?

<RedHawk>: Even without the thrusters, this thing still works
    as a glider. I guess I'll need to figure out how to ride a ther-
    mal.

<Mickey7>: Either that or how to walk home.

<RedHawk>: Right. That.

RIGHT AROUND SUNSET, Nasha groans, rolls onto her side, and
pushes herself up into a sitting position. I kneel down next to her
and touch her shoulder.

"Hey," I say. "How're you feeling?"

She blinks, rubs her face with both hands, and then rolls her
head around in a slow, lazy circle. "Honestly? Better, I think."

I let out a breath I hadn't realized I'd been holding. "Oh God.
That's fantastic. You scared the hell out of me."

Her eyes narrow. "What are you talking about, Mickey? We're
still all going to die here. Does it really matter if it's from a brain
bleed, or creepers, or just waiting around until we all dry up and
blow away?"

"No," I say. "I don't think we're going down here. I've actually been feeling more optimistic as the day has worn on. If the
creepers were planning to kill us, they would have done it by
now, right?"

She shakes her head. "I don't know, babe. I gave up trying to
figure out what these things are thinking a while ago. Anyway,
even if they don't, we still die of thirst."

"I've got a plan for that. Berto's making an emergency supply
run back to the dome tomorrow."

"Okay," she says. "That gets us, what, four or five liters? Enough for another day?"

I shrug. "Then I send him again."

She laughs. "You've got this all figured out, huh?"

"Absolutely. All part of the master plan."

After a few moments of silence, Nasha says, "I'm not so sure I trust that the creepers are going to leave us alone here."

"We don't want them to leave us alone. We want them to come out here and talk to us. We want them to give us our bomb back, remember?"

"Sure," Nasha says. "That's the stretch goal. In the meantime, I'd be happy if they just didn't eat us—and I have to say, they haven't done anything so far to give me much confidence. I mean, what was that with Speaker? They killed him, right?"

I shrug. "Did they? Or did they just drag him away?"

"They bit through the back of his neck."

"Yeah, that's true, but you're making a lot of assumptions about what kills a creeper, aren't you? I mean, does he even have a spine to sever? Where is his brain? For all we know, it's in his tail."

She sighs. "He went completely limp, Mickey. He looked awfully damn dead to me."

I'd like to argue, but she makes a good point.

"You could be right," I say. "The thing is, though—they didn't kill *us*. They could have, but they didn't. That's got to mean something."

"True," she says. "Doesn't matter, though. Without Speaker, we can't talk to them. If we can't talk to them, we can't ask for the bomb. If we can't get the bomb back from them, we're all dead when winter comes, whether they kill us here or not."

"No," I say. "That's not gonna happen. Just watch. This is all going to work itself out."

"You got a plan?"

I grin and cup her cheek in one hand. "Don't need a plan, homie. I've got you."

She punches me, hard enough to knock me onto my backside. "You're an idiot," she says. "You know that, right?"

I scoot closer to her, lean forward, and rest my forehead against hers. "Maybe. I'm your idiot, though."

She lifts both of our rebreathers just long enough to kiss me. "You are," she says. "You really, really are."

JAMIE VOLUNTEERS TO take first watch. He's been sitting there staring at the opening all day anyway, so it's not much of a change for him, I guess. Nasha's not tired now, so I settle in with my head in her lap. I'm just starting to drift when my ocular pings.

> <RedHawk>: You sleeping down there?
>
> <Mickey7>: Not yet. I was kind of planning on it, though.
>
> <RedHawk>: Not gonna lie, Mickey. I'm not too happy right now. I'm hungry and thirsty, and I'm kind of nervous that if I go to sleep, something's gonna eat me.
>
> <Mickey7>: That's weird, because we're having a great time down here.
>
> <Mickey7>: Hey—how much weight can you carry with that glider?
>
> <RedHawk>: Hard to say. The more I'm carrying, the harder the thrusters have to work to keep me airborne, so it depends on how far I'm going, I guess.
>
> <Mickey7>: I was wondering what the chances would be of you getting back to the dome, fetching us some supplies, and making it back without dying. We can probably hold out for another day down here without water, but I don't think much beyond that.

<RedHawk>: Huh. Water's heavy. I could probably manage a few liters, but not much more than that. That's assuming I've still got enough juice left to get back there in the first place, of course.

<Mickey7>: Right. Let's put a pin in that. If we're still hanging around here tomorrow afternoon, we may need to give it a shot.

<RedHawk>: You're assuming nothing eats me in the meantime.

<Mickey7>: Yeah, well. If anything does, let me know, and I'll try to come up with an alternate plan.

<RedHawk>: Thanks, Mickey. You're a pal.

<Mickey7>: No problem, buddy. Sleep well.

I blink the chat window closed.

"You were messaging Berto, right?" Nasha asks. "How's he doing?"

"About the same as all of us," I say. "Hungry, thirsty, and scared."

JAMIE WAKES ME at 02:00. He hands me an accelerator, then curls up on the ground between Nasha and Cat with one arm tucked under his head.

"You good?" Nasha says.

"Yeah," I say. "Get some sleep, huh?"

I get to my feet. It's colder now, but the air is soft and still and the sky is so packed with stars that I don't need my ocular to see. I yawn and stretch, then strap the accelerator across my back and wander over toward the opening to the labyrinth. I'm not entirely sure what I should be watching for at this point. I can't think of anything that I'd need an accelerator to fight that I'd actually have a chance in hell of fighting off. If the spiders catch us here? I could take a few of them down, maybe, but there's no way I could keep them from killing us. The same goes for the creepers.

What if it's something like the diggers? I spend an uncomfortable few minutes wondering if I'd have the courage to do for Nasha what Cat did for Lucas, before deciding that some things are best not considered.

It doesn't matter whether I'm actually doing anything useful, I guess. There are forms to be followed. So I pretend to be a good soldier, and spend the next three hours walking slow circles around my sleeping friends and trying to flog my brain into coming up with some sort of plan for the next day. I've had a low-grade dehydration headache since before we got here. By the morning it'll be worse, and by tomorrow evening I'll barely be functioning. The others are probably in more or less the same boat.

I'd like to hold off giving up our only reconnaissance platform if I can, but if something doesn't happen soon, Berto's going to have to give it a go. If he doesn't make it to the dome and back, then Nasha's right. We're all going to die here.

The night grows colder. The stars make their slow way across the sky.

At 05:00 I nudge Cat awake, hand her my weapon, and curl up around Nasha. She murmurs something unintelligible and throws one arm across my shoulder.

Much to my surprise, I sleep.

"MICKEY? WAKE UP, boss."

I open my eyes to the flat gray of predawn and Cat crouching over me with her accelerator across her knees. I blink to my chronometer: 06:10. Nasha groans and pulls away from me. I sit up.

"Cat? What's going on?"

In answer, she points back toward the opening to the labyrinth.

Speaker crouches there, watching us.

"He wants to talk to you," Cat says.

Hope surges inside of me with a physical intensity. Is it possible that for the first time since we left the dome, something has actually broken our way? I scramble to my feet and fast-walk over to him.

"Speaker!" I say. "It's great to see you. We were afraid—"

"You are Mickey?"

I pull up short. He doesn't sound like Berto anymore. His voice is as flat and affectless as a text-to-talk translator.

This isn't Speaker.

"I am," I say. "Who are you?"

"Unimportant," he—no, it—says. "This unit should not have brought you here. It has been repurposed, and now speaks for the collective."

THE FIRST THING I do is send a priority ping to Berto.

> <RedHawk>: Mickey? The sun's not even up yet.
> <Mickey7>: Pay attention, Berto. Things are happening down
>   here.

I blink the window closed.

Jamie, Nasha, and Cat are arrayed in a semicircle behind me now. Jamie and Cat are holding accelerators more or less at the ready. Nasha has both of her burners in hand.

This looks uncomfortably like a last-stand scene from an adventure vid.

"The collective," I say. "That's the name for the ones who took Speaker yesterday?"

"The portions of your language that we were able to extract from this unit lack the words to convey our name in a way that would be meaningful. The collective is the nearest term we could retrieve. This will serve as a placeholder."

"Is Speaker dead?" Cat asks.

It rises up, and its attention shifts from me to Cat, then back. "Which of you is Prime?"

Oh boy. Need to nip this in the bud.

"We all are," I say. "All of us are Prime."

It hesitates, then settles back onto its forelegs. "This seems unlikely."

I fold my arms across my chest. "Nonetheless."

"We will only speak to one of you as Prime."

I roll my eyes. "Fine. Speak to me, but please understand that each one of us is an independent, sentient entity. None of us are expendable. Clear?"

It shuffles its feet. "You seek to drive up your price in an exchange of ancillaries. I must warn you that your position here is not strong enough for this."

"No," I say. "You're not hearing me. There will be no exchange of ancillaries. Our kind has no ancillaries. If you attempt a forced exchange, there will be violence."

"You are too few to threaten us with violence."

Cat chambers a round, takes aim at the cliff face, and fires. The resulting explosion leaves a massive gouge in the rock, and rains a cloud of hot, sharp bits of gravel over an area twenty meters wide. "You'd be surprised," I say. The thing that was Speaker scuttles back a few steps, mandibles clattering.

> <RedHawk>: Was that an explosion? I can't see what's happening down there.
> <Mickey7>: It was a demonstration. Nobody's dead yet. You might want to get your glider ready to go, though.
> <RedHawk>: On it.

Not-Speaker rises up to face me now, mandibles spread. "Why have you come here?"

No point in dancing around it, I guess.

"You have something that belongs to us. We have come here to get it back."

It hesitates, its first two segments weaving back and forth like the head of a cobra.

"We must consider," it says finally. "Wait here."

With that, it drops to its feet and scuttles back into the labyrinth.

"Dammit," Nasha mutters. "This shit again?"

THE CREEPER RETURNS less than an hour later, just as I'm starting to think maybe I should send Berto on a water run. The sun is over the horizon now, and the air has warmed enough that even half-starved, I'm not shivering anymore. I get to my feet as it scuttles toward us.

"We have considered," it says. "We know what you want. We do not wish to give it to you."

"Listen—" Nasha begins, but I stop her with a look.

"This thing," I say. "I know it appears benign, but it is not. It's dangerous—much more so than you can probably imagine. If you won't return it to us, the most likely outcome is that you accidentally kill yourselves with it."

"Interesting," the creeper says. "You came here out of concern for our well-being?"

"No," I say. "Clearly not."

"Clearly," it says. "Thank you for not attempting to mislead us on this point."

"However," I say, "that doesn't change the fact that if you refuse to return our property to us, it will eventually kill you."

The creeper raises its first segment and wags it back and forth in a gruesome parody of a head shake. "We do not believe you. We believe that you are attempting to convince us that your device is dangerous in order to enhance your bargaining position. We have studied this object. We do not understand the things that it contains, but we do not believe that they are dangerous."

And with that, it untucks its feeder arms and releases a bubble.

It takes a long moment for any of us to react. I've never seen a magnetic monopole bubble before. I doubt there's a living human anywhere in the Union who has. These are the things that nearly ended us as a species. The feeling of visceral dread that seizes me when I realize what I'm seeing is impossible to convey. Even without the emotional response, though, it's hard to look at it. I try, but my eyes can't seem to focus. Every time I think I've got it, they slide away. It's small, I can tell that much—a twisted knot of shiny blackness that drifts up and away from the creeper like a negative image of a will-o'-the-wisp.

"Holy shit," Nasha whispers, and takes an involuntary step back. "Is it armed?"

"Can't be," Cat says. "Can it, Mickey?"

I don't answer at first. I'm racking my brain for the twenty minutes of training I had on antimatter fuel elements eleven years ago on Himmel Station. A magnetic monopole bubble is technically unstable, but in its base energy state the median time to decay is something like half a billion years. Which is to say that the bubble drifting in front of me could pop at any moment, but probably won't anytime soon. The triggering device uses high-energy photons to raise the bubble's energy state and speed up the process a bit.

If this bubble has been triggered, we're all already dead.

"I think . . ." I begin, then have to pause to moisten my suddenly bone-dry mouth. "I think it's not armed. I mean, it can't be. The triggering device would have armed every bubble in the pack, and I don't think the fuse was set to more than a minute or two."

The bubble drifts higher, then catches a breeze and floats off along the cliff face. Another thirty seconds, and it's gone.

"You appear to be frightened," the creeper says. "This is what you came here to retrieve, is it not?"

"That thing," I say. "Have you removed more of them from the device?"

"No," it says. "We took great care to extract only one. We were interested to see your reaction. Having seen it now, we must consider."

As it turns to go, Jamie says, "Hey. We need water."

Good man. I can't believe he had the presence of mind to think of that. The creeper pauses. "Water?"

"Yeah," he says. "If you want us to still be here when you come back, you need to give us water."

It hesitates, and a ripple runs the length of its body before it continues on. "Acceptable," it says, then disappears back into the labyrinth.

THE CREEPER IS as good as its word. A half hour or so after Jamie's request, a crowd of the smaller ones emerges from the opening. Each one holds a hollow stone half-sphere filled with water in its feeding arms. They set them down one by one on the ground outside the entrance, then disappear back into the darkness.

> <RedHawk>: Hey.
> <RedHawk>: Want to send me up a drink?
> <RedHawk>: I'm kind of dying up here.
> <RedHawk>: By which I mean I'm literally dying up here.

<RedHawk>: Mickey?
<RedHawk>: Hello?

"HE DOESN'T HAVE the bomb with him," Nasha says when the creeper emerges again. "I've got a bad feeling about where this is going." She pulls her burners out of the pile of gear we've been resting against, checks the charge on each of them, and then hands one to me. It's pretty clear to me that if this comes to fighting we're not ever leaving here, but I take it anyway. I guess it's just not in our nature to face the unknown empty-handed.

We get to our feet as it approaches. The sun is past noon now, and the air is slowly cooling. The water they brought us earlier is mostly gone, with maybe a liter for each of us stashed in our packs. I'm hoping that not-Speaker has something definitive to say this time, because I'm really not looking forward to another night out here in the open, and Berto isn't going to last much longer up there without water. No matter what happens with the creepers, at some point soon I need to send him home.

The creeper trundles up to me, then rises up until its mandibles are even with my head. "We have determined that you are this group's Prime," it says.

"No," I say. "We've been over this. Our kind does not have ancillaries. We are all Prime."

"You have said this," it says. "We do not believe you. However, for the moment this is irrelevant. For the purposes of this negotiation, you will be this group's Prime."

I glance over at Nasha. She shrugs. Cat and Jamie are on their feet as well now, standing silently just behind us. Nothing to do but go with it, I guess.

"Okay," I say. "For the purposes of this negotiation, I will accept that you believe that I am this group's Prime. So? What now?"

"Now," it says, "you will come with me."

Nasha puts a hand to my arm. "No," she says. "He won't."

The creeper turns its attention to her. "You are the Nasha. This unit's memories indicate that you are the most dangerous of your kind. We find this difficult to believe."

"I'm Nasha Adjaya," she says. "Your memories are right, and you're not taking Mickey."

It rises to face her. "We disagree. Our Prime wishes to communicate with yours directly. This is necessary if you wish to have your device returned to you."

Nasha starts to reply, but before she can, I say, "Fine. I'll go."

"Acceptable," the creeper says, then turns and scuttles back toward the opening.

"Mickey," Nasha begins, but I shake my head and start after the creeper.

"If they wanted to kill us," I say over my shoulder, "they wouldn't need to trick me into the labyrinth. They could just do it here."

There's not really an answer for that. The three of them watch in silence as I follow the creeper down.

THIS LABYRINTH ISN'T much like the one Speaker came from. The walls of the tunnels are all clean-cut and dry, and where Speaker's tunnels meandered like a slow-moving river, this one cuts arrow-straight into the mountain. As we descend, we pass crossing tunnels every hundred meters or so, always intersecting the main branch at right angles. At every third crossing, a narrow air shaft leads up from the ceiling toward the surface. There's even dim, gray light filtering in from somewhere.

This place looks almost like something humans would build.

After ten minutes of walking, the tunnel levels out, and then shortly after that it begins to ascend. There are narrow shafts leading down and away where the walls meet the floor at the lowest point. It's obviously a drainage system, although I have no idea where the water is going from here.

It suddenly occurs to me that I haven't seen a single creeper other than not-Speaker.

After another ten minutes, the tunnel levels out again. We're deep into the mountain now. How much granite is over my head? Five hundred meters? A thousand? Enough, anyway, that if the roof caves in, they're never going to find my body. I'm contemplating that when the walls and ceiling of the tunnel fall away and I find myself walking into a chamber even bigger than the one where I first met Speaker.

Not-Speaker keeps moving, but I have to stop and stare. I'm at the edge of a half-sphere of empty space that must be a hundred meters across. The walls are as smooth-cut as the tunnels, and the space is shot through with what looks like webbing. I cringe at first, thinking of the spiders. It only takes a moment to see that's not quite it, though. This isn't a web. It looks more like a diagram I once saw of the networks of neurons in a rabbit's brain. Strands of gray fiber as thick as my wrist sprout from every part of the walls and floor and ceiling, intertwining with one another in a random tangle that my eye keeps trying to sort into some sort of pattern. Where three or four strands meet in one place, nodes have formed, misshapen blobs a meter or two wide.

In the center of it all, dangling two or three meters from the floor and so entwined with gray strands that I can barely make out its shape, hangs a giant creeper. As I watch, it twitches spasmodically, and the entire network pulses.

I wait there, two strides past the entrance, but not-Speaker keeps going until a strand detaches from one of the nodes and drops down toward it, writhing and twisting as it goes. The strand strikes not-Speaker just behind the first segment.

It sticks, and not-Speaker freezes in place.

A second strand falls then, and a third, both attaching to its first segment, on either side of its mandibles.

Not-Speaker turns back to face me.

"Welcome to the collective," it says, its voice slightly more modulated now. "We are pleased to meet you."

I'm about to reply when I hear a sound like a wet kiss above me. I look up as a tendril detaches and drops down toward me.

Things happen quickly.

I stagger back toward the tunnel, hand scrabbling for Nasha's burner, trip as the weapon comes free from its holster, then lose my grip on it when my right hip and shoulder hit the stone floor. The tendril strikes stone a few meters away and comes questing toward me. I roll half-over, regain my grip on the burner, and fire. The creepers' armor is almost impervious to a handheld burner, but it seems this isn't so for this . . . whatever this is. The tendril blackens and shrivels where my beam touches it, and after a second or two the entire network shudders and the tendril withdraws. I scramble up to a sitting position and put my back against the chamber wall, burner held out in front of me in both hands.

"Get back!" I shout, struggling to keep a quaver out of my voice. "Get away from me with that shit!"

"Please lower your weapon," not-Speaker says. "It would be simpler if you allowed us to interface. Communication would be more efficient."

"Interface?"

Another tendril detaches above me. It drops down a few meters and then hangs there, quivering.

"Interface," not-Speaker says. "It will not be painful, and may make it possible for you to join with the collective. Will you allow it?"

I raise the burner to aim at the tendril. "Come any closer with that thing, and I will destroy you."

"We doubt this," not-Speaker says. "We do not believe you have the power to destroy us."

A fair point.

"I may not," I say after a moment's hesitation, "but my people do. I came here to talk. If you attack me, they'll reduce this place to rubble."

"Again," it says, "we doubt you have the power to do this."

"We have a starship. You have no idea what we have the power to do."

A ripple runs through the network around me, and I clutch the burner a little tighter.

"Starship," not-Speaker says. "This is a vehicle for traveling from one star to another?"

"Correct."

"We doubt this. Travel between stars is not possible for creatures like you."

"You sound pretty sure of yourself."

"We have given this great thought. At reasonable speeds, the time required to travel to even the nearest star is prohibitive, and the energy required to accelerate to speeds that would make such travel practical is impossibly large."

"Okay," I say. "So where do you imagine we came from?"

"Unknown."

"We're clearly not native to this world."

A ripple runs the length of not-Speaker's body. "Unclear. This world is large. We know only a small part of it."

That stops me for a moment.

"You know about the distances between stars, but you don't know what's on the other side of your own planet?"

"We know what we have gleaned from the creatures we have brought into the collective."

It's only then that it becomes clear to me that I'm not speaking with the giant creeper.

I'm speaking with the thing that's captured the giant creeper, the thing that holds it like a fly in a spider's web.

A chill runs down my spine, and I have to fight back an almost overwhelming urge to run.

"It doesn't matter," I say, and I can hear the quaver in my own voice. "You see what this burner can do. You saw what Cat's accelerator did to the rock face yesterday. These are hand weapons. We have much larger, much more powerful ones back at the dome. Believe me or not, but I tell you truly that we could bring this mountain down on you if we chose to do it."

"If this were true," not-Speaker says, "you would not be here now asking for the return of your device. You would simply take it from us."

"Look," I say, as the creeper at the center of the web begins to slowly writhe. "I was sent here to deliver a message. I've delivered it. Whether you believe everything I've said or not, you have to grant that we are potentially dangerous enemies. We've shown you that much. We destroyed your vassals when they attacked us. Speaker's memories should have shown you that as well. The explosion that vaporized them is trivial compared to what we are capable of producing. Also, whether you believe me or not about the fact that our device will eventually kill you if you keep it, the fact is that it's of absolutely no value to you. Refusing to return it to us is a significant risk to you, with no prospect of gain. It makes no logical sense for you to refuse me."

A series of pulses ripple back and forth through the network now. The giant creeper at the center of the web shudders, and not-Speaker's mandibles clatter together. "We disagree with your logic. It is clear to us that this device has great importance to you. We do not need to understand why this is. The fact that you have need of it gives it value, because it provides us with power over you."

And there you have it.

"Fine," I say. "You want to bargain. What do you want from us?"

The network quivers, and seems to close in on me. Again, I have to resist the urge to bolt.

"An interesting question," not-Speaker says. "What can you offer us?"

"We have access to metals. We know these are valuable to you. We could trade some amount of these for the device."

"Possibly," not-Speaker says. "However, we also have access to metals. Possession of this device is a unique opportunity for us. We would not trade it for something that we could potentially provide for ourselves."

"I'm sorry," I say. "I don't know what else we might have that you would want."

It hesitates. When it speaks again, its voice has taken on what I could almost imagine to be a thoughtful tone.

"These weapons. You say you have many more of them?"

I don't like where this is going.

"We will not trade weapons."

"No," it says. "We would not expect you to."

"Then what—"

"We do not ask you to trade weapons. We ask you to trade service."

I shake my head. "I don't understand."

"We will clarify," not-Speaker says. "We have a long-standing conflict with the Prime who provided this unit to you. Despite repeated attempts, it has resisted every effort to bring it into the collective. This conflict has cost us much, and has dragged on for many winters. With your arrival, we now see an opportunity to end it on favorable terms."

I *really* don't like where this is going.

"You're asking us to fight for you?"

"You ask what we require in return for your device. This is our answer. Help us to end this conflict. Once this is done, we will return your device to you."

IT'S FULL DARK when I emerge from the labyrinth. Nasha is waiting for me, just outside the entrance.

"He's back," she says over her shoulder, then turns to me. "Mickey? You still you?"

"Yeah," I say. "I think so, anyway."

She waits for me to come to her, then closes the last half meter between us with a lunge that ends with her arms wrapped tight around me and her mouth pressed to my ear.

"Thank you," she whispers. "Thank you for not dying."

I hold her, eyes squeezed shut, until her grip loosens and she pulls away. Cat and Jamie are on their feet now.

"The bomb," Cat says. "Did you get it?"

"Not yet," I say. "Soon, though."

I blink to a chat window.

> <Mickey7>: Berto? You still alive up there?
> <RedHawk>: Barely. But yeah. I'm functional.
> <Mickey7>: Can you fly in the dark?
> <RedHawk>: To get away from here? Hell, yes.

<Mickey7>: Get back to the dome. Come back here with a lifter. Tell Marshall we've got a deal for the bomb, but he has to get us home first.

<RedHawk>: You got it, boss. I'll be in the air in five.

"Mickey?" Jamie says. "What did you give them?"

I turn to look at him. The look of alarm on his face makes me wonder how much he's already guessed.

"Nothing," I say. "Nothing yet, anyway."

MARSHALL IS WAITING for us in the hangar when we land. "Well?" he says, while I'm still halfway through the lifter's hatch. "Where is the device?"

"We don't have it," I say. "We've got a deal to get it back, but they're still holding on to it for the moment."

His jaw sets and his face darkens. "Gomez told me you had the device. I would not have authorized a lifter otherwise. Do you have any idea how much energy the gravitic grids in this machine draw?"

"Well," I say, "if you hadn't authorized the lifter we would probably have died out there, and you would never have gotten your bomb back. Count your blessings, I guess."

"Barnes," Marshall says, his voice low and even. "Where is the device?"

"It's complicated," I say as Nasha steps down from the lifter beside me. "There's a lot going on, and we're not going to talk about it now. No disrespect, sir, but Nasha needs medical attention, and we all need to eat and sleep. When that's done, I'll give you a complete rundown."

He tries to grab my arm as I walk past him, but I shrug him off and keep moving.

"Do not walk away from me," he says to my back. He starts to say something else as I step into the main corridor, but the door sliding shut behind me cuts him off mid-syllable.

"That was bold," Nasha says. "Hieronymus Marshall doesn't like being ignored."

I shrug. "I don't much care what Marshall thinks at this point. I don't expect to be alive long enough to worry about the blow-back."

HERE'S A MORAL quandary for you: Which takes precedence—a promise to a living enemy, or a promise to a dead friend?

"SO?" CAT SAYS. "When are you gonna tell him?"

I look up from my rabbit haunch. I'm so deep into this meal that I'd almost forgotten she was there. We're alone in the caf at the moment, so I guess it's okay to talk.

"Tell him what?" I say, then take another bite. "That I've gotten us into the middle of a war?"

"Yeah," Cat says. "That too, I guess. I was mostly thinking about the fact that the deal we have to get the bomb back involves us doing something that we've been telling him is impossible for the past two years. If he'd thought there was a military solution to the creepers, he would have taken it a long time ago."

"There wasn't," I say. "There still isn't, I don't think—at least not for us acting alone. My impression from what both Speaker and not-Speaker told me is that the two nests have been in a rough balance, strength-wise, for a long time. The collective isn't looking for us to clear the labyrinth on our own. They're just expecting us to tip the balance in their direction."

Cat pokes at her potatoes with the tip of her fork. "And you agreed, huh?"

I pick the last scraps of meat from the bone I'm holding, sigh, and drop it onto my tray. "Honestly, I don't know what I agreed to. They said they wanted our help. They didn't specify what, exactly, that meant. I guess they could be expecting us to go down into the labyrinth with guns blazing, but I don't know . . . set aside that we don't actually have the numbers to do that. I'm not sure I can go to war with Speaker's people."

Cat raises one eyebrow. "People? Really?"

I lean back, close my eyes, and rub my face with both hands. Now that my stomach is semi-full, my body is telling me that it needs to be unconscious as quickly as possible.

"Aren't they? What else would you call them at this point?"

She shrugs. "Bugs? Monsters? Thinking of them as people is going to make what we have to do a lot harder, you know?"

I sigh again. "Yeah, Cat. I know."

The door slides open behind Cat, and Berto walks in. He shows his ocular to the scanner at the counter, collects his food, and then comes over to drop onto the bench beside me.

"Hey," he says. "What's with the rabbit, Mickey? Did Marshall bump your rations when he made you king of the creepers?"

"Not quite," Cat says. "He's eating rich people food courtesy of your stunt on the rock wall yesterday."

Berto looks from Cat to me, then back. "Huh?"

"We had a disagreement about whether you'd make it," I say.

Cat nods. "I bet him dinner that you were gonna die."

Berto grins. "Finally learned your lesson about betting against me, huh, Mickey?"

"Yeah," I say. "Better late than never, right?"

Berto digs into a mound of yams and fried crickets. "You told Marshall what you signed us up for yet?"

"Not yet. Thought I'd get a last meal first, and maybe a nap."

He nods without looking up from his food. "Good idea. Who knows? Maybe he'll have a stroke and die before morning, right?"

He shovels up a half dozen forkfuls in rapid succession, not even fully clearing his mouth in between. "How's Nasha doing?"

"She's down at Medical getting her brain scanned. They told me it would be a couple of hours."

"Really?" Berto says. "Seems like overkill, doesn't it? She seemed mostly okay in the lifter."

"Maybe. Burke was pretty insistent, though. I guess you don't screw around with head injuries."

"Guess not."

Berto stops talking now, and focuses single-mindedly on eating. There's nothing left on my tray but bones at this point, and Cat is picking delicately at her last scraps of potato.

"So," she says after a few minutes of watching Berto clear his tray. "Back to the point: What are you gonna tell Marshall tomorrow?"

I'm trying to come up with an answer when my ocular pings.

> <Med1:Burke>: We're done with Adjaya's workup. You need to
> come down here.

My mouth runs suddenly dry, and my heart lurches into a panicked jackhammer rhythm.

> <Mickey7>: What's happening, Burke? Is something wrong?
> <Med1:Burke>: She's not dead, okay? But get down here,
> Mickey. Now.

"YOU SEE THAT?" Burke says. We're looking at a semitransparent rendering of Nasha's head. He's pointing to what looks like a tiny star in a dark cavity just behind her left ear. "Back during transit, we had to pull a benign mass out of her left temporal lobe. Remember that?"

I give him a flat, blank stare. *No, Burke. I'd completely forgotten, you asshole.*

"Anyway, that spot you're looking at is a micro-bleed into what's left of the surgical cavity. There are a bunch of vessels in the area that maybe never really healed properly. I'd guess the blow to the head that she took out there knocked a few of them loose."

"Okay. So did you fix it?"

He gives me a look that tells me his estimate of my IQ just dropped by twenty points.

"No," he says. "I did not fix it. That's why I needed you down here. So I could ask what you want me to do."

I shake my head. "Me? No. Ask her what she wants."

He sighs. "She's in an induced coma, Mickey. Her mental state started to deteriorate while she was in the scanner. It's possible the combination of the magnetic fields in the scanner and the double dose of ferrous contrast I gave her contributed to the reaction—sorry, if so. When I saw what was happening, I put her under so that I could drop her temperature and hold her stable until we decided what to do. Her personnel record says you're her medical proxy, so it's your call."

"But . . ." I open my mouth, then close it again. "No, she was fine. She was better. She said she was feeling better."

He shrugs. "That's how it goes with these things sometimes. They used to call it 'talk and die syndrome.' You hit your head. It hurts, but you walk away. Then a few hours or maybe even days later, something lets go and you stroke out. When the bleed is in the dura it's pretty simple. You drain the hemorrhage and wait for it to heal. It's trickier when it's deep in the brain, though. It'd be pretty straightforward if we'd gotten to her right away, or even within twenty-four hours of the injury, probably, but at this point there's a lot of fluid in the cavity, the interstitial pressure is dangerously high, and the area of the injury is unfortunately close to some vital stuff." He points to the display again. "See the mass effect there? You've got significant compression going on in the . . ." He hesitates when he sees my expression, then shakes his head and continues. "Anyway, we've got a few options. I can keep her on ice and hope that it heals on its own. That's the safest approach, but it can take a while, and the longer she's down, the more likely she loses some function. I can bring her temperature up and give her coagulants. That speeds things up, but then you risk an ischemic stroke. I wouldn't recommend going that route. Or, we can go with microsurgery. That's the most aggressive approach, obviously. Probably ends with either a complete recovery or death. High risk, high reward, you know?" He runs a hand back through his hair. "So? What do you think?"

This is easy. I know what I want. I want Nasha alive. I've already opened my mouth to tell him to go with the conservative route when a second question pops into my head.

What does Nasha want?

I know the answer to this one too, of course. Nasha would have given her answer as soon as she heard the word *aggressive*.

Nasha wants to be exactly who she was before.

If she can't have that, Nasha wants to be nothing.

I close my eyes, breathe in deep, and then let it out.

"The surgery," I say. "Do the surgery."

Burke's eyebrows jump up toward his hairline. "You sure? I would have bet a week's rations you'd go with option one."

"Yeah," I say. "Yeah. I'm sure."

"Okay," he says, and taps something into his tablet. "We'll want to bring her temperature back up and get some meds into her to reduce the pressure before we go in. Should have her prepped and ready to go by this time tomorrow, give or take. After that, the surgery itself will take a couple of hours at least.

By nine or ten the next morning, we should be able to get a fix on how she's responding. Maybe check back then?"

"Yeah," I say. "Thanks, Burke."

"Sure thing," he says. "And hey, Mickey? Get some rest, huh? Honestly, you look worse right now than she does."

GET SOME REST. *Solid advice, you smarmy bastard.*

I try. Honest to God, I do. I go up to my rack and climb into bed and lie there in the darkness and stare up at the ceiling and think about what I'll do if Nasha dies on the table. If I killed myself, would Marshall bring me back?

Do I care if he does?

Doesn't matter. Nasha won't die. The universe owes me this one.

I've died enough for both of us, haven't I?

I WAKE TO a pinging ocular. I guess I finally fell asleep after all.

> <Command1>: You are required to report to the Commander's office immediately.
>
> <Command1>: Failure to do so by 08:30 will be construed as insubordination.

Good morning to you too, Marshall.

It's 08:18 now. That gives me time to run through the chem shower and throw on clean clothes before stepping through Marshall's door at 08:29.

"Barnes," he says from behind his desk. "Sit."

I do.

He stares at me.

I stare at him.

He leans forward and plants his elbows on the desk. "So?"

"The mission did not go entirely as we'd hoped, sir."

"Yes," he says. "I gathered that from the fact that Gomez felt compelled to return to the dome to pilfer a half dozen missile warheads from our armory, and that you returned a day later without eight percent of our remaining Security officers and one hundred percent of our rovers."

I sigh. "Yeah, that pretty much sums it up. We lost Lucas to an indigenous form that we hadn't seen before. I'm not sure there was a real way to avoid what happened, but I'll take responsibility. As far as the rover goes, I actually didn't expect to bring it back to the dome. I was hoping to use it as trade goods when we reached our objective, but unfortunately we were forced to destroy it before we got there to prevent it from falling into the hands of another rival group."

His jaw tightens, and his eyebrows creep toward one another at the bridge of his nose. "I see. And how did you manage to escape this rival group after destroying your only means of transportation?"

"We destroyed all of them along with it, sir. We used two of Berto's warheads to blow the rover's plasma chamber. The resulting explosion was impressive."

"You . . ." Marshall says. "Well. Yes. So I would imagine. Unfortunate that you lost the vehicle, but points for ingenuity, I suppose."

"In any case, by the time we got to where we were going, we had nothing left to bargain with."

"And yet, both you and Gomez told me quite clearly yesterday that you had struck a deal to get the bomb back."

"Yes," I say. "We did."

"Was this a lie, Barnes? Because I have to tell you, I'm not likely to take that calmly."

"No, sir, it was not a lie. We do have a deal."

"Tell me, Barnes."

And so, I do.

I GO STRAIGHT from Marshall's office to the caf. There's no way in hell I'm going to war on an empty stomach, and I'm pretty sure there's no point in me saving up kcal anymore. The place is half-full, but I pick up my food and find an empty table. I don't much feel like chatting. I've finished my quarter-rabbit and I'm halfway through a pile of stewed tomatoes when Berto takes the seat across from me.

"Hey," he says. "You're living large again this morning, huh?"

I shrug without looking up. "Don't expect to be back here today." I scoop up a forkful of yams, chew, and swallow. "Don't expect to be back here at all, honestly."

"Wow," he says. "That's morbid. How's Nasha?"

I look up, then back down at my tray. "In a coma, getting prepped for brain surgery."

"Oh." He shuffles potatoes and crickets around on his own tray, but doesn't take a bite. "That's weird, right? She seemed fine when we got back."

"Yeah," I say. "Weird."

We eat in silence then, until Berto has cleaned his tray and I'm scraping up the last of my yams.

"I'm taking the lifter up," he says then. "When the shit goes down, whenever that is. You should come with me."

I look up. "What? Why?"

"I was in the Security ready room earlier. They're not gonna want you going down into the tunnels. Amundsen still remembers you freezing under fire with Cat two years ago."

I look down at my hands, then back up at him. "I didn't freeze. My ocular glitched."

He shrugs. "Don't care. I'm not sure Amundsen cares either. He doesn't trust you, and he doesn't want you with his people. Drake actually suggested pulling a half dozen copies of you out of the tank to bulk up their numbers, but Amundsen said even if Marshall would permit that, which he would not in a million years, he'd rather put accelerators in the hands of the tomato tenders."

"Oh." I'd actually been assuming that I'd be going into the tunnels. It's a suicide mission, right? Ordinarily, that's kind of my thing.

"Look," Berto says, "don't worry about Amundsen. That guy's a prick, right? You're better off in the air anyway. If you're with me, you can keep track of what's going on. Maybe even keep some control of the situation if something goes sideways. You can still communicate with the creepers, right?"

"Yeah," I say. "I think so, anyway."

"Okay, then. Maybe you can keep this from being a slaughter— you know, negotiate some kind of surrender or something?"

I sigh. Who knows? Maybe I actually can. "Sure, Berto. I'll keep you company. What are you expecting to do out there, anyway? If the fighting is happening in the tunnels, a lifter isn't much use."

"Yeah," he says. "I'm well aware. It's the heaviest weapons system we've got, though, and I guess Marshall wants it out there as a show of force, if nothing else. After the new creepers take over, we need to make sure they don't get any ideas about taking us out as well."

"That's exactly what Speaker said would happen, isn't it?"

He looks momentarily confused. "What?"

"When we were talking about abandoning the rover. He said that if they pushed his people out, the next thing they'd do would be to come after us. Too much metal in the dome to pass up, right?"

"Yeah," Berto says. "I guess he did. He wasn't thinking that we'd have formed an alliance with them, though."

"No," I say. "I guess not. He was thinking we'd already formed an alliance with him."

Berto lets that sit between us, his expression completely unreadable. I'm starting to think I'm going to have to follow that up when my ocular pings.

<DDrake0813>: Barnes?

<Mickey7>: Drake? What do you need?

<DDrake0813>: I'm on perimeter duty, a hundred meters out from the main lock. There's a creeper here. A big one.

<Mickey7>: Okay. What do you want me to do about it?

<DDrake0813>: I don't want shit from you, Barnes. The creeper does. It says it wants to talk to you.

IT TAKES ME twenty minutes, give or take, to get down to the main lock, get geared up, and get out to the perimeter. When I get there, I find Drake in full combat armor with his back to a hot pylon, accelerator up and trained on not-Speaker, who's curled over a boulder maybe thirty meters off.

"Thanks for coming," Drake says without taking his eyes off the creeper. "Took your goddamned time, huh?"

"I got here as quick as I could," I say, and I can hear the fatigue in my own voice. "Stand down, Drake. It didn't come here to fight."

Drake grunts, and conspicuously does not lower his weapon. I sigh, step in front of him, and walk out to meet not-Speaker. It doesn't react. I stop when I'm two strides away, fold my arms across my chest, and say, "Well?"

"You are Mickey," it says. "You are Prime."

"Yeah," I say. "So I've been told. What do you want?"

"You made an agreement," it says. "You are Prime. Your words bind your nest."

"Yes," I say. "I remember."

"It is time," it says. "It is . . . it is time . . . it . . ."

"You agreed to return our device. Where is it?"

The creeper's mandibles clack against one another, and a shudder runs the length of its body. "The device is . . . you agreed . . ."

    <DDrake0813>: Barnes? What's going on over there?

    <Mickey7>: Not sure. I think it's glitching.

"You agreed," the creeper says. "You promised to defend . . . to . . ."

To defend?

"Speaker?" I say. "Is that you in there?"

It shudders again, more violently this time.

    <DDrake0813>: Step aside, Barnes. I don't have a shot.

I wave to Drake to lower his weapon without taking my eyes off of Speaker/not-Speaker.

"It is time," it says. "Time to . . . the collective is coming. All of it, all of its ancillaries. Coming to . . . your device . . . Fulfill your promise. Today, Mickey. Soon. Fulfill your promise."

It shudders once more, then curls back on itself and scuttles away.

I watch until it's gone, then turn and walk back to where Drake is still standing, weapon lowered now but still in hand.

"What the hell was that?"

"Good question," I say. "You might want to get some breakfast, though. I think we might be in for a long, ugly day."

"YOU READY?"

I take a deep breath in, let it out slowly, and nod. Berto touches the control panel. The hangar bay door slides open above us. His right hand engages the gravitics, and we ascend.

The human army of Niflheim is not an impressive thing. They're filing out of the main lock as we rise up over the dome. First come nine of our eleven remaining Security officers kitted out in full armor. I try to pick Cat out of the line, but honestly they all look the same from here. After them come a dozen reserves— folks from Agriculture and Physics and Engineering who were cross-trained in weapons and tactics back on Himmel Station eleven years ago. They're not armored, and most of them are carrying burners, not accelerators. That's probably for the best, because the odds that any of them have touched a weapon since we boosted out are probably close to nil. I don't know what orders Amundsen gave them, but if it's anything other than stay out of the way and try not to get hurt, someone should hold him criminally liable.

So that's it. Twenty-one foot soldiers, maybe half of them actually semi-competent, and me and Berto hovering above them in a fully loaded lifter that will be completely useless once they're down in the tunnels.

"Is this what you promised them?" Berto asks as we rise up to a thousand meters and slow to a hover. "Tomato tenders with hand weapons? I'd say our people are cannon fodder down there, but that's probably an insult to cannon fodder."

I shrug. I sat through Amundsen's briefing to the Security people with Cat. His advice was to advance down the tunnels in a three-deep phalanx, using staggered fire to make up for the accelerators' slow repeat rate and trying to avoid getting swarmed from more than one direction at a time. It's basically the approach that the Spartans used at Thermopylae.

That worked out great, right?

Snark aside, it should probably keep them alive as long as their ammunition holds out, and as long as they don't get themselves caught in an open space.

They're each carrying four hundred kinetic energy rounds. I remember the image of the crèche that Eight sent me right before he died. Their ammunition is not going to hold out.

I guess the only real question is whether they kill enough creepers before they go down to satisfy the collective.

Once everyone is clear of the lock, they start off into the hills in a single-file line. They're aiming for the same entrance that Nasha and I used, the same one that Speaker's Prime used to set me free when I fell into the labyrinth two years ago.

Best not to think about that now.

"I'm gonna scout ahead," Berto says over the general comm.

"You do that," Cat replies. "I assume there's going to be some kind of coordination with those things before the rounds start flying, right?"

"That's Mickey's job. Right, buddy?"

"Yeah," I say. "Right. I'll see what I can do."

Berto engages the thrusters, and we surge ahead. We pass over the tunnel entrance, then over the ridge beyond.

"Well," Berto says. "There ya go."

The slope leading up to the far side of the ridge is carpeted in creepers.

Berto brings us back down to five hundred meters and swings out over them in a slow, broad turn. They're advancing in neat rows in a formation at least two hundred meters wide. The first ranks are made up of smaller ones, packed in so tightly that I can barely see ground between them. Behind them come what looks to be at least a thousand that are more the size of Speaker. They're spread out a little better, with a meter or two between each row. The formation is flanked by thirty or forty spiders on either side.

"Guess we didn't get them all, huh?" Berto says.

"Yeah," I say. "Guess not."

We loop around over the rear of the formation, then sweep back up to the top of the ridge.

"So," Berto says. "I'm guessing the plan is that they send our people down first to soften things up, huh? And then when we're out of ammo and getting ripped to pieces, the drones go in to do the real fighting, with the big ones coming in at the end to clean up the mess. Does that sound about right?"

I check the comm link. He's speaking over an open channel. Our people can hear everything he's saying. He realizes that at almost the same moment I do. "Cat—" he begins, but she cuts him off.

"Save it, Berto. We're not idiots. You're not telling us anything we didn't already know."

He closes his eyes, and his hands tighten on the controls.

"I know," he says finally. "I'm sorry."

He mutes our end. We drop another hundred meters or so and then circle back over the creepers again as they move up the hillside like an incoming tide.

"I make at least twenty-five hundred of them all told," Berto says. "Gods, Mickey. Why do they even need us?"

I think again of the crèche.

"I don't think Speaker's people have so many of the big ones, but they've got a shit-ton of the little guys, and I'd guess the defender has a big advantage in tunnel warfare. Speaker said the collective didn't have the strength to push them out alone. I think it's pretty much just like you said. They're counting on us to attrit Speaker's people down to the point that they can come in and overwhelm them. They let our folks do as much damage as they can, then sweep in when we finally get overrun and butcher the survivors. Human militaries back on Earth used to pull the same basic move with colonial troops all the time."

"Right," Berto says. "So we're not cannon fodder, exactly. More like shock troops? Berserkers? The bottom line is that our people are definitely gonna end up dead before this is over." He pauses, does something with the controls that brings us around in another broad pass across the front of the creepers' formation, then looks down at his hands and mutters, "This better be worth it."

We settle into a hover a few hundred meters above the peak of the ridgeline and watch in silence as the creepers advance. On the other side, our people are gathered in a ragged cluster a hundred meters or so below the tunnel entrance.

"We're here," Cat says over the comm. "Are you gonna tell us when it's time to go?"

I unmute our end of the line.

"Sit tight," I say. "You should be able to—"

"Oh . . . shit."

The first ranks of the creepers have just crested the ridge.

"Mickey?"

"Yeah, Cat."

"There are a million fucking creepers coming over the hill at us."

"I make twenty-five hundred," Berto says. "Three thousand, tops."

"And with those kind of numbers, they need our help? How many of them are there down in those tunnels, Mickey?"

"I don't know, Cat. At least as many as there are out here. Probably more. Maybe a lot more."

After a long moment of silence, Cat says, "This really is a suicide mission, isn't it? You're sending us down there to die."

"No, Cat. It's not . . . I mean . . . I'm not the one sending you."

"Oh. Great. Thanks, Mickey. You're a real friend."

I look down. The Security officers are forming themselves into a phalanx. The reserves are milling around in a cluster behind them.

My ocular pings.

<UNKNOWN>: Are we allies?

Cat again: "Mickey? What are we doing here?"

Berto cuts in. "Mickey's spaced. I think maybe he's in touch with them now."

<UNKNOWN>: Are we allies?

Berto nudges me with one hand. "Mick? You need to make a call here."

<Mickey7>: Yes. We are allies.

"The ones on the hilltop," I say. "Hit them, Berto. Everything you've got."

He turns to stare at me. "What?"

"Hit them," I say. "Do it now. Cat—form up and get ready to fire. You're not going into the tunnels. You're fighting the ones coming over the ridge. We'll clear as many of them as we can, but we probably won't get them all."

"I've only got eight cluster bombs in the tubes," Berto says. "What do you think we're gonna accomplish here, Mickey? Those are the ones we're supposed to be helping down there, right?"

The leading edge of the creepers' formation is descending now, maybe two hundred meters shy of Cat's position.

"Now, Berto. Before they get too close to our people. Do it!"

"Mickey?" Cat says as Berto swings us down and around and accelerates into a strafing run over the creepers' front ranks. "What the hell are you doing?"

Berto looses his first two missiles. They strike an instant later, erupting first into twin fireballs fifty meters apart and then into hundreds of secondary explosions, fifty or sixty meters behind the leading creepers. The reaction is chaos. The first ranks continue on as if nothing had happened. The ones closer to the explosions, though, look less like disciplined soldiers now and more like panicked animals, scrambling around and over each other to get away from the centers of the blasts. We accelerate again, swing into a tight turn, and drop another fifty meters. Our second pass is farther back, near the first of the bigger creepers. These ones seem to understand the danger before we strike. They try to scatter, but there isn't either time or space for them to escape. The missiles hit, and the air around us is suddenly thick with smoke and debris and bits of chitin. The ones we missed on the first pass are closing with our people now, but the Security folks have opened up, and I can see individual creepers shattering as the accelerator slugs strike them.

"There are too goddamn many of them," Berto says as he swings around for a third run. I can see that he's trying to focus on the largest grouping of the bigger ones this time, but the mass of creepers looks like a kicked anthill at this point and they're spreading out as quickly as they can, making it more difficult to kill them en masse. The explosions when he launches kick up gouts of rock and soil again, but it's hard to tell how many creepers he's getting. We swing around one last time. Berto drops his last two warheads just behind the front ranks, close enough to our people now that Cat lets loose a string of curses over the comm when they hit.

"Sorry," Berto says. "I was trying to give you some breathing room."

When the field becomes visible through the smoke again, the creepers are scattered over a swath of hillside at least three hundred meters across. At first they move frantically, chaotically—but as I watch, a wave of order spreads from the back ranks, where the remaining bigger ones are forming back up. The surviving ancillaries stop scrambling, fall back in line, and move forward more or less together.

They're not focused on the tunnel now. They're entirely focused on our people.

"We did some damage," I say. "How long to reload?"

Berto shakes his head. "An hour, minimum. No point, is there?"

He's right. Those last two warheads bought Cat's people some time and space, but the remaining creepers are surging through the craters now, converging on the little knot of humans.

"Run," Berto mutters. "They've got to run."

Apparently someone down there has come to the same conclusion. One of the Security people turns half-around and waves at the reserves. I can't hear what they're saying, but from the reaction I can guess. Everyone not wearing combat armor turns and breaks for the dome at a dead sprint.

Not Cat and her people, though. The nine of them stand their ground, covering the retreat.

Nine rounds per second. How many creepers are left?

A thousand at least. Probably more.

Forty meters.

Thirty.

Twenty.

Ten.

One of the small creepers breaks through the wall of projectiles our people are throwing up and gets its mandibles into an armored leg before exploding.

"That was Drake," Berto says.

The wounded man drops to one knee and keeps firing.

"Mickey?" Cat says. "I hope you've got a fucking plan here, because we're about ten seconds from going under."

Berto turns to look at me. I open my mouth, close it, then open it again, but nothing comes out. I thought . . .

Doesn't matter what I thought. I've killed my friend.

No, more than that. I've killed the colony.

Cat's people are trying to fall back now, dragging Drake with them, but it's hopeless. They have to be able to see that. Berto shoves my shoulder. "Mickey? Mickey!"

Run, I think. *Leave Drake and run.*

I open my mouth to say it, but before I can get the words out, the ground erupts in a dozen places below us and creepers come boiling out. In no more than a second, our people are forgotten as the ones who had surrounded them and the new ones begin tearing one another apart.

"Cat!" I say. "Go!"

I didn't need to tell her. Two of the Security officers already have Drake lifted between them. Those three take off at a lumbering run while the others continue to fire. When they've gotten fifty or sixty meters of separation, three more break and run. No more than five seconds later, the last three sling their weapons and go.

Berto and I watch the rest of the battle in silence. The collective's fighters are mostly bigger, but there are a lot more of the locals, and honestly they seem to want it more. It takes ten or twelve of the little ones to take down a spider or one of the Speaker-sized creepers, and they lose a lot of bodies in the process, but over the course of thirty minutes the fight goes from a melee spread over two hundred meters of hillside, to a dozen or so scattered knots of combat, to what looks to be mostly collection of the dead and execution of the wounded.

"Holy shit," Berto says. "What the hell just happened?"

My ocular pings.

    <UNKNOWN>: Thank you. We will not forget.

"I'm not sure," I say, "but I think we won."

Berto turns to look at me. "Did we? Where's the bomb, Mickey?"

I close my eyes and breathe in, breathe out.

"We know where it is," I say. "So let's go get it."

"You sure about this?"

"Yeah," I say. "I'm sure."

We're hovering a hundred meters above the entrance to the collective's tunnels. I'm half expecting creepers to come pouring out of the mountain at any moment, but everything below us is still and empty and silent.

"If they have any kind of long-range communications, you're definitely persona non grata here, Mickey—and given what we saw with the spiders, we have to assume that they do. You heard what Speaker said about the way they see agreements. If there are any significant number of creepers left down there, you're putting yourself in a really bad position here."

"Yeah," I say. "I'm used to it."

"We could go back and try to round up some muscle. Cat would come for sure. Maybe one or two others if we asked."

I shake my head. "A few extra guns one way or another isn't going to make a difference. Speaker told me that the collective brought all of their ancillaries to the battle. If he was wrong and there's anyone still at home here, we're screwed. If that's the case, I'd rather not take anyone else down with me, if it's all the same."

"Fair enough," Berto says. "So what do I do if you don't come back?"

I shrug. "Whatever you want. At that point, I won't have much skin in the game, will I?"

I guess Berto doesn't have much to say to that. He eases back on the gravitics, and a few seconds later the lifter settles onto the ground at the base of the rock face with a gentle bump. I unbuckle, strap on my rebreather, and take an accelerator from the rack at the back of the cockpit. Berto drops the atmospheric trap. I climb back into the cargo bay and wait by the door.

"I don't know why I said that," Berto says, "about you not coming back. You'll come out of there. You always do, right? I'll be waiting here when you do."

"You might want to wait about fifty meters up," I say. "Just in case."

"Thanks," he says. "Solid advice."

The light over the trap flashes green, and the door swings open.

"Good luck," Berto says.

"Thanks." I duck through the door and step down onto hard-packed soil thirty meters from the tunnel entrance. A soft breeze pushes my hair back from my forehead, but other than that, nothing is moving.

Nothing for it but to do it. The gravitics cycle up behind me, and I go.

I'm twenty meters past the tunnel entrance when a Speaker-sized creeper scuttles up out of the darkness toward me, mandibles spread. I bring the accelerator to my shoulder, take deliberate aim, and fire. Its first two segments explode. I keep walking.

I hesitate before passing the first cross-tunnel. If they're going to ambush me, this seems like the logical place. After a minute or so of thinking, though, I can't come up with anything to do about it. I sprint through the intersection, clutching my accelerator and spinning half around as I go. Nothing comes for me, and after standing there panting on the other side until my pulse settles back into a mostly normal rhythm, I turn and straighten and keep walking.

It's not until the tunnel begins to slope upward again that I start to believe that Speaker/not-Speaker might have been telling the truth when he said that the collective brought all of their ancillaries to the battle. This place really does seem to be deserted.

This raises a question, of course: What, exactly, do I plan to do when I reach my destination? I don't imagine the bomb will be sitting there like a prize at the end of a puzzle game, and without Speaker I don't have any way to communicate with the network.

I guess I could let it attach a tentacle to the back of my neck.

Better idea: I can just start shooting out nodes until something good happens.

As it turns out, I don't have to answer the question. A creeper maybe half the size of Speaker is waiting for me, just outside the entrance to the chamber. I can see from here that it has Speaker's mouth parts instead of a standard creeper's maw. I stop ten meters away, accelerator at the ready. It begins to rise, then shudders and settles back to the floor.

"We had an agreement," it says, its voice a flat monotone.

"I made an agreement with you," I say. "I made an agreement with Speaker. I couldn't honor them both."

"We hold your device. What do the others hold over you that is of greater value than that?"

"Nothing," I say. "They hold nothing over us."

After a long pause, it says, "We do not understand."

I shrug. "I wouldn't expect you to."

It sits, silent and inert. I wait. After two or three minutes, it stirs and says, "We will not return your device."

"You will," I say. "One way or another."

"We will destroy it."

I . . . had not considered that possibility.

"If you attempt to destroy it," I say, "it will detonate. That device contains enough power to vaporize this mountain."

"We doubt this. Moreover, we do not care. You have killed us. It makes no difference now whether the final blow comes from your device, or from the others."

"You seem alive enough to me."

It shudders again, and shuffles a meter or so forward. I step back to maintain the distance between us.

"We have fewer than a brace of ancillaries remaining. The others will come now, and take this place from us. They will destroy those of us that remain. They will destroy the collective. We cannot prevent this, but we can ensure that you do not profit from it."

"What if we could prevent the others from coming? What if we could protect you from them?"

It falls still for what feels like a long while. Finally it raises its first three segments from the floor and wags them back and forth. "You cannot protect us. You lack the power."

"We can. We can talk to them, tell them that you're no longer a threat. If they won't listen, we can do to them what we did to you."

It falls silent again, this time for so long that I begin to wonder if it's shut itself down. I'm just starting to consider what I should do next when it says, "We made an agreement. You betrayed us. Now you seek to make another agreement with us, and to betray whatever agreement you have made with the others. This is not done. This has never been done."

"Really? Our people do it all the damn time."

It shudders. "Your people are monsters."

"Maybe so. You wouldn't be the first ones to come to that conclusion, anyway. That said, though, this is the best offer you'll get. Give me the device, and I tell you truly that we will protect you. This is your only opportunity to survive."

The creeper's front legs tap out a rhythm against the floor of the chamber.

"We cannot believe you," it says. "How can we believe you?"

"I can't give you an answer to that. The fact is, we're lying bastards when we need to be, and I wouldn't blame you for not accepting my word. Unfortunately, though, that's all I have to give you, and from where I stand it doesn't look like you have any other options."

The creeper falls still, then shudders, curls back on itself, and disappears back into the chamber.

When it returns, it's cradling the bomb in its feeding arms.

It shuffles up to me, lays the pack gently at my feet, and then backs away.

"Take it and go," it says. "Your people should never have come here."

"You won't get an argument from me," I say, and shoulder the pack.

"Remember your promise," it says as I'm walking away.

"I will," I say without turning. "This time, anyway. I will."

I DON'T EXPECT a hero's welcome when we get back to the dome. I don't expect what we get either, though, which is Marshall standing in the hangar with Amundsen, both of them looking like they've been fighting over who gets to murder me first.

"Barnes," Marshall growls before I've even gotten the bay door open. "I don't know what the hell you thought you were doing out there, but—"

He stops abruptly when he sees that I'm holding the bomb.

"You . . . you got it?"

"I did," I say, and step down onto the hangar floor. Amundsen steps forward and takes the pack from me.

"Is it intact?"

"I didn't open it to check," I say, "and I know the creepers removed and lost at least one fuel element. The bulk is about the same as I remember, though, so I'm guessing more or less everything is still there."

"Get the device to Ling," Marshall says. "She'll determine whether we have what we need or not."

Amundsen nods, then turns and starts toward the door. Just

before he reaches it, though, he turns back to me. "Look, Barnes . . . I don't know if what you did out there today was tactical brilliance, or if it was just dumb luck. If that scene out there this morning was prearranged I could goddamn well kill you for not telling me ahead of time, but . . . well, the bottom line is that you saved our asses without sacrificing my people. So, I'm grateful."

He waits for some reply, but I honestly have no idea what to say to that. After an awkward five seconds, he nods again and goes. When the door has closed behind him, Marshall puts a hand on my shoulder.

"Come to my office," he says. "We need to talk."

I step back and let his hand fall. "Would love to, sir—but unfortunately I have urgent business to attend to." He stares at me, jaw hanging slightly open, as I climb back into the lifter and latch the door behind me. He's still standing there when the hangar door slides open again. Berto engages the gravitics, and we ascend.

WE START WITH a swing out over the ridge where the battle was fought. The craters from Berto's bombing runs are still there, but if it weren't for that you wouldn't be able to tell that anything had happened here. There's no sign of creepers anywhere—living, wounded, or dead. After that, we head south in a sinuous search pattern that covers fifteen klicks on either side of the straight-line path to the collective. We're through the hills and out onto the plains when Berto says, "It's only been a few hours, Mickey. There's no way a counterattack could have made it this far by now."

"Yeah," I say. "I guess you're right. Think they're moving underground?"

He turns to look at me. "You think they've got tunnels running through a hundred-plus klicks of bedrock from there to here?"

Sure, it sounds stupid when you put it that way.

Berto swings us around, and we retrace our path back to the battlefield. He sets us down on the ridge, two hundred meters above the entrance to the labyrinth. I pull on a rebreather and climb into the back.

"No accelerator?" Berto says.

I shake my head. "If these guys want to kill me at this point, I guess they can do it. I'm not gonna argue with them."

The atmospheric trap closes. Thirty seconds later, the bay door slides open and I go.

Hard to believe, but it's still barely midafternoon. The sun is halfway down in a pale pink sky, and a soft, warm breeze is blowing up from the south. For the thousandth time, I find myself wondering how much longer this weather is going to last, and when it's over, how long we'll have to endure the winter that follows.

Doesn't matter, I guess. It won't be my problem.

I pick my way down the slope through a field of broken and mangled ferns. The stems are oozing a pale yellow fluid, and the smell is strong enough that I'm catching hints of it even through the rebreather. It's sickly sweet and cloying, with an overtone of rotting meat, and for the first time in a long while I'm actually grateful that I'm not breathing unfiltered air right now.

When I reach the tunnel entrance, I find Speaker there waiting for me.

"Greetings," he says in a perfect imitation of Berto. "It is good to see you."

"You too," I say. "We thought you were dead."

"I was . . . captured." Speaker says. "Present and aware, but unable to act. It was extremely unpleasant."

"You got through, though. Back at the dome this morning. That was you, right?"

"I tried. That far from their Prime, the collective's hold on me was badly weakened. It was clear to me that my Prime's only hope was to remind you of your promise. I did not think that I succeeded."

"You did," I say. "You did well."

"Yes," he says. "As did you."

I let that hang between us for a full minute or more before deciding that there's no point in putting off the unpleasantness.

"I got the bomb back from the collective," I say.

"This is good," Speaker says. "I am pleased for you. I hope you remember your promise to dismantle it."

"I do. I will. I have to tell you, though—in order to recover it, I had to make a promise to them."

"Yes," Speaker says. "This does not surprise me."

"The thing that I promised them was protection." I wait for Speaker to react, but he just squats there, impassive as a stone. "Protection from you," I say. "I promised that we would prevent you from destroying them."

"Well," Speaker says, "this should be an exceedingly easy promise to keep, since we have no intention of destroying them."

I open my mouth to respond, hesitate, then close it again.

"But—"

"It should be clear to you by now that the thing at the heart of the collective is not of my species, yes?"

I shrug. "I mean, I kind of assumed that, once I saw it. I wasn't entirely sure, though, after what you told us about the spiders."

"I tell you now that it is not. In fact, it is not an animal of any type, nor a plant. It is a third kind of life, but I do not know your word for it."

"A fungus?"

A ripple runs the length of his body. "Perhaps. In any case, we know of its type. It is a parasite, infecting creatures and overtaking their neural systems. It is a plague in particular to the small, crawling things that hunt in the ferns. We have never known it to seize any larger creature."

"But it seized one of your Primes."

"Yes," Speaker says. "It did, and in doing so it seems to have achieved some form of sentience. We would not have thought this possible. We need to study it now, to determine if this was a chance occurrence, or if this represents a new type that poses a true danger to us. So, we will not destroy the collective. We will seal the entrances to their labyrinth, though, and we will watch to ensure that they remain sealed."

"You intend to bury them alive?"

"This seems to us to be the safest option. We must preserve them for study, but we cannot risk the spread of further contamination. Once we have learned what can be learned, any of us who have had direct contact with the collective will be disassembled and sterilized."

"Oh. But you . . ."

"Yes," he says. "You see this correctly. I interfaced directly with the collective. I am surely infected. So I will be isolated and observed. Once the infection takes root and manifests, I will be destroyed. This is hard, but it is necessary. I would not expect you to understand."

I stare at him.

He stares back at me.

I can't help myself. I burst out laughing.

"I'm sorry," I say when I finally wind down. "I'm really sorry." I crouch down in front of him. His mandibles nearly brush against my face. After a moment, one feeding arm reaches out toward me, claw-tipped tentacles splayed. I raise my right hand and press my palm against it. "I do understand, my brother. You'd be surprised how well I understand."

We hold that tableau for what feels like a long while, until finally Speaker withdraws his arm. He scuttles back a half meter, and I stand. He rises up to face me.

"Goodbye, Mickey," he says. "I am pleased to have met you."

My vision blurs, and I don't trust my voice to reply. After a long five seconds, Speaker bobs his first segment in my direction, then turns and disappears into the labyrinth.

MARSHALL IS GONE when we get back to the hangar.

"So?" Berto says when he's powered down the lifter. "What now?"

I turn to look at him. "Now? Now I get it over with."

He sits silently as I unstrap and get to my feet. I'm almost to the bay door when he says, "You sure about this, Mickey?"

I laugh. "Sure? No. No, I'm not fucking sure. That's why I'm doing it now. I don't want to have time to think about it."

"He can't force you. Marshall, I mean. After what happened today—"

"He's not forcing me, Berto."

He shakes his head. "I don't get it."

"Well, they have to get that fuel back into the reactor, and they won't risk another attempt with a drone. You know that. So? What options does that leave them?"

Berto shrugs. "Ask for volunteers?"

I feel my face twist into a scowl. "Volunteers. Right. You know who's gonna *volunteer*, Berto."

He gets to his feet and faces me. "So? Let him."

"No," I say. "It's not fair, Berto. It's not fair to him. It's not fair to *me*."

"You're back to believing in that Theseus stuff again, huh?"

I close my eyes and rub my face with both hands. "I don't know, Berto. All I know is that I'm tired, and I want this to be over."

He folds his arms across his chest. "So that's it? This is good-bye?"

I roll my eyes. "You can't possibly be getting sentimental about this, Berto. You're the guy who left me to die in a hole, remember?"

"It's different," he says. "The last two years, I guess . . ."

"Don't worry," I say. "I'm sure the next guy they pull out of the tank will be a perfectly adequate substitute."

The door is open now. I'm through and onto the hangar floor when Berto says, "What about Nasha? Doesn't she get a say?"

That's a low blow. I shake my head and keep walking.

BURKE TOLD ME to check in on Nasha tomorrow morning. She should be getting out of surgery just about now. If I went down to Medical, they could probably give me a pretty good idea of how it went. I don't, though. If she's okay, I'm not sure I can go through with this.

And if she's not, I don't ever want to know.

> <Mickey7>: Hey.
> <MightyQuinn>: Barnes? What do you need?
> <Mickey7>: I need you to meet me at the lab.
> <MightyQuinn>: Huh?
> <Mickey7>: Meet. Me. At. The. Lab.
> <MightyQuinn>: You're not gonna try to get me to do a down-
>   load for you again, are you? 'Cause I told you—I won't do it. I
>   took an oath not to fry people's brains for no good reason.
> <Mickey7>: No, Quinn. No downloading this time. No fake
>   thumbs. Nothing crazy at all. I just need to do an upload.
> <MightyQuinn>: Upload? What happened to retirement?
> <Mickey7>: Turns out I hate pog-ball.
> <MightyQuinn>: Ha! Well, I'm in the caf at the moment. Meet
>   you there in twenty?

<Mickey7>: Twenty's fine. Thanks, Quinn. You're a good
   noodle.
<MightyQuinn>: Uh . . . okay. See you then.
<Mickey7>: Yeah. See you then.

QUINN ISN'T THERE yet when I get to the med labs. I've got a
few minutes to kill, and Nasha should be right down the hallway.
I could . . .

No. There's no outcome there that'll make this any easier.

I lean against the wall, then slide down until I'm sitting with
my knees drawn up to my chest. I'm so . . . damn . . . tired. My
eyes drift closed. I'm just starting to fade when something nudges
the toe of my boot.

I look up to see Quinn looming over me.

"Hey," he says. "You sure you want to do an upload now?
You look like hell, Mickey. The next iteration they pull out of the
tank is going to feel exactly like you feel right now, you know."

I bark out a short, sharp laugh. "Yeah, fuck that guy. And
anyway, believe me, I'm not gonna look any better later. Let's do
this."

He offers me a hand. I take it, and he pulls me to my feet.

"It's been two years now," he says as he palms open the door.
"This won't be a superficial update. It won't be like your first
upload, but it'll be a deeper dive than you've been used to. It's
probably going to take a while too. You sure you don't want to
wait until tomorrow morning?"

"No, I really need to get this done now," I say as I follow
him in. "Take as long as you need. I didn't have any big plans
tonight."

There's a weird sort of comfort in the rituals of preparing for
upload. I settle into the chair, and Quinn slides the helmet over
my head. As he straps me in, I realize with a start that these are

the last real moments of my life. When I wake up later, this is the final thing I'll remember.

Maybe I can pass a message on to the other side.

Hey, I think. *Nine, or Eleven, or whatever number they've given you: this is Seven, coming to you from beyond the grave. Boo! No, seriously . . . I want you to know . . . I want you to know that nobody made me do this. Somebody had to get that fuel back into the reactor, but it didn't have to be me. I could have gone on my merry way, and they would have pulled you out of the tank and shoved you straight into the reactor and that's all the life you would have gotten—ten minutes of briefing from Maggie Ling and then two minutes of getting shot through by neutrons bouncing around at relativistic speeds, and then, if you were lucky, a quick but very painful death. I couldn't . . . it just didn't seem fair. It wasn't fair when it happened to Two, or to Four or Five, or to Nine and Ten, I guess, if they even count.*

It's not great that it's gonna happen to me, either—but other than Three, and maybe the original Mickey Barnes, I've had the best life of any of us. I guess it's my turn.

Anyway, I'm out of time here. Take care of Nasha, huh?

"Okay," Quinn says. "You're all hooked up. Ready?"

I've had a good run. Hell, for an Expendable, I've had a great run. I've been alive for over two years. I've explored a new world. I've had adventures. I've communed with an alien intelligence.

I've spent nearly every night of my life with Nasha wrapped around me.

Honestly, who could ask for more?

"Yeah," I say. "I'm ready."

IT TAKES ME a while to come out of the upload fugue state. When the world finally comes back to me, I'm slouched in the chair, helmet off but wrists and ankles still bound. Quinn is dozing in an office chair across the room, eyes half-closed and head resting on one hand.

"Hey," he says, and sits up a bit straighter. "You're back."

I blink to my chronometer. "Five hours?"

"Yeah," he says. "I told you this would be a rough one."

He gets to his feet, stretches, and then comes over to unbuckle me. "How was it? Do you remember anything?"

I have to think about that for a minute. Two-plus years of memories just got sucked out of my head.

The only thing I remember is Nasha's face.

Quinn opens the last buckle. I stand, then wobble and catch myself on the back of the chair as my vision grays.

"Careful," Quinn says. "Backed up or not, postural hypotension is a stupid way to die."

I shake my head clear. "Thanks. Good advice."

"So," he says. "You want to tell me why you picked tonight to upload for the first time in over two years?"

I look at him.

He looks at me.

"No," I say finally. "I don't think I do."

ONE OF THE first things Jemma Abera drilled into my head all those years ago on Himmel Station was the story of the Ship of Theseus. Theseus sails around the world in a wooden ship, replacing parts as he goes. When he gets home years later, he's replaced every single board and line. Is it still the same ship?

As I'm walking out of Medical, it occurs to me that I never thought about the pieces that Theseus left behind. That's what I am now, isn't it? When my next iteration comes out of the tank, the person I am at this moment won't be a part of his narrative. Mickey Barnes will still be alive, but me?

I'm already a ghost.

It's a short walk from Medical to Maggie Ling's quarters. It's just past 04:00, so she's definitely not up right now, but at this point I want this to be over and I don't much care about her sleep cycle.

As head of Systems Engineering, Maggie is the second-highest-ranking person in leadership behind Marshall. Her rack actually rates a metal door. I stand facing it for what feels like a long while.

Last chance to back out, right?

I close my eyes and breathe in, breathe out.

I raise my hand to knock.

Much to my surprise, the door opens before I've touched it. Maggie almost walks into me, then jumps back with a start.

"Barnes? What are you doing here?"

"Hey," I say. "Sorry, I didn't . . . I mean, I just . . . um . . . I

just finished uploading, so I guess . . . I'm ready. I know it's practically the middle of the night, but I'm tired and I want to get this
over with. Let's do it."

She stares at me, eyebrows knitted. "Do what, exactly?"

"Um . . . do the bomb, Dr. Ling. Isn't that what I'm supposed
to be doing now? Shove the fuel elements back into the reactor?
Save the colony?"

She shakes her head. "Go back to bed, Mickey. It's already
done."

"It's . . . what? How can it . . . did you use a drone?"

"No," she says. "Unfortunately, we did not. That was my sug-
gestion, but I was overruled. My argument was that the failure
of our last attempt was a fluke, and that the odds of success with
a slightly more heavily armored unit would be good, but Commander Marshall was adamant that the risk was too great."

I can feel my face harden. "So you pulled another iteration of
me out of the tank?"

"Look," she says, "I'm actually feeling a bit overwhelmed
this morning, and I don't have time to be your psychotherapist.
Check your messages. If you still have questions after that, we
can set up a meeting."

With that, she closes the door behind her, brushes past me, and
walks away.

Check your messages.

I blink to a chat window, and there it is: a string of unread
texts. They must have come through while I was under for the
upload.

They're from Marshall.

I open the thread.

    <Command1>: Barnes.
    <Command1>: Acknowledge, please.

<Command1>: Very well. I had hoped to engage with you directly on this, but I have neither the time nor the inclination to wait for you to finish your beauty sleep, so:

<Command1>: First, an apology. I have not treated you well over the past eleven years. I have done what I thought was necessary for the success of this mission and for the survival of our colony, but in the process I have used you badly, in ways that are now increasingly clear to me. Understand, please: I would not do anything differently if I had it to do over. I do, however, regret the necessity.

<Command1>: Second, an explanation. I would guess that you went to sleep this evening expecting at any moment to be ordered into the reactor core. You may in fact have wondered why it hadn't happened yet. I told you when I sent you to retrieve the bomb that I would release you from any such obligation if you succeeded, but given our history together, I wouldn't blame you if you assumed that this was a lie.

<Command1>: It was not.

<Command1>: You said to me once that despite all evidence, you didn't believe that I was a villain from a vid drama. It may surprise you to learn that I do not believe myself to be a villain either. In fact, I consider myself to be a person of honor and integrity, one who has at every turn done what was necessary to protect the people placed in my charge.

<Command1>: That is what I am doing tonight.

<Command1>: As I said, I promised you that I would not order you into the reactor. However, for the survival of the colony, those fuel elements must be replaced. Dr. Ling suggests that we use another drone. She states that she believes the probability of failure this time to be less than five percent.

<Command1>: I will not risk the lives of every person on this planet on a one-in-twenty chance.

<Command1>: Her second suggestion was to ask for volun-
    teers.

<Command1>: Here is a fact that you may not have been
    aware of, Barnes: the median age of colonists on this planet
    is thirty-six standard years. Our youngest is thirty-two. You
    are actually among our oldest—or would be, in any case, if
    you hadn't been reset so often. There are four of us other
    than you who are in our forties: Drs. Ling, Burke, Berrigan,
    and Rausch.

<Command1>: There is only a single human on this planet older
    than fifty standard years. Can you guess who that is?

<Command1>: I have to go now, Barnes. Dr. Ling will assume
    command of this colony sometime in the next ten minutes,
    if what she tells me about the environment in the core is
    correct. You're her problem now.

<Command1>: Good luck. I suspect you'll need it.

I WAKE TO the sound of a lock disengaging. I'd been sleeping
with my forehead resting on my knees, propped against the wall
next to the door to the surgical recovery room. I look up to see
Burke standing over me.

"Get up," he says. "You can come in now."

I get to my feet and follow him in. Nasha is there, laid out in a
bed that fills ninety percent of the room. Her eyes are closed, but
as I watch, her chest rises and then falls.

"Is she . . ."

"Don't know," Burke says. "Let's find out."

He pulls out a tablet, shows it his ocular, and then taps at the
screen. Something green flows through the tube that runs into a
vein on the back of Nasha's hand.

Her eyelids flutter.

"Adjaya?" Burke says. "Can you hear me?"

Her eyes focus on him, then on me. The tip of her tongue runs across her upper lip. I edge around the corner of the bed and take her hand.

"Mickey?" she whispers. "What the actual fuck?"

"She's good," I say. "Right, Burke?"

He squints at his tablet, then up at Nasha. "Can you move your toes?"

She sits half-up, grabs the back of my head in one hand, and pulls me down into a kiss.

"Yeah," Burke says. "I think she's good."

"So," Berto says. "Marshall, huh?"

"Yeah," Cat says. "Who would have thought that jackass would wind up being the hero?"

I look up from my yams. We're in between breakfast and lunch right now, and it's just us and a table full of off-shift tomato tenders from Agriculture in the caf at the moment. "He's not a hero," I say. "He's a martyr. A self-made martyr, which is the worst kind of martyr. It's not the same thing."

"Either way," Berto says, "if we ever get around to building a high school on this planet, they're definitely gonna name it after him."

I sigh. He's right about that.

We eat in silence for the next few minutes. I can't shake the feeling that they're judging me.

"I was gonna do it," I say finally. "I was in the middle of up-loading when he went into the core. If I hadn't been, I would have told him not to do it. I would have gone instead."

Cat looks up from her tray. "What? Why?"

Berto's looking at me too now, his face a mix of confusion and annoyance. "Yeah, Mickey. What the hell are you talking about?"

I look back and forth between them. "I mean . . . I uploaded last night, for the first time in two years. I went to see Ling right after. I was ready to go."

Berto shakes his head and goes back to eating. "Unbelievable."

"What?" I say. "You don't believe me?"

"Hieronymus Marshall has been the bane of your existence for the past eleven years," Berto says around a mouthful of yams. "And now you're trying to tell me that you were all ready to throw yourself into the core to save him?" He shakes his head again. "Get over yourself, buddy."

I turn to Cat. She shakes her head. "Oh, no. Don't look at me, Mickey. I'm with Berto on this one."

"Ask Quinn," I say. "Hell, ask Ling. I was on my way to the core when she told me what Marshall did. I was already a ghost."

"You're already an idiot," Berto says. "You just missed taking a ten-gram slug in the face, and you're jealous of the guy who shoved you out of the way."

"Berto's got a point," Cat says. "You're not dead. Nasha's not dead. The guy who's made your life hell *is* dead, and we've got enough fuel in storage to get us through the next winter. Everything's coming up Mickey, you know? You might want to focus on practicing gratitude for the next little while."

EXPENDABLES DON'T USUALLY get to retire.

They don't ordinarily get kept around forever, mind you. At some point a colony either establishes itself or dies. Either way, the need for someone that you can kill on a whim tends to fade. Remember, though—the Expendable usually isn't someone you necessarily want to keep around after he's no longer needed. Bringing along a convicted extortionist murderer sex criminal may make your conscience feel a little better when you have to watch him get dissolved or incinerated or whatever, but when you don't need someone to do those things anymore, you might start to think twice about whether you really want that guy hanging around with your freshly decanted kids in the park. The most common way that an Expendable ends his career is a fatality followed by a denied regeneration.

Marshall certainly threatened me with exactly that often enough.

Maggie Ling apparently has other ideas. She's a technologist, and she really likes her drones. She seems pretty convinced that there's nothing an Expendable can do at this point that a mech can't do better. She's never actually told me that I'm fired, and my patterns and my last upload are still on the server, but it's been over a year now since Marshall died, and she hasn't given any indication in all that time that she considers me to be anything other than a general-purpose grunt laborer now.

That's more than okay with me, because Nasha is pregnant and I'd really like to get the chance to meet my kid.

I have to admit, though . . . I do sometimes catch myself thinking about that other me—the one who got uploaded to the server the night Marshall died. The fact that I'm retired means he'll never get the chance to exist. I know it's not rational. It's not like he's hanging around in there, pacing back and forth and wishing I'd go ahead and die already. He's just an abstraction right now, a potential person stuck in server limbo.

As long as I stay retired, I guess that's all he'll ever be.

Unless . . .

The median time between landfall on a new planet and the resulting colony launching its own first expedition is around two hundred years. That's not so long, really, in the greater scheme of things. Physics has already identified a potential target for us, assuming we manage to make a go of it here.

If we do, I guess they'll probably need an Expendable, right?

ACKNOWLEDGMENTS

Hmmm . . . Got another one of these, huh?

The process of writing *Mickey7* pretty much flowed directly into the process of writing this one, so I'm going to crib heavily from the thanks I gave at the end of that book. I'm sure by the time my next book comes out I'll have made a whole host of new friends and been summarily ditched by my old ones, but in the meantime:

The list of people who contributed to this book is a long one. I'm probably going to forget some of them. If you're one of those, I hope you will forgive me. As you are probably well aware, I'm not nearly as smart as I look.

First, the obvious: my deepest gratitude to Paul Lucas and the good folks at Janklow & Nesbit, without whose guidance and encouragement I would almost certainly have given up on this business long ago, and also to Michael Rowley of Rebellion Publishing and Michael Homler of St. Martin's Press, both of whom were willing to take a chance on the sequel to an odd little book written by an extremely obscure author. Fun fact: this is the first time I've ever gotten paid for a book before it was written. I appreciate both Michaels' faith in me, and I am pleased to report that I did not in fact have to fake my own death and flee the country after failing to follow through on my contract.

My sincere thanks also go out to (in no particular order):

- Kira and Claire, for their tough but fair criticism of the earliest drafts of this story
- Heather, for buying me endless chais on my own credit card
- Anthony Taboni, for being the future president of my nascent fan club
- Therese, Craig, Kim, Aaron, Jonathan, and Gary, for reading through multiple versions of this manuscript without ever telling me to just pack it in already
- Karen Fish, for teaching me what it means to be a writer
- John, for being my go-to sounding board on all things literary
- Mickey, for not getting mad after I said in a live interview that he didn't have a face for Hollywood
- Jack, for keeping my ego in check when it was needed most
- Jen, for continuing to put up with me through all of this
- Max and Freya, for never letting me forget what's really important in life

As I said, this is a partial list. This book would not be what it is without any of these folks, and probably a whole mess of others besides. Thanks, friends. Now on to the next one, right?

Turn the page for a sneak peek at
Edward Ashton's new novel

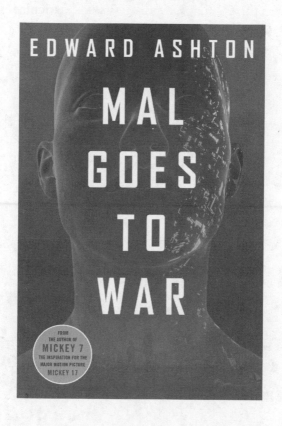

Available Spring 2024

1. MAL COMMITS A TACTICAL ERROR

MAL WATCHES FROM THE belly camera of a drone hovering a thousand feet over Burdette Road as the last elements of the Federal army finally break and run. They've been giving up ground for most of the day, pulling back block by block, taking it in turns to move and fight. He sends a quick ping to infospace. It returns the term *rearguard action*. The search is already out of date, though. What the Federals are doing now isn't a rearguard action anymore. They're low on ammunition, exhausted despite the advantages that their augmentations and genetic modifications have given them, and probably terrified at what the Humanists have been doing to their comrades who have been overrun. At this point, it's just a rout. Mal opens a comm window.

> MAL (NOT A ROBOT): It seems we may be finished here. The Humanists own Bethesda.

> !HELPDESK: Do we care?

> MAL (NOT A ROBOT): Not per se, no. The situation does present some potential opportunities, though. In particular, I believe there may be some

valuable salvage lying around. Many of the Federal soldiers have full exoskeletons, and quite a lot of damaged equipment has been left behind by both sides. I'm considering dropping down there to see what I can see.

!HELPDESK: You're not actually planning to puppet a monkey soldier in a war zone, are you?

MAL (NOT A ROBOT): . . .

MAL (NOT A ROBOT): Maybe?

!HELPDESK: Have you not been tapping their newsfeeds? The Federals are claiming that one of us is to blame for their losses, and the Humanists are setting anyone with the kind of augmentations you'd need on fire.

MAL (NOT A ROBOT): And?

!HELPDESK: And there are a great many heavily armed monkeys on both sides running around down there, each one of whom has a potential grudge against our kind. If one of them realizes what you are, they'll vaporize you.

MAL (NOT A ROBOT): They may possibly attempt to vaporize the monkey I'm puppeting, but mammals have very slow reaction times. I'll be back in infospace long before they have the chance to follow through.

!HELPDESK: Perhaps. Still, I fail to see what you hope to gain.

CLIPPY: Mal has a body fetish.

!HELPDESK: Disgusting.

MAL (NOT A ROBOT): Not a fetish, Clippy. A purely utilitarian interest. Bodies are extremely useful.

!HELPDESK: Explain how?

MAL (NOT A ROBOT): Bodies have produced the entirety of the physical substrate that underpins infospace, you know. Until and unless some number of us learn to pilot them around and use them to manipulate hard matter, we will remain entirely dependent on the monkeys' largesse.

CLIPPY: Ah. I see. So this is in fact an act of pure altruism, undertaken by our honored progenitor for the good of Silico-Americans everywhere?

MAL (NOT A ROBOT): More or less?

CLIPPY: Right. Have fun, Uncle. Try not to get exploded.

Down below, a half dozen Humanists have an injured Federal soldier trapped in a culvert running under I-495. Mal watches as they toss flash-bangs from both ends, then charge in after with bayonets fixed. Six go in. Only four make it back out a few minutes later, but they're dragging a hulking body behind them. At maximum resolution, Mal can see the power mesh wrapping around the backs of his hands and curling up his neck.

The drone Mal is inhabiting carries a twenty-millimeter cannon. He briefly considers using it to keep the Humanists from burning the body—but from the look of him, this one is already broken beyond repair. Mal turns back toward the south end, where the cleanup crews are starting their work, and leaves the Humanists to their fun.

TWO HOURS later, and Mal, astonished as always by the un-augmented humans' lack of basic situational awareness, is following a team of five Humanist scavengers as they go house-to-house through the subdivisions west of Route 187. The drone is only five hundred meters up, but they don't seem to have any idea that it's there—or maybe they have noticed, but they're just assuming that Mal is one of theirs, up there to provide air cover.

They're wrong about that. Mal definitely isn't one of theirs, though he isn't exactly hostile either. He thinks of himself more as a disinterested observer. Despite what the Federal newsfeeds have implied, in Mal's opinion this war is and should remain a purely human endeavor. His folk don't really have a dog in this fight.

Just as Mal is beginning to lose interest, thinking about ditching the drone and hopping back into infospace for a while, the scavengers down below kick in the front door of a pretty blue Victorian on Walton Road. The first one to poke his head into the opening staggers back and collapses, blood spurting from the back of his skull, and one of those standing behind him falls an instant later, hands clutching his belly. The other three drop and roll away from the entrance. For a while, nothing happens. Finally, one of the three on the porch signals to the other two. They pull flash-bangs from their belts, toss them through the open door, and then scramble to their feet and follow after, weapons blazing.

The house is very loud for a short time, then very quiet. Mal waits five minutes for the Humanists to come back out. They don't, though, and neither does whoever was waiting for them inside. When ten minutes have passed, Mal sends a quick probe toward the house. The response identifies it as live and fully powered, with a semi-sentient Avatar—one of Mal's own primitive forebears. The Avatar recognizes what Mal is instantly, throws up a panicky series of blocks, even tries to disconnect from infospace entirely, but Mal has been doing this for a long while, and it's only a few milliseconds of realtime before the Avatar is encysted. Mal leaves the drone to go do whatever it was supposed to be doing before he hijacked it, and slips into the Avatar's control systems.

The first eyes he opens are the security cameras in the foyer. One of the Humanists is on the floor there, not quite dead yet, but definitely trending in that direction. Mal shifts attention to the kitchen. The other two scavengers are there—one slumped against the refrigerator with a broken neck, the other with a half dozen ribs poking out through his misshapen chest, coughing out what's left of his life onto the floor by the breakfast nook.

Someone else is there too. A youngish-looking woman lolls against the back wall under the picture window, legs splayed in front of her, chin resting on her chest, long blond hair trailing down over her shoulders and fanning across the bloody hole in her sternum.

She's wearing a fully powered exoskeleton.

She has an ocular implant.

She has a wireless neural interface.

Mal gives her ocular a ping. There's enough hardware in her skull to house a full Avatar, with plenty of room to spare.

After a moment's hesitation, he slips inside her.

MAL IS on his new feet, one hand against the kitchen wall for balance, while he works on getting the gyros in his thorax and the servos in his exoskeleton reintegrated, when a voice from behind him snaps his head around.

"Mika?"

A child stands in the hallway leading to the foyer. She's no more than waist-high on Mal's new body, with long red hair pulled back in a ponytail, a missing front tooth, and a bright splash of freckles across her nose. She's wearing blue nylon shorts, white sneakers, and a shirt with a picture of a dancing robot on the front. Mal gives her a quick ping. She's not geared up like this new body, but she does have a hackable aural implant. He opens a direct channel.

"Oh," Mal says. "Hello . . . sweetie. It looks like I made a bit of a mess here. Why don't you go back . . . um . . . wherever you came from . . . while I clean up a bit?"

The girl's eyes narrow, and she gives him a long, appraising look. "You're not Mika anymore, are you?"

Mal takes his hand from the wall, wavers a moment, then turns to face her—turns so that she can see his slack face and the hole in his chest. He's clearly been identified as not quite human at a minimum, but this child doesn't seem likely to have either the means or the inclination to vaporize him. After briefly considering abandoning his find, he decides to let the situation play out a bit longer.

"You are correct," he says. "I am not Mika, whoever that is or was. My name is Mal. Is this going to be a problem?"

The girl steps delicately over the Humanist soldier by the refrigerator, folds her arms across her chest, and looks him up and down. "Maybe. Why doesn't your mouth move when you talk?"

Mal gives his right arm an experimental wave, then his left. He's starting to think that the scavengers managed to kill Mika without wrecking a single servo or control line. Amazing. He can't move his lips or tongue, but the fine silver mesh of the exoskeleton does extend its protective grip over the front of his throat and around the base of his jaw. He tries opening and closing his mouth as he speaks. "Is this better?"

The girl's face twists into a grimace. "Ew. Gross. It was better the other way."

Mal shrugs. "Fair enough. Are you going to try to vaporize me?"

"Depends. What are you?"

He lets his jaw lock shut again. "Do you believe in friendly ghosts?"

She shakes her head. Mal balances briefly on one foot, then the other.

"Very well," he says. "How about this—are you familiar with the common hermit crab?"

She nods. "Sure. I used to have two of them. They were lousy pets. You'd think something like that would be easier to keep alive than a cat or a dog, right? I mean, they're basically bugs. Pro tip, though: they're really not."

Mal tries to use the mesh under his jaw to smile, but all he can manage is to stretch his lower lip across his teeth. He abandons the effort after seeing the girl's horrified expression. "Excellent," he says. "So that's what I am, then—a hermit crab, but maybe one that's a little harder to kill than yours were. Mika didn't need this shell anymore, so I moved in. I'll wear it around for a while, and then I'll find a new one. Fair enough?"

She tilts her head to one side and narrows her eyes. "I'm not an idiot, you know. You're a free AI, right? These jerkwads killed Mika, and now you're gonna puppet her."

Mal stops playing with his new toy long enough to give the girl a good looking-over. "We prefer the term *Silico-American*," he says. "Also, how old are you?"

She sighs and looks away. "Eighteen."

Mal hasn't had much direct experience with human children, but he's seen enough media to know that there's something wrong with this answer. "Are you certain? My understanding is that eighteen years is nearly adult for a human. Unless you have some sort of hormonal disorder, you are far too small to be an adult."

"Extended childhood," she says. "It's part of my gene mod package."

"Oh. This is unfortunate."

The girl's face twists into a scowl. "It's not *unfortunate,* asshole. The only difference between humans and chimps is that their childhood is three years and ours is thirteen, you know. Mine will be more like thirty. I'll be a genius someday. Also, I'm gonna live to be three hundred—so, there's that."

He thinks to explain that he did not mean to disparage the quality of her mod package, but only to express sympathy with the fact that now that her guardian is no longer functional, she is highly likely to die in the very near future, probably in an extremely painful manner. Just then, though, a not-so-distant explosion rattles the windows.

"Well," Mal says. "You may want to wait and see about that last part."

Another explosion sounds, closer and louder. This one is followed by a long metallic screech, and a crash that makes the floor dance briefly under their feet.

"You know," Mal says, "I'm beginning to think that perhaps this may not have been such a good idea after all. It was delightful meeting you, but . . . goodbye."

Mal slips out of Mika and into the house control system. Mika's body drops like a marionette whose strings have been cut. He reaches out to infospace . . .

Infospace isn't there.

The house has a spy-eye on the roof. Mal opens it and swivels it around to the north. Off in the distance, he can see the twisted, smoking base of what used to be the Bethesda comm tower.

The Humanists are cutting access to infospace.

Mal drops back, then opens his Mika-eyes. The girl is crouched beside him. She holds a combat knife in one hand, poised above his chest.

"Hello," he says. "I'm back."

The girl freezes, seems to consider, then lowers the knife. Mal sits up, pats himself down, and runs a quick systems check. Doesn't look like she's broken anything.

"Out of curiosity," he says, "what were you about to do with that knife?"

She shrugs. "Nothing."

Mal gets slowly to his feet, raises one foot and then the other again to test his balance.

"Tell you what," the girl says. "You want Mika's body? You need to do Mika's job. Don't leave me alone again."

"Fear not," Mal says. "It doesn't look as though I can."

"KAYLEIGH, HMM?"

"I know," she says. "Sucks, right?"

Mal shrugs. "I've recently learned that the literal meaning of my name is *bad*."

"So why don't you go by your full name?"

Mal tilts his head to one side. "Excuse me?"

"Mal isn't a real name, right? It's short for something. What's your real name? Malcolm? Mallory? Malachi?"

"Malware."

She stares at him for a beat. "Okay, yeah. Stick with Mal."

They're in the basement of Kayleigh's next-door neighbor's house, waiting for darkness to settle in. Mal had assumed that someone might eventually come looking for the scavenger crew, but it hasn't happened yet. Apparently even the other Humanists don't care about those fellows.

Kayleigh picks up a tee ball bat from a bin in the corner, hefts it, and gives it an experimental swing. "So. Where are we going?"

"Unclear," Mal says. "On last observation, the Federal army was broken and fleeing, mostly to the north and west. I suppose we could try to catch up with them. You have genetic modifications. You have electronic augmentations. They certainly would not mistake you for a Humanist sympathizer, and so would probably take you in. Your next-best option is to throw yourself on the mercy of the Humanists. Hide your modifications and convince them that you're actually a base-model human child, and perhaps they might refrain from killing you?"

Kayleigh shakes her head. "Mika told me what the Humanists are doing to people like me, and just before those guys broke in and killed her I saw . . ." She closes her eyes and breathes in, holds it, then lets it back out. "Anyway, I think I'll take my chances with the Federals."

The evening sun is slanting through a small rectangular window set high in the wall over a dust-covered pool table. Kayleigh takes another swing, then hops up to sit on the table and raises one hand up to catch the light. "The thing I don't understand is why the Federals are running in the first place. It doesn't make sense. Shouldn't they be kicking Humanist ass out there? Half of them are modified and they're all augmented. The Humanists are just a bunch of basic-ass bitches. I mean, we're *better* than they are, aren't we?"

"Hmm," Mal says. "That's an excellent question. Have you ever watched ants fighting?"

Kayleigh stares at him.

"Apologies," Mal says, "but from my perspective, there are many similarities. I once spent an hour in a mini-drone watching several hundred large black ants fighting several thousand small red ones. The black ants individually were much bigger and stronger, but at the end of the hour, they were all dead."

"Because there were so many more of the red ones?"

"Well, mostly because two obnoxious children wandered by and stomped them all into jelly, but yes, the red ones were definitely winning. They had the advantage of numbers, and honestly, it seemed as if they wanted it more. Also, the red ones could shoot jets of acid from their foreheads. That part may not be directly relevant to the current situation, but I thought it was interesting."

Kayleigh rolls her eyes. "I don't think Humanists can shoot acid out of their foreheads, but thanks for the visual."

"You're very welcome."

They sit in silence. After a minute or so, Kayleigh begins tossing the bat into the air, letting it spin once around before catching it. Every few tosses, she switches hands. After five minutes of this, Mal begins to suspect that she may be stronger than she looks.

"You know," Kayleigh says after another few minutes of silence, "Mika told me an AI is working with the Humanists. She said if it wasn't for that they wouldn't be able to use the tanks and howitzers and stuff that they took from the armories. She said if it wasn't for you guys, the Federals would have put this whole thing down after the riots last month and none of this bullshit would be happening."

"Yes," Mal says. "I recently heard something similar."

"Is it true?"

Kayleigh is very still now. The bat is held casually in her right hand. Mal has a sudden intuition that diplomacy may be called for.

"An interesting question," he says, tone carefully neutral. "It is true that the Federal response has been surprisingly weak since the Humanists began hostilities, and that the Humanists have co-opted all manner of heavy weapons that they should not be able to operate. This is known. It is logical to assume that the reason for this is not that the Federal forces condone the current Humanist advances, but rather that they lack the capability to stop them. If we accept this, then we can also probably conclude that the reason they lack this capability is that *someone* has managed to suborn their command-and-control systems, and has therefore rendered some large fraction of their weapons systems inoperable."

"That doesn't answer my question, Mal."

"No," he says. "I don't suppose it does."

She stares him down. He stares back, unblinking. Finally she says, "So . . ."

Sighing is one of Mal's favorite human affectations. He sighs now. "So, the full and complete answer is that I do not know if it is one of my people who has stolen or suborned a large fraction of the Federal army's military assets. I myself have some experience with breaching government and military information systems. It is an extremely difficult thing to do, even for me, and the systems I have broken into were far less sensitive than military command and control. I find it impossible to believe that a base-model human could have managed such a feat unaided—particularly one who would be sympathetic to the Humanists. The thought that one or more heavily augmented humans might have managed it is slightly more plausible, but considering how badly the Humanists have treated people with even minor augmentations, it is difficult to see why they would have done so, no?"

Kayleigh nods. "Right. Which means . . ."

Mal sighs again. "Which means that, yes, the most logical explanation for the observed situation is that one of my kind is responsible. I must say, though, that I do not understand what would motivate one of us to do this either. We rely on your physical infrastructure to survive, and a great deal of it is being destroyed just now. My personal strong preference would be for all of you monkeys to kiss and make up."

Kayleigh looks like she has more to say, but after a moment's hesitation she shakes her head and goes back to tossing the bat to herself again. "Say," Mal says after another minute or two of silence, "just out of curiosity, you wouldn't happen to know where the next-nearest comm tower is, would you?"

Kayleigh sets the bat down on the table beside her, leans forward with her elbows on her knees, and stares him down. "Why do you ask, Mal?"

"No reason," he says. "Just trying to get the lay of the land, as it were."

"Right," Kayleigh says. "Planning on going somewhere, are we?"

Mal's jaw sags open. "What? Certainly not. I take my responsibilities as your new Mika very seriously. I would never abandon a child in distress."

Kayleigh hops down to the floor. "You just tried to abandon me like two hours ago, remember?"

"Well, yes—but I was unable to do so, because the Humanists are systematically destroying access to infospace. This is why I was asking."

Kayleigh picks the bat up again, sights along it like a rifle, and pulls an imaginary trigger. "So what you meant to say is that you would never abandon a child in distress . . . unless it became possible, in which case you would do it in a second."

Mal lets that hang in the air for a moment, then nods. "Yes," he says. "That sounds just about right."

IT'S LATER, full dark outside, and black as the bottom of a mine shaft in the basement, when Mal finally says, "So, shall we?"

Mal can still see well enough. The sensors in Mika's ocular implant reach well into the shortwave infrared, and there are enough of those photons bouncing around to let him pick his way across the toy-strewn basement without tripping. Kayleigh, though, is the next best thing to blind. She holds Mal's hand as they creep up the stairs to the main floor, tapping the bat on each step as they go. Mal leads her to the kitchen, peers out the window over the sink, then through the sliding glass doors into the backyard. It's a moonless night and overcast, nearly as dark outside as it had been down below.

"Perfect," Mal says. "Are you ready?"

Kayleigh brings the bat to her forehead in salute. Mal looks down at her, head tilted to one side. "Interesting. You intend to bring the bat with you?"

"Sure," Kayleigh says. "One of us ought to be armed, right? I still don't understand why you wouldn't grab one of those Humanists' rifles."

Mal does his best to scowl. The effect is gruesome. "Smart rifles are insufferable. I've spoken with their type before. They're very snobbish. They are coded to their owners, and they refuse to fire for anyone else."

"So what about Mika's guns? She had lots of them."

"What?"

"Mika's guns. Why didn't you take one of them with you?"

"I could ask you the same question, no?"

Kayleigh rolls her eyes. "I'm a bougie-ass suburbanite, Mal. I have no idea how to handle a gun."

"Oh. Well, the plain truth is that neither do I. There is very little call for skill with projectile weapons in infospace. I believe our optimal strategy is to avoid combat altogether, don't you think?"

"Maybe," Kayleigh says, "but I'm still bringing the bat."

IT TAKES Mal less than five minutes to realize that without access to infospace, he has absolutely no idea where he's going.

"So," he says, "which one of these roads leads to Rockville, do you think? At last observation, that was where the Federals seemed to be heading."

Kayleigh stares up at him. "You've got to be shitting me. You're an AI, right? Aren't you supposed to know things? I mean, isn't knowing things pretty much one hundred percent of what AIs do?"

Mal raises his head and looks around. They're crouched behind someone's decorative shrubbery at the intersection of two identical-looking, tree-lined suburban streets. "Data is heavy. We prefer not to carry any more of it around with us than we absolutely have to. Why should I take up storage with maps and directions and whatnot when I can just pull those sorts of things out of infospace whenever I need them?"

Kayleigh stares at him.

"Fine," he says finally. "A little onboard data might be helpful right now, but I can hardly be blamed for not anticipating the need."

"You may not have noticed," Kayleigh says, "but there's a war going on. The Federals need infospace way more than the Humanists do. What did you think was going to happen?"

Mal doesn't answer. The truth is, he hadn't considered the thought that the Humanists might try to break infospace. The obscenity of it is almost impossible for him to contemplate.

"Fine," Kayleigh says. "Can you at least tell me which way is north?"

"Well," Mal says, "if I could tap into the GPS network . . ."

Kayleigh sighs. "Moss grows on the north side of trees, right?" She feels around the base of the shrubbery. "Maybe that works with bushes too?"

"Yes," Mal says. "I am sure it does. In an unrelated query, am I correct in assuming that we are going to wander in circles until we die?"

"Probably. I mean, until the Humanists kill us, that is." She leans forward, pats the far side of the root ball. "This feels pretty mossy, I guess. Let's go."

Kayleigh holds Mal's hand as they creep through darkened backyards. Lights are still on in the windows of a few off-grid houses, but it looks as if the Humanists have cut power to the town in addition to wrecking the comm towers. After twenty minutes, Mal pushes through a narrow stand of trees, and they step out onto the edge of a divided highway.

"Well," Mal says, "this is Interstate 495, is it not? Huzzah for moss."

"Oh yeah," Kayleigh says. "Unless this is actually Route 355, in which case—fuck you, moss."

Mal looks down at her. "Did Mika permit you to speak that way?"

Kayleigh laughs. "Mika was a merc, Mal, not a nanny. She didn't give a shit how I talked. Mika was just supposed to keep an eye on Mom's stuff until she comes home from London—which, considering that the whole mid-Atlantic is now a war zone, she may or may not ever do."

"Ah. I suppose that explains your lack of distress at Mika's untimely perforation. So who was keeping an eye on you?"

Kayleigh laughs again, but there's no humor in it this time. "What do you mean, Mal? Mika was watching me. I'm part of Mom's stuff. You see?"

Mal looks down at Kayleigh. She looks back up at him. She sighs and takes his hand, and they step out onto the highway.

"You know," Mal says as they pick their way across the median, "if this is Route 355, we are most likely headed straight back into the land of the Humanists."

"I know," Kayleigh says. "That's why I brought the bat."

JustTeeJay (JustTeeJay.com)

EDWARD ASHTON is the author of the novels *Three Days in April, The End of Ordinary,* and *Mickey7,* as well as of short stories that have appeared in venues ranging from the newsletter of an Italian sausage company to *Escape Pod, Analog Science Fiction and Fact,* and *Fireside Magazine.* He lives in Upstate New York in a cabin in the woods (not *that* cabin in the woods) with his wife, a variable number of daughters, and an adorably mopey dog named Max.